Emily Perkins was born in 1970. She lives in New Zealand.

NOVEL ABOUT MY WIFE

Tom Stone is madly in love with his wife Ann, an Australian in self-imposed exile in London. Expecting their first child, they buy a semi-derelict house in Hackney despite their spiralling money troubles. But soon Ann becomes convinced that a local homeless man is shadowing her — she spends hours cleaning the house, and sits up all night talking with a feverish passion. As their child grows, Tom senses an impending threat. Their home seems beset with vermin, smells and strange noises. On the verge of losing the house, Tom makes a decision that he hopes will save their lives.

EMILY PERKINS

NOVEL ABOUT
MY WIFE

Complete and Unabridged

ULVERSCROFT
Leicester

First published in Great Britain in 2008 by
Bloomsbury Publishing Plc
London

First Large Print Edition
published 2009
by arrangement with
Bloomsbury Publishing Plc
London

British Library CIP Data

Perkins, Emily, *1970 –*
  Novel about my wife
  1. Pregnant women- -Psychology- -Fiction.
  2. Hackney (London, England)- -Social conditions
  - -Fiction. 3. Psychological fiction.
  4. Large type books.
  I. Title
  823.9′2–dc22

  ISBN 978–1–84782–670–1

Published by
F. A. Thorpe (Publishing)
Anstey, Leicestershire

Set by Words & Graphics Ltd.
Anstey, Leicestershire
Printed and bound in Great Britain by
T. J. International Ltd., Padstow, Cornwall

This book is printed on acid-free paper

For Karl

If I could build her again using words, I would: starting at her long, painted feet and working up, shading in every cell and gap and space for breath until her pulse couldn't help but kick back in to life. Her hip bones, her red knuckles, the soft skin of her thighs, her fine crackle of hair. (That long red hair. The shock of it spread out on the floor.) I loved her boredom, her glazed look, her dark laugh, her eyes. The way she moved around things, gliding, very near. The warmth that emanated from her skin. Everybody gives up warmth but with Ann it had a special quality, as though she was heat seeking heat, threatening to touch you in the spirit of danger, on a dare. She'd stand in the gutter, off the kerb, while she was waiting to cross the road. Buses skimmed past. She didn't flinch.

She wasn't one of those women who hate their feet, who hate their bodies, the kind who turn the sight of their ass in broad daylight into a state secret. (God, you just find yourself dying for a glimpse, you'll do anything to get it, hover outside the bathroom door, hide under a table, pull back the sheets when she's sleeping.) Ann didn't care. Her body was open for viewing. It was one of the ways she distracted you from what was inside her head.

And her feet weren't perfect: they were long and dry, with knobbly toes and a verruca on one heel which never went away because she refused to do anything but laugh about it. She liked pedicures, massage, that slightly sickening world of female self-obsession, and went in for toenail polish in dark, back-off shades. The lightning bolt scar on her right arm was a bubble-edged disaster, a memento of youth that she kept covered up. What you couldn't take your eyes off were her legs. She had a sexy stance and walk, sort of hollow around the waist and jutty at the hips, shoulders slumped forwards. Now that I see it written down it makes her sound like a gorilla, but was more sort of slutty flapper. Bear with me.

She was a mould-maker; that was her job, to take casts of people's bodies, the parts of their bodies that were ill and needed radiating to kill cancer cells or shrink tumours. This wasn't what she'd had in mind during her sculpture major at the Slade but it brought its own satisfactions. A little plaster-dusted room at St Bartholomew's Hospital very like a studio, the Hogarth diorama she could visit there each day, the walk to work under St John's Gate. She loved the historical location, the feeling it gave her of being part of something, of belonging. It was a raggle-taggle version of the past that Ann had, she picked up scraps about the Knights Templar or pilgrims, eighteenth-century pleasure gardens, I don't know, there was no grand scheme in her mind, no connecting dots. She said she needed the feeling of stone at her back, even if it was in ruins.

I can't look at Ann in terms of the bare bones. She was this kind of person, she was that. Her parents were whatever, the house she grew up in was blah — it isn't going to work. Partly because there's so much I don't know. It was Ann's mystery I fell for, her genuine mystery, not the cultivated kind so many of the English girls had. Those girls, I can give you their bare bones: mummy and daddy still together, decent schools, hopes of working in television, a pesky brush with the law over shoplifting, an affair with a drug dealer, a lost night waking into a frightened morning (where am I, what is that mark on the floor, I don't have the tube fare, where the fuck are my jeans) that is better left unexcavated and so she puts the bad-girl days behind her. She flounders for a bit. Drops the media dream and retrains, funded by the parents, in something useful to society (can't think what that might be), in which instance she is out of my orbit and we'll never cross paths again. Or she pursues the dream with renewed vigour, pulls contacts to get a job on the women's section of a broadsheet supplement, acquires a new edge, drops the milliners and jewellery designers that she went to school with and goes out to bands at night. Then she meets me, or someone like me, at the launch for a new short film and bang. A few movies, a Malaysian meal or two, the introduce-to-friends dinner party, three months of electric fucking, one mid-week trip to a foreign city and then the writing on the wall. They're paper, those girls, and Ann was flesh.

I'd like to be inside her somehow, to strap her ribcage on over my own and see the world from behind her skin like the serial killer in a lurid film. Breathe with her breath, hear and smell with her senses, taste the inside of her mouth, speak with her voice. A clear Perspex mask of her head, big holes gaping for eyes and mouth, sits in the corner of my office. She had a radiotherapy trainee do it, lay the cling film over her face, cover her with the cold gypsoma strips, piece by tightening piece

— so she would understand how her brain tumour patients feel. Plaster has plastic memory. Ann found it magical. These aren't death masks, she'd say, they are the opposite. I borrowed her glassy head for one of my creatures, back when I was trying to please Alan Tranter, trying to go commercial. Now I want more than this transparent mould from Ann; want to make her so real that I can hold her. *Tshh* — quiet. Shut off the radio. Close the window on the neighbours, muffle those clangouring workmen in the street below. I'm trying to hear her speak. It isn't going to be easy, for a man more used to writing about vampires than about spirit, flesh and blood. But I'd like to know what the hell else I'm meant to do.

* * *

A long time after the accident, as though she was experiencing *déjà vu*, Ann swore that she had dreamed about it — being on the derailed train — before it happened. I couldn't tell if this was true or whether she was trying, after the event, to turn what was really a disturbing memory into a premonition of some kind — into something with meaning. Why she would do that was unclear, but by that stage I didn't know why she would do or say a lot of things. Kate was listening too; perhaps it was the day of the exorcism.

'It was dark,' she said, as though seeing a warning film playing in her head, 'but emergency fluorescents flickered, lighting the passengers in odd blues and yellows. There was the toasty smell of smoke or burning hair. Most people stayed calm. We followed the instructions that came over the tannoy system.' When she spoke she still sounded like herself. She'd kept her careful, covered-over accent.

'All of us walking forwards over the rails towards the next stop felt, some people said at the hospital later, a weird sort of achievement, camaraderie, the pleasure of an ordeal survived. You knew that it was better to be down there, in the hot dark mess of it all, than one of the thousands of passengers whose journey was delayed. All above your head were men and women with nothing to show for it. You could imagine them, limp-armed and impotent at the grilled-shut tube entrances, late now for meetings and lunch dates, travellers bound for Stansted making frantic useless mobile phone calls to airline check-in voicemail, no money for taxis, losing their holidays, no way now of catching their aeroplanes out.' Ann's eyes were glassy.

She was on holiday from herself; she didn't need an aeroplane.

When she was thrown from her seat to the other side of the underground train, hitting her head on the yellow metal pole, Ann's first thought was for the baby. The lights went out and a sharp object jabbed her in the temple (it was the corner of another woman's briefcase) and she realised she wasn't being attacked but that something had gone wrong. 'This is it! This is it!' shouted a female voice and she thought, don't be so stupid, of course it's not. Then through the darkness she smelled smoke and quickly felt it stinging her eyes, robbing her, for the moment, of her remaining vision, and she wondered if perhaps the hysterical woman was right. Ann was three months pregnant with our baby, that astonishing baby, and I assumed she had left work early so as to miss rush hour: she'd been feeling sick, headachy and exhausted, but because she didn't yet show nobody knew to give up a seat for her on a crowded train. Londoners do give up seats on trains, despite what other people think of us. I made a habit of it after the morning when Ann phoned me from work, her voice bumpy like she was saying the words aloud for the first time, which she was. She had been pregnant before, but not to me; not to anybody she would tell.

And there she was in her carriage, sitting on the worn tartan cover of the bench seat, where a billion tired, impatient, resigned people had sat before, coming home early, so I thought, because she was in need of comfort, in need of rest. Earlier at Farringdon station, waiting for the train to arrive, she had watched two immigration officers approach a couple of men who were speaking to each other in what sounded like Arabic. One of the men started to walk away and an officer followed him, stepping around and into his path so he couldn't go forwards. For a few seconds they performed a ludicrous dance, until the man took a wallet from his jacket and shoved it into the immigration officer's face. 'I really resent this,' he said in a loud, accented voice, gesturing so that everyone near him on the platform turned to look. 'Papers, he wants, here they are.' The officer made a point of looking methodically through the wallet, his face expressionless. 'All in order?' the foreigner asked as he shoved the wallet back inside his suit jacket. 'Good. I'm so pleased.' His friend came towards him and took his elbow. They walked off down the platform arm in arm, the questioned man shaking his head in silence.

While this was happening a train had

pulled up, and passengers had got on and off, and it had driven off again. Ann had not moved. The other immigration officer tried to stare her down, and she knew it was rude to stop and gawp, but she also felt it was her duty. It shouldn't be normal, she said to me later, shaking her head just as she had demonstrated the questioned man's gesture. It isn't right. The officials left the platform. More travellers arrived and waited. It was too crowded to see what had happened to the other two men. Ann got on to the next train. This was the one that, deep underground in a lightless tunnel, bucked its tracks and derailed.

There was screaming at first, panicking and total darkness, the 'This is it' woman and others like her. A man flicked his lighter — a sudden, oddly Christmassy glow, the tips of his fingers translucent pink, the O of his face in orange. 'Put it out!' shouted a half-carriageful of voices. It was nearly twenty minutes before the passengers were allowed to move. People made indescribable noises, Ann said, words of outrage and fear, banging on immobile windows, worrying that the air was running out or whether there were chemicals in it. But what were *you* doing, I asked her, while all of this was going on?

'I started by not wanting to breathe too

much, because of the baby, so I didn't want to talk or join in.' As she described the scene she sat with her elbows on her knees, her head in her hands, flicking quick glances at me through her fingers, and I understood that this was how she had been on the train. 'By the time I did want to join in it was too late, we were moving.'

Of the two hundred and ninety-six passengers that clambered through the darkness towards the light of Liverpool Street station, twenty-eight suffered serious cuts and bruises and seven were later admitted to hospital. (She had made it to the *Evening Standard* late edition, along with an archive photograph of a derailed train, on-the-street interviews with dazed survivors, and the politics of outrage: '2.39 P.M. — THE WAKING NIGHTMARE'.) Ann had been sitting at the back of the train, and had to make her way forwards through all of the carriages and out the emergency doors at the side of the driver's cabin. She could hear nothing behind her yet had the feeling that someone was there, in the darkness, just waiting for her to move on. The dark space at her back had a presence, she told me, an occupied quality. It was the darkness that stopped her from turning and looking to see. When she finally left the train she inhaled deeply with relief, but dust quickly entered her mouth and throat, thrust in like a cobweb mitten. Decades of it had been thrown up by the impact, soft felt-like layers of human hair and skin cells, so thick that all around her people choked on it. A man just ahead wheezed asthmatically. Ann fumbled in her handbag for her inhaler, which for once she had with her, and passed it up to him. This, she thought later, must have been when she lost her phone. She didn't hear it fall: the tunnel was full of the echoing voice of the driver, issuing instructions through a loud-hailer, and the smaller human sounds of muttering and griping, complaints about the state of the railways, the state of the country, the state of the world. Somebody mentioned Al-Qaeda and somebody else snapped at him to shut up. There were the sounds of pushing and skidding feet — two men were actually fighting down there, Ann laughed, swearing at each other, fuck you, no fuck you, scuffling over whether or not they were victims of a terrorist attack. A third man boomed at them to break it up, in the voice of schoolyard authority, and the tussle subsided.

It was hot and dizzying in the tunnel. Some people cried out that they could see sparks and flames; others shouted at them to just keep moving. Somehow Ann was now in the middle of the shuffling crowd, being jostled and pushed into the slower, cautious people in front of her. Although she wanted to be out, to push through, climb over people towards the open air, Ann thought she might faint or be sick, so she stepped aside and bent over for a minute, by the hot dark wall, to try and get oxygen into her head. People bumped her as they passed. It seemed to go on a long time, this moment — doubled over in the dark, covered with soot and dust, preventing herself from clutching at passing arms. Then a man's voice came towards her, trying to stay low and calm, comforting his crying child.

'Can I help?' Ann asked, pulled out of herself.

'He's done something to his wrist,' the man said. 'Can you carry anything?'

Ann took his bags and the man lifted his boy into his arms.

Later in the grot of the Royal London Ann waited with the man while his son's wrist was put in a splint. He lent her his mobile phone and she called me. There had been fire engines, she told me when I arrived, when I finally found her waiting for an ultrasound scan in the obstetrics department. She still had soot smeared on her face and hands, and blood — somebody else's — in small brown spots on her blouse. People had sat around at the station and later the hospital A & E centre dazed, bleeding, getting bandaged. The man with the boy had gone home. She still had his mobile phone. She was going to wait for him to ring, if he remembered that she'd borrowed it. 'Let's turn it off now,' I said, looking at the picture by the sonographer's door: a mobile phone with a red diagonal line through it.

We could see the baby's heartbeat. Ann and I laughed at the same time — I had the huge ballooning sensation of being given something undeserved — blood rushed to my face in a hot sweet tingle. The baby was a transparent pulsing bean in a sea of grey whorls. I squeezed Ann's hand. There were tears in her eyes; she looked suddenly much younger. When I kissed the side of her face I could smell the sweat and dust, and I had to resist an uncharacteristic urge to wrap my arms tightly round her, to cling to her in gratitude and relief.

'Hang on,' the sonographer said. 'What's that? You've got something there.'

'What is it?' Ann gripped my hand hard.

The woman pushed the monitor deeper into Ann's belly. Now we could see it, a thick mass of tissue, enormous next to the embryo, ten or fifteen times its size.

'Don't cry,' the sonographer said to Ann, as though she were a silly little girl. 'It's just a fibroid. Baby's fine.'

'But that thing's so big,' Ann said, her voice off-balance. 'Look at it.' Her smudged face was tight and worried. It was hard to comprehend that the murky image on the screen was showing us the inside of Ann.

'It's nothing,' the woman said, wiping the transparent jelly from Ann's stomach with a paper towel. 'It can't hurt you.'

★ ★ ★

Together Ann and I drove round to return the mobile phone to the father from the train. He lived in Hampstead, a part of London I pretended was too fuddy-duddy for me but secretly aspired to. I tried to take a clever short cut, and we got lost on the way and narrowly avoided a navigation fight. Our laughter, as we turned into street after street of bigger and bigger houses, was thin with envy. Ann brushed invisible creases out of her sleeves and reapplied her lipstick in the glove box mirror. Outside the tall wide house — the wrought iron gate, the polished railings, the sheeny windows bouncing light — we sat silently, bracing ourselves for strangers. On their doorstep Ann squeezed my arm and nodded at the pile of champagne bottles in the recycling bin. When Simon, this man who'd shared the intense hours of the derailment with Ann, came to the door I smiled tersely and gripped his hand, which was, I noted gratefully, neither clammy nor vice-like. We stepped into his house.

There are few situations more uncomfortable than entering a stranger's house; beyond university you really shouldn't be expected to meet new people. I found myself checking out the woman standing behind him in the hallway and comparing her to Ann. She had that insane Birkenstock look, tanned skin, no make-up and lots of single white streaks through her straight long black hair giving her an unnerving Medusa-like quality. Her eyes, a wild sort of orangey-brown, stared in eager greeting as she wiped her hands on her denim apron and stepped forwards to say hello. An invisible hand pushed at my chest. I found myself looking for an exit. Her name was Kate; she introduced her husband, Ann's crash cohort, as 'my partner Simon', and their children, preposterously, as Titus and Ruby-Lou. 'After circus performers, do you think, or porn stars?' Ann snorted and rolled her eyes on the drive home. It was a break in the frosty silence between us. 'You're cross with me aren't you,' she asked, once I was safely laughing about the children of these people we didn't know. If there was one habit of Ann's I didn't like, it was her persistent need to smoke out bad feeling and dispel it with this little-girl routine. I was more than cross with her; I was outraged, and didn't want to be cajoled out of it.

We'd been sitting in Kate and Simon's kitchen, Ann having accepted, despite my significant no-no-no eye contact, their offer of a drink. Now press-ganged into it, I'd gone for tea, figuring it was quicker to make, but Ann wanted coffee and we had to wait while Simon faffed around with some fancy espresso machine that he'd brought back from Italy. He actually told us that: 'I brought this back from Italy.' 'Congratulations,' I managed not to say. We'd been introduced to Titus, his bandaged wrist and Ruby-Lou who were now off cruising the Internet or watching Looney Tunes while pretending to practice the clarinet or whatever eight-year-olds did.

'Two cappucini coming up,' said Simon, which confirmed my hatred of him — it's ridiculous to fuss about the niceties of another language when you're not even on foreign soil. And then Kate asked whether Ann was going to seek counselling about the accident. I laughed, but Ann seemed to take her seriously.

'I don't know,' she said, 'I hadn't thought about it. What about you?' she asked Simon. 'What about Titus?'

Simon had his back to us, frothing milk, but you could hear the pride in his voice. 'Kate's a therapist. She's helping us through it.'

'Oh. Wow. That's great.'

'Are you allowed to treat your own family?' I asked.

'Oh yes, I treat them all the time,' Kate said, in what I had hopefully thought was a stoner's voice but now took to be a very irritating, all-seeing tone of wisdom.

'What kind of thing do you talk about? If you don't mind my asking.' Ann was clearly fascinated.

Kate looked perplexed. 'What do you mean?'

'Sorry, it's presumptuous, sorry.' Ann laughed, shaking her head in that charming way she had as though amused by her own stupidity. We were all silent for a few seconds. She could handle it.

While Simon spoke he dabbed a finger around in his cappuccino froth. A flashing vision of him aged three sitting on a sandy beach, tentative and curious. Perhaps he wasn't so hateful. 'We were going to Bethnal Green, to the Museum of Childhood.' Of course they were. 'They've got a brilliant collection of old — ' He must have sensed something in the air, my rising urge to laugh, perhaps, as he cleared his throat and said, 'I did wonder if the tube is safe these days, we'd not taken the children on it for months after the bombings.'

'But that's crazy,' said Ann. 'You can't blame yourself.'

'Were you on your way home from work?' Kate asked.

'Well,' said Ann, sipping her coffee, 'I'm pregnant.'

I stared at her. We hadn't even told my parents. Kate and Simon cooed congratulations and delight. What were we doing here around this unknown kitchen table? I stood, patting my pockets for cigarettes, and was about to excuse myself into the back garden, when Ann said, 'But I left work early . . . because of . . . ' She examined her hands. 'This guy who's been following me.'

I sat back down.

'Really?' said Kate, unable to disguise her curiosity. 'Do you know him?'

Ann looked at me, guilty. This was the first I'd ever heard of him. 'No. But I recognise him.'

'Who is he?' I asked, not caring that the question made it obvious to Kate and Simon I knew nothing at all about this situation. 'When's he been following you?'

'Black or white?' asked Simon.

She hesitated. 'He's a black.'

The racist-sounding use of the article alarmed me. Would she phrase the sentence in quite such a way if she were telling Tonia? Tonia would not have asked Simon's question. And he would never have asked it if she'd been in the room. I hated him all over again, turning the four of us into a bunch of middle-class anxious white people with that simple 'Black or white?' (All right, that's exactly what we were, but how rude of him to point it out.)

'I've seen him in the playground across the road from our house. Just sitting on his own. Do you know the guy? He's disturbed, you know, not right. He wears, like, a hood and a really heavy coat, he's skinny but all,' her fingers were gesturing claws, 'shaggy some-how.'

'Are you sure it's always the same guy?'

'Oh it's him.' She was certain. 'It's always the same guy. Hunched over. But like he's watching.'

This spooky touch was unlike Ann. I laughed. 'There are one or two hood-wearing creeps in London.' I often stared out at the so-called playground, an oval stretch of tarry rubber on which was planted one broken seesaw and a pair of swings. Older children came out like imps in the night and pushed the swings over and over the bars that held them so that they hung way out of reach on shortened, looped chains. They left broken bottles, takeaway fried chicken boxes, plastic bags and dead lighters, but I'd never seen them do it, and I'd never seen this man.

'Once I thought he was following me to the tube, but then I decided I was paranoid.'

There were bright spots of red in Ann's cheeks. Simon and Kate were staring at her. We ignored the muffled thuds and shrieks of Titus and Ruby-Lou fighting upstairs.

'And then on the day of the crash, I saw him at my work.'

Kate asked where she worked.

'At the radiotherapy department at Barts. I see lots of people who don't look well, and you know, homeless people get cancer too, I mean I'm used to a range. But he wasn't there for treatment, I'm sure of it.'

'Did he actually come in?'

'He just stood outside with the smokers, where the ambulances pull in. He watched me when I arrived and he was still there when I went for lunch. In the afternoons I work upstairs so I went in the back way, but then I couldn't stop thinking about whether he was still there or not.'

I envisaged Ann's upstairs room — the pressing machine where she made the latex moulds of people's heads and arms and hips and torsos from her plaster casts. The white shelves, laden with these rubber parts, and the sinister, transparent (sinister because they were transparent?) masks of individual faces that all looked exactly the same. Ann went into a kind of zone in the afternoons, I knew from trying to call her and getting a distracted version of her voice on the end of the line, disembodied and somehow floating. Now, in this house of people we didn't know, she looked the way that voice sounded.

'How did he look at you?' This was Simon.

'Not directly. He keeps his head ducked down. So I asked one of the nurses to check for me and she said he was there, this was about two o'clock. And I really started freaking out, so I cleaned up and left early, out the back. And got stuck on the train.'

'He keeps his head ducked? Have you seen him since?'

Ann nodded silently. A tear rolled down her face.

'For Christ's sake Ann, why didn't you say anything?' I asked. 'We should call the police.'

She shook her head. 'He hasn't done anything. He's sort of forlorn.'

I couldn't understand her. For a cavernous second I had the feeling she was making it all up. I said, 'If you see him again you've got to tell me. He can't just follow you around, he's probably a psychopath.' I glared at Kate. Wasn't she the nutcase professional?

'Oh, before I forget.' Ann passed Simon his mobile phone.

'I'll take your number,' Kate said. 'We're very grateful you weren't opportunist phone-thieving teenagers.'

Ann laughed. 'There were all sorts on that train.'

After Kate punched our phone number into Simon's mobile, Simon handed Ann a small rectangle. 'Here. Have my card. I hardly ever get to hand it out.'

She looked at it. 'Oh, how completely weird! You're a writer too.'

I couldn't get out of there fast enough.

'You're cross with me,' she said in the car, and I pulled over and unbuckled my seat belt and said, 'Why didn't you tell me?'

'I'm sorry.'

'What if anything happened to you? What if he — I just — don't understand why you wouldn't tell me.'

She shook her head. 'I don't know. Because

you'd want to do something, call the cops, or move house, or confront him — I guess — I don't know.'

'I don't understand you.'

'Don't say that!' She laughed, surprising me, my Ann again. 'That's your job. You have to understand.'

I started the car and pulled out into the traffic.

'Do you know him?' By this she meant Simon, did I know his work? Yes I did know his fucking work. Oh, get a grip, Tom, I told myself, you are too old for envy to be in the slightest bit wolfishly attractive on you. And what did I envy? His solid career on *Holby City, Casualty* and *EastEnders*? He was television. There'd been that usual awkwardness as we paid each other our respects, him feigning surprise that I'd heard of him, me genuinely relieved he didn't draw a blank when my one decent credit was mentioned by Ann. The wives were our mouthpieces, Kate reporting that Simon was the new story editor on *Casualty* and Ann responding with the name of my film. Résumés delivered, at last each of us spoke for ourselves.

'Yes I read somewhere you'd gone back to run the show, I hear it's doing very well, you're up in the ratings, congratulations.' I 'read somewhere', I 'hear', was I going out of my way to be clear I'd never actually watched the show?

His turn: 'The class-divide romance, I remember. Whirlwind produced it. You doing anything else for them?' Clever. No indication as to whether he'd seen it or, if he had, what he thought. I'd had enough wrong-footing for one morning.

'And,' he went on, 'weren't you doing something with Hallie?'

John Halliburton. Wide-boy Australian producer of attempted blockbusters. Simon must have heard of the meltdown in Fiji, the humiliating way I'd got the flick. 'Do you know Hallie?' I asked, glacially. I shot a quick glance in Ann's direction. She had stood, and was asking Kate about their garden.

'Well not really — seen him round the traps, you know — out in LA last month, met him at a party, he's . . . ' He had the grace to drop the end of his sentence into his coffee cup. Faker, calling Hallie by his nickname when they were only on canapé terms.

This time, Ann responded to my stare. 'We really must leave you in peace.'

Just as my first film was coming out, I'd briefly — *briefly!* — had a fair bit of currency as a 'hot new screenwriter'. Then it opened to reviews that revealed it to be the kind of 'right on' British feature everybody thought they should go to but nobody did. (I actually stood in a queue at Steve Hatt and heard this exchange: 'Have you seen that new film, the council estate love story one?' Shrugging of shoulders, sucking in of air over teeth: 'No . . . I know I should, but . . . ' 'I know what you mean.' 'If I'm going to pay for a babysitter I'd honestly rather do something fun.') Anyway, in that window of hotness I'd signed a contract to write a script for John Halliburton. The story was set at a luxury resort in Fiji, which was taken over by machete-wielding locals during one of that country's many recent military coups. It was in danger of being one of those stories where the plea 'but this really *happened*' doesn't make the outlandishness of the situation any more believable. I was drawn to it for a number of reasons, not least the research trip to the resort that Hallie was spunking for. Ann had just moved in to my Camden flat, and if I switched the business class flight for two economies I could take her too.

Driving down the tree-lined Hampstead street I poked again at my jealousy, like checking a new cavity in your mouth with your tongue, and was pleased to discover that yes, indeed, there was no longer anything there. I thought myself a master at side-stepping such emotion, the king of rationalisation: so-and-so was older than me and therefore more experienced, or was more commercial, or more alternative, or was a woman and so didn't count as direct competition, or was a different bloody star sign. Probably I could have talked myself out of any grinding competitive urges with anyone other than an identical twin brother, and as he didn't exist I was home free. Ann approved of this absence in me of what she termed 'alpha bullshit', as long as it didn't interfere with my drive, my will to succeed in general. Since the pregnancy there had been a few treacherously light exchanges about money-earning capacity and the mortgage. We both lay awake some nights, listening to the other's breathing, trying to discover sleep through the electric field of tension in the air. I was running out of tricks to play on my insomnia.

'No,' I said, 'I've heard of him. *Casualty*. Fuck.' I had taken a wrong turning and was faced with one of those idiotic bollarded streets without warning.

'She was interesting.'

'Can you just look at the A-Z for me? I hate Hampstead.'

Her head was bent over the map, but I could see she was suppressing laughter.

'I do! It's a stupid maze where wildly successful television writers and their freaky all-seeing wives live with circus midgets they pass off as their own children.' It was a pleasure to make Ann laugh. She really gave in to it, enough to make me laugh too, even while negotiating a ten-point U-turn between smugly clean German cars. 'If you see that man following you again you've to tell me Ann, you promise.'

'I will. I promise. I'm sure it's just coincidence.' She looked happy.

⋆　⋆　⋆

Some facts are known. We met. Fell in love. Went to Fiji. Were married. We lived together in the house in Daley Street and we had our baby. Ann died. Now I live alone with Arlo, who is four, and I can barely remember the last three and a half years. A rented flat. The move to Muswell Hill. A series of nannies: the Romanian, the Canadian, the Russian, the droopy-haired Danish girl crying as she fled the house. One of them saying, 'You cannot speak to me like that.' The Romanian's boyfriend coming with aftershaved pals to collect her things, his gaze at me through rheumy eyes, *don't start*, as if I could. Somewhere, in all that, Arlo learning to walk, feed himself, use the lavatory. Arlo talking. Arlo singing in his birdy voice, perched on a stool in the back garden while I cut his coppery-red hair. It has felt, lately, since Arlo started school, as though the haze is lifting — as though Ann is coming back to me. So that is why I'm writing this. There are the known knowns, as a politician might say. Other things I can only take a stab at. What Ann thought. What Ann felt. What happened to her when I was not around. For this I need fiction, the *grrrt* of the paper rolling into the old typewriter I've hung on to since my student days. I like this arrangement, the computer for what I know, the typewriter for everything I'm not so sure of. Fiji.

N.A.M.W. 01.07

They arrive, after travelling for a day and a half, so much sea they all but hang motionless above it, and it is the middle of the night. The passengers limp off the plane on to a covered, raised walkway without walls. Ann feels the heat like a hand pressing a warm damp cloth over her nose and mouth. Dense, rubbery air envelops them. Against the fading white noise from the plane engines, a bird makes the creak of a screen door. Frangipani, even with all this asphalt, all these big machines. In a room floored in linoleum fans whirr; the overhead lights are dim, economies are being made.

A band of men wearing traditional skirts plays the guitar. Ann and Tom walk towards the blackness of night at the end of the hall. Dark carved wooden masks, shop windows of raffia bags and coconut soap, car-hire logos in flat primary colours. A man loops a shell necklace over Ann's head. He leads them to a car with windows of tinted glass.

'It looks like a politician's car,' says Ann.

'You can see out,' the driver tells her, 'but no one can see in.'

They can't see out. The roads are marked by cat's-eyes. 'On our left are some sugar cane fields. Sugar cane is Fiji's secondary industry.' After what, Ann nearly asks, then realises — tourism, them. 'Sugar cane crops are still harvested by hand. It is hard, rough work. I am Fijian Indian. We have a slave history, brought here by your people' (a light, wry emphasis on the *your*) 'as indentured labour, and we still cannot buy land.' It makes Ann feel better, this all being said out loud.

'Nadi,' the driver says, 'your first stop.' Ann makes out colonial buildings lining the road under the small icy glow of the streetlights. He says something about the dry side of the island and the average rainfall and she has a vision of the wet side of the island being the underneath of it, as though it were a floating disc, and there was a mirror world on this underwater side with buildings and upside-down people and sugar cane growing down into the sea.

Work, the day after Ann's revelation about her stalker, went sluggishly, like walking forwards in a nightmare, weights attached to your feet. My sleep had been disturbed by visions of Ann's drowning body, her arms outstretched, cross-like, a meaty red hand holding her face under the water until the air bubbles stopped coming. She lay next to me in the bed, deeply asleep with the swallowed-up exhaustion of early pregnancy. At five a.m. I began to think of my tax self-assessment. I didn't sleep again.

The very early morning is supposed to be the best time to write but I looked at my screenplay in despair. The who-gives-a-fuck element was at an all-time high. I was working on a script, strictly a money job that had started as a romantic comedy but now needed to become a horror 'for reasons of zeitgeist', as the producer, who wore his blond hair in spiky dreadlocks, described it. Who were these people and why was I doing it? How had I come so far from what had made me want to write film scripts in the first place? I sat in my office on the middle floor of the house, rocking in the hideous ergonomic chair, periodically banging my head lightly on the desk. The idea was to get enough girls, twists and sudden flashes of knives in to please a bloodthirsty audience of young misogynists; naturally I wanted to do better, only lately, even achieving that small goal seemed beyond me. I wasted at least two hours inserting religious imagery, knowing that without the story in place it was an indulgent exercise. After a period scanning the Internet for film industry gossip I heard Ann walking around downstairs, and gratefully went to make her breakfast.

She was trying to leave the house, unable to find her wallet, tired smudges under her eyes, skirt crumpled, hair awry, when the phone rang.

'Alan, hi.' The man who was paying me to write.

Ann looked at me questioningly and brought the sofa cushion that was in her hand to her chest. I turned away from her as I accepted Alan's invitation to coffee. He suggested a café in Islington that was always full of young people writing manuscripts and talking about technology I had never heard of.

'What did he want?' Ann asked, panting lightly, which she often did now with the oxygen uptake difficulties of pregnancy, having resumed her search for the wallet.

'I don't know. To meet up.' He wants to fire me! I was screaming inside, but for fear of making it true by saying it aloud, kept my mouth shut. I fished in the pocket of Ann's raincoat hanging from a peg in the hall. 'Here.' Her wallet. She took it, and the tiny beginnings of tears welled up in her eyes.

'I'm losing my mind,' she said, and tried to laugh.

'Don't be stupid. You're hormonal.'

We embraced. I pulled her long slim back towards me, feeling the small invisible hardness of the pregnancy against my middle. Then suddenly I found myself on my knees in front of Ann, my arms around what was still only just her waist, kissing through the fine wool layers of Ann's clothes. Our baby. Ann's long, fine-boned hand rested softly on my head.

★ ★ ★

I'm the kind of man who is attractive to a certain type of woman. This is not bragging: she's not damaged exactly, but borderline fucked; needs reassurance but resents this lack in herself and constantly plays against it. Self-deprecating, but when she lacerates others you see the tentacles and double-row teeth of her inner self. Her sexual centre is in her eyes. She's easy to fuck. Responsive, a bit perverse, sometimes lazy. But I'm not complaining. Despite having been married to Ann for four years, I can still see them coming, red-dotting me at parties, thinking I don't know what's in their minds, feverish and bright with drink, ready to provoke. Ann entered my life like this, only she somehow stayed a step ahead.

The usual rule for a man like me is that your primary relationship is not enough, that you get bored of the mysterious wide-eyed not-quite-beauty who started off aloof and self-possessed and turned out to want to know your whereabouts all the time. Such a cheat, and in my last relationship I'd often allowed my feelings of aggrieved betrayal to justify inviting another ambitious young brunette out for a drink. They went a long way on the promise of nothing, these girls, though I got a nasty shock when a particularly neurotic one, Rebecca the journalist, began writing to me at home. Mobile phones and email count for nothing when you're dealing with a woman who imagines herself a nineteenth-century literary heroine, and a wronged one at that.

I was living with Bridget then; she was

older than me and I'd once worshipped her. She frightened me, which is always compelling. In her omnipotent way she got wind of the girl's obsession just as I was about to tell Rebecca to stop writing. It's true I had let it go on. Who wouldn't, once they'd been described as 'saturnine'? (OK, it was within the mildly over-the-top phrase 'my saturnine lord', but still. It isn't every day.) I had to plead ignorance and beg forgiveness at the same time, and was not convincing on either count, and although Bridget let me stay it was the true beginning of the end. Not long after that I met Ann.

Ann was tall, rangy, with thick red hair she wore tied back. She was Australian and though I'd never been to that country I understood from a mutual friend that Ann had 'the Sydney look'. This observation wasn't passed back to her; she had done her best to shake her roots. She never talked about home and sometimes I wondered what she did bloody well remember: it was as though she'd been hit with the amnesia stick on landing at Heathrow. The description referred to Ann's penchant for skinny jeans and skirts in varying shades of black, big boots and eyeliner that winged over her top lids in the style of a fifties film star. The whole effect was don't fuck with me, and stopped crucially short of gothic. Our sex life had ground to a halt the moment her pregnancy hormones kicked in (when, by the way, her wardrobe underwent a dramatic change too and she seemed constantly swathed in layers of gauzy, floating natural fibres). Our 'sex life' — how can that bloodless phrase encompass something so wrist-bitingly, bruisingly tender, the cold press of steel, the light scrape of a knife edge, the warming security of bonds, the long, long gazes between us? It took me by surprise, I admit it, but I didn't pass judgement on how Ann wanted to be fucked. She was tough.

★ ★ ★

I got to the café first and was able to spend a good paranoid couple of minutes checking out the fashions of those younger than myself and wondering what Alan wanted to meet up for. The third coffee of the day is always a mistake, but it was that or one of those chai abominations that taste like liquidised baby food. I was not afraid of Alan but I was very, very afraid of the sack. I'd take anything to avoid it; he could switch genres as many times as he liked, he could ask me to dramatise the phone directory, he could demand a part for his wife, I didn't care: I was his writing bitch and would hang on to that prestigious position till my fingernails bled.

A woman sat on her own in the booth across from me. She had the look a little of neurasthenic Rebecca: huge eyes, an oddly small rosy mouth, something about her pale arms that looked squishy to the touch as though she had other people to do the tiresome stuff like handle her money and cut up her food. She was reading an old paperback, exactly the kind of thing Rebecca would have pulled out in public: *Under the Volcano* perhaps, or *Wide Sargasso Sea*. I tried to see the front cover without her noticing.

'Hi.' Alan had changed his look. The matted peroxide tufts were gone, and in their place was a surprisingly corporate hairdo. Had he finally understood he was too posh and too white to pull off the dreads? Had he given up hope of ever being cool? Had his wife put her foot down? Alan was talking about her, about his wife, but I couldn't concentrate. First there was the hair, then a fat woman joined Rebecca's *doppelgänger* at the other table. Fat women always keep their friends waiting, I have noticed, it is a symptom of their anger. The Rebecca lookalike's novel was *The Yellow Wallpaper*. I pitied her boyfriend; undoubtedly she had one, a skinny bespectacled fellow who cooked Thai food. She caught me staring at her.

Alan said, 'So that's made a huge difference, obviously.'

'Sorry?' I came to rudely. 'This music, I couldn't hear what you just said.'

'The pregnancy. Everything's been so insecure with the company and now with the baby, it's too precarious. I need something more reliable. The advertising gig is perfect. Tom, I'm going to take it.'

'A job in advertising?'

'A creative at Clock. Yes. I'm nearly thirty, I'm bloody lucky they'll have me.'

'You're leaving producing?'

'Yes.'

'Because Ann's having a baby?' I was outraged, discriminated against. 'That doesn't make a blind bit of difference to my writing, I'll still come up with the goods.' All the time I spoke my mind was spiralling down the tube of no Alan, no producer, no backer for the script, Ann, the baby, no money, no money, no money.

'*My* baby. Sally's pregnant, didn't you hear me?' He blew steam off his coffee. It might have been the vapour from dry ice, so cold was the air that slowly swept over me.

'Alan, that's great.' I knew their story: miscarriage after miscarriage, an empty round of IVF, the specialists, the hormone injections, the slow dropping away from friends who had children, the desolation of it all. Ann and I had felt guilty and awkward about our easy, almost accidental pregnancy. More than ten years older, we were meant to be the dried-up, wizened ones unable to conceive. This was wonderful news for them. And of course he wanted to take a more secure job. But oh my God. 'The script, Alan, it's so close. This draft is it, I can feel it.' Bullshit. I was trying to save my life.

'We'll pay you for this draft of course.'

'But after that?'

Alan shrugged. 'Sorry Tom. I wanted to tell you in person.' The betrayer's plea for lenience, the calling card of finer feeling.

'And what if it is — you know, what if this is a great script, can you just walk away from it?'

'I'm not producing any more. It's a mug's game. You wouldn't do it.' A pathetic attempt at consolation. 'Nearly thirty', he had said, 'bloody lucky they'll have me'. 'Even without the baby, I . . . Well. That's it.'

Alan had a business partner, an older woman, canny, with an ex-drinker's inability to be fazed by anything. 'What about Rosemary? And Cheryl?' The company assistant, she of the roll-your-own voice and poky hips. 'How are things going, Cheryl?' you'd ask, and she'd say briskly, 'Tits-up, the film industry is tits-up as per usual,' which always (as it was meant to do) made you think of Cheryl's tits, small and high but remarkably present in her skinny high street T-shirts. The last Christmas party she'd sat on her desk, queen of all she surveyed, one springy leg swung over the other. The look she sent out under her half-closed lids, equal parts come-on and disdain, pierced me like a wire. I remember actually squeezing my fingernails into my palms to survive the moment. The Rebecca lookalike was staring at me staring at her. I felt sick, as though I had been unfaithful to Ann and this was the ever-dreaded tap on the shoulder from the fidelity police.

'Cheryl's staying on.'

'With Rosemary?'

'Yes. Before you ask, Rose has looked over the projects I've got in development. She's only taking over one.' I willed his mouth to form the word, 'Yours.' He said, 'Joe Baxter's.' Joe Baxter was twenty-six. He had once written a lovely script that was slightly reminiscent of my first screenplay, the council estate thing that I now regarded with some embarrassment. Other people must have seen the similarities too because Alan couldn't get

Joe's script off the ground. He gave it to me, at Joe's request, to see if I could suggest any improvements. There was nothing to say: the writing was tight, the characters surprising and real, the jokes true. It made me laugh out loud and want to cry in all the right places and when I put it down I knew it would never get made. This sort of thing had already been done. There wasn't enough of either the blue flame of originality or the satisfying clicking into place of a perfectly executed genre piece. A small voice inside asked whether my film, its commercial failure, hadn't scuppered Joe's chances. A successful movie spawns imitators. But Joe's script was no homage; it was probably, the voice whispered, better than mine. I wrote Joe a letter praising his work in some detail, and suggesting he use the script as a sample piece to generate commissions. He would have, I told him, a good career in film, and I believed it. I didn't say what else I believed, which was that he had sent me the script not to garner my critical notes but this very praise, and to let me know he was most definitely on the block. Part of me was flattered he thought me important enough to receive his smoke signals. Now he was the sole survivor of Tranter's defection to the dark side.

'What is it, the council estate project?'

'A new one.'

'That was quick.'

'It's early days.'

'Can I take the project anywhere else? The rights are mine?'

'Yes of course.' Magnanimous now. 'The rights revert to you.'

Through pursed lips I blew out slowly, deflating the paper bag of self. Without knowing it was coming I began, helplessly, to laugh.

'Tom, Tom. Take it easy.'

'Oh, God!' Trying to finish and polish this draft and then hock a hybrid script that had been misguided from its inception, that only Alan had faith in and I had taken on in the cynical hope of a proper pay day at the end. Selling the house we'd only been in six months, incurring all over again the legal fees, the estate agent's fees. Losing space, losing time. Where would we go? Not Andy and Tonia's, no. My parents', never. A smaller place, a flat? Where would we get a mortgage now? Ann resuming work as soon as she'd had the baby? Telling Ann? Again. It had happened again. I was that guy. Laughter keened from my throat. Though I was shaking my head, covering my stretched face with both hands, I couldn't stop. The Rebecca woman brushed past me on her way out the door, clutching her coat tightly as though whatever I had might be contagious. At last the laughter tipped into a light fearful sob, and this humiliation enabled me to lasso the emotion, squash it with a couple of shuddering breaths. Sit still. I shrunk down in the booth, wiped my face with the flat of my hand. 'OK,' I said. 'All right.'

★　★　★

Ann lay downstairs on the sofa, her long legs over the end, her eyes closed, an effigy from a fairy tale. I poured a beer and sat and watched her, the faint purply lines on her eyelids, the smudged eyeliner, the saliva glistening in the corner of her slightly open mouth. She'd been off sex since she got pregnant. I didn't know whether or not this was normal and couldn't think of anyone to ask. The one time we tried it she said she didn't like the alcohol on my breath. She was dry. We persevered but it didn't seem worth going through again. I was hoping for a second trimester transformation.

She woke suddenly, with a deep intake of breath. I put down my drink. Her head jerked towards me and she clutched a pillow to her at the same time. For some reason neither of us spoke. She sat up and flicked her gaze around the room, her head darting like a bird's, as though sure somebody else was there.

'What?' I said, and coughed to clear my throat. 'What is it?'

'Nothing.' She stood, then sat down again. 'I thought there was someone in the room.'

'Only me.'

Ann told me her dream. It is not my usual practice to listen to other people's dreams. I can't bear the female penchant for analysing these sleep-time ramblings as though they contain messages of meaning. Horoscope bullshit, palm reader lies. This time I paid attention. She was still in the dream's grip, speaking almost in a monotone, holding my arm as though afraid.

When she first woke her voice often sounded more Australian than usual. Ann assimilated successfully when she came to this country over twenty years ago. It was a survival move, she told me, defence against being treated like a colonial bozo by arrogant parochial shit-heads like me. Shit-head, wanker, prick (prek, she said it) — these endearments were common to her, she swore like a posh girl. I have met self-appointed upper-class Australians, with their landed gentry airs and Aryan physiques; they wear linen in varying degrees of beige, their shirt collars up, have suntans and streaked blond hair and speak with pretentious rounded twangs, shushing 's's. They maintain the same old right school, right surname nonsense essential to any strain of society that considers itself superior. In their case it is an especial curse, coming as most of them do from looters, killers and thieves, and that's just what they did once they got there, never mind what got them sent in the first place. Ann wasn't one of those.

Some facts are known. She was born in Australia in the mid-1960s. At the point in time that I'm describing, this was all I knew about her life before she landed on these shores, aged seventeen, full of fury and adventure, in the heyday of New Romanticism. Like everyone of her generation she was enraged with the world as it was. She enjoyed the anger; it powered her forwards through her reinvention. Scrupulously she avoided other Australians, the squatted flats of Earl's Court, the lair-ups and random homesick sex. She was no longer 'En Weals' but Ann Wells, who with her drawled vowels and fishnet gloves, tilted chin and smoky eyes, defied anyone who challenged her right to be here.

I was at university at this time, getting sat on by fat lesbians who were in love with

Hélène Cixous but couldn't find anyone to fuck them. If Ann and I had met then, we speculated later, we would probably have gone to bed together and then behaved inhumanly towards each other as quickly as possible. It was my emaciated phase, when cheekbones were at a higher social premium than having a friend who knew Simple Minds (I could tick this box too), and perfecting your angst-ridden bastard routine was guaranteed to get you laid. This was where the puddle-eyed screwy girls entered my life and where I learned that the tougher they acted, the more you could get away with because they couldn't be seen to care. When I fell in love with Ann I fell way out of my depth. Too late, I discovered that in her the toughness was all true and all a lie, both at the same time.

It is surprisingly, disappointingly hard for me not to ramble on about myself, when my (self-assigned; perhaps this is the problem) task is to figure out how Ann got us both here. I'd have thought years of reading other people's thinly veiled autobiography in screenplay form for a hundred-odd quid a pop would have put me off the personal. The wandering down lonely streets, the unattainable beauty, the mother fixation and, worst of all, the obligatory masturbation scene. So often have I had to put down my tea in disgust at other people's compulsion to tell the world their dirty little secrets. But here I am just like everybody else, wanting all the detail, picking over the laundry, not content with what is in front of me now, sniffing hard with my face right up against the past.

Ann became a waitress in one of the champagne-spilling, Camembert-frying restaurants of the day. Before long she was managing the place, greeting people at the door with the unsmiling facial rigor mortis that we all suffered from back then. She was, briefly, at the centre of things, where all the right music was played and drugs were taken and styles were worn; she was someone you had to know. The lifestyle, playing at dressing up, suited her. It was as far from Pokesville Australia as she could imagine. By the time the summer of love hit, she like everyone was bored with looking bored and she leapt on the new drugs, the ones that made her look happy. There were always boyfriends, often older, attached, but nothing serious, and then one day she realised that she wanted to go to Paris but that her UK visa had expired, and so she got married. In the Marylebone Registry Office, upstairs amongst the faux marble columns and oak-panelled walls, at eleven o'clock in the morning she became

Mrs Lincoln. It surprised me, this, that she would change her name. Some facts are known.

Ann didn't live with her husband. She never had sex with him. The deal was that he and his boyfriend could set up in Australia in a couple of years' time, and she'd go out and act as his wife until the authorities put the right stamp in his passport. Knowing now what I do about Ann's attitude to her country of birth, I wonder if she ever really planned to follow through, or if the crossed fingers she held behind her back during the ceremony were more about the emigration promise than the wedding vows.

Tonia told me about the crossed fingers. She had met Ann when both were working as artists' models at a Slade life drawing class. In my limited experience, a certain type of woman becomes a life model. She has a history with class-A drugs and finds it hard to understand why the students don't lovingly render her tattoos. Ann and Tonia were still young; they had serious nightlife habits to support; Tonia supplied the drugs and Ann had the scars. Over the weeks, in the five-minute interval between classes, as one dressed and the other stripped (look I know it's not supposed to be sexual, but it just is), they exchanged first covert glances, then

47

nods, then began to speak. They must have been gorgeous then, rake-thin laughing girls, Ann with that tumble of hair and the faint slice marks on her long blue-white thighs, Tonia's dark brown limbs arranged at angles over the white-sheeted podium, shadows in the cleft of her collarbone as she leaned forwards . . . Oh, it's so wrong to think about your wife's best friend in this way, but as the young say nowadays, it's so right . . . Tonia lived near the campus, in a filthy enormous Peckham squat with an indefinite number of people: before too long Ann started sleeping with one of them, Useless Bill, who pretended to be a film-maker but was more a professional ashtray; he smoked roll-ups incessantly and rubbed the leavings on his rank-smelling grey jeans. I like to think the sheer pointlessness of Useless Bill's existence was the catalyst for Ann's next move, which was to surprise herself, and everyone she knew, by enrolling in a foundation course at Camberwell College of Arts.

Several years later Ann went, reluctantly, to her husband's funeral. He had never got to Australia: hepatitis caught from needle sharing kept him at home and eventually a fungal infection killed him. He and Ann had lost touch but his partner called and gave her the news. 'Dress like a widow,' Sam told her.

'Martin would like that.' So when I first laid eyes on Ann her face was obscured under a black net veil, her tall slim figure encased in a 1940s suit, black high heels sinking into the cold graveside mud. Martin was buried in Bournemouth, where he had been living and then half-living, and afterwards we — those who had been his friends, his family — congregated at the draughty beach hut he had shared with Sam, grey winter waves crashing just outside. It was there that Ann took her hat off and I saw all of her red hair, gathered into a heavy pile at the nape of her neck. She was thirty then and at her most striking, her face solemn and white, a properly sombre note against the multicoloured fairy lights and glowing tulips Sam had draped around the place as decoration.

I was there with Bridget: we no longer lived together but through her I vaguely knew Sam, and paying respects to his dead boyfriend seemed like the right thing to do. But really the wake was intolerable, pervaded as it was with a sullen sort of tragedy despite the Santa's grotto feel: another good man gone too soon, why Lord why, sort of thing. Martin had belonged to a tight little community of university friends, of whom Bridget was one. Perhaps I envied them their ease with one another, as though they all belonged to the same special race, but since they walked around glum because the race had dwindled, it was not what I would call a fun send-off. Through the fug of cigarette smoke and sea damp I made my way to Sam and asked who was the woman with red hair and he said, 'Martin's wife.' We weren't introduced but when I overheard her making her excuses, explaining that she had to take the train, I offered her a lift back to London and left Bridget hugging Sam, promising she wouldn't leave until after the weekend. As I left, my hand hovering near the small of Ann's back, Bridget gave me the most disgusted of her extensive array of disgusted looks. She knew me.

Who was Ann then? Mostly what I remember is that getting together with her plunged me into a bout of deep insecurity. Who was she? Who cared? Who was *I*, who dared to think she might want to be with me? Every morning after we slept together I would wake amazed that I'd escaped being transformed into a lion or placed under some other kind of curse. In fact getting her into bed — or across the kitchen table — was the easy part. It was getting into her mind that required a technique I apparently lacked. For the longest time she seemed not to give a shit about me, while I lost every shred of dignity phoning her several times a day, booking tickets to plays that I thought would impress her, cooking extravagant and frankly homosexual fish dinners because she was a part-time vegetarian, and generally haunting her life like a sad old ghost who doesn't know when to stop.

For a year and a half we took turns visiting each other at night. At that time she had a cheap lease on a place in Clerkenwell, near the hospital where she would later work, just before the area became fashionable. I used to walk down from Camden on sooty summer evenings, find her in her tiny studio flat surrounded by small piles of moulded wax and human hair, slip her sandals on to her long bare feet and gently push her out the door. We'd drink everywhere, in the new gastropubs and the Fleet Street holes and the tapas bars behind Tottenham Court Road, making ourselves wavy, smudged, emerging into tepid air as though into warm water, leaping recklessly on to the number 19 home just as it was pulling away. Ann pulled away, she tried it, she was so totally convincing I was on the verge of giving up, and then — she must have sensed my withdrawal, felt the silence of the phone as the nights went by while I didn't call her, now a week, now a month

— she appeared in the doorway of my flat, ears red, hands thrust into her trench coat pockets, and told me in a quick, angry voice that she loved me. Behind her, across the road, wind shook the tree blossoms. She scowled. Was I so fucking rude that I wasn't going to invite her in? My mouth filled with a new taste. The beginnings of tears shuddered on her lower lids. Every part of my body was pent with the weeks of restraining myself from contacting Ann but still I drew the moment out, not wanting her to have it so easy. Hate, love.

'Good,' I finally said. 'Because I don't ever want to go a day without seeing you again.'

★ ★ ★

'I've got the sack.' I blurted it, taking a perverse pleasure in the phrase. There was a tense moment when we both waited for me to say, 'Again,' but I wasn't going to blame Ann and once she realised that, perhaps, she laughed. Not in desperation as I had at the café with Alan, but lightly. Where was her panic, the fizzing anxiety of three a.m.?

'Your face!' she said, and laughed again. She told me I would get another contract, we had had gaps before, she wasn't finishing work for another five or six months and something was guaranteed to turn up by then.

I squeezed her arms. 'You're amazing.' It was true, she could make anything better. She edged out of the embrace and went to phone Tonia from the back step. The cool autumn night flowed into the kitchen. I closed the back door.

This was what we had become, after the first symbiotic year of our living together: a couple who needed another couple to be around. Tonia and Andy, the man she had got together with back in the life model days, had no children either. We all behaved, the four of us, as though we had a tacit agreement not to do it, that childlessness was our lifestyle choice. No ties, no banal obsession with schools and jabs and bodily functions, no ugly great family car. We all hated kiddie bores, we socialised with them sometimes but would never stoop to asking after their offspring or remembering their preposterous names (poor little Savannah, showing every sign of growing up to be more lumpen blob than Southern belle; pity snaggle-toothed Indigo and speccy white Sylvester!) Our holidays together were filled with novel reading and explorations, mountain walks and tennis games and one couple clearing off into whatever neighbouring town while the other enjoyed a do-not-disturb afternoon in bed. We stopped short of nicknames, but only just. Considering all this Tonia and Andy took the news of Ann's pregnancy well. There was just one shaky fortnight when we didn't hear from them and I did think, here we go. I was amazed by how upset that made me. Not, of course, to the degree where I lay awake at night thinking we'd made a mistake, or wishing we had the friendship back instead of the child ahead. Then Andy called and said they'd still be our friends if we promised never to buy an SUV or use the sentence, 'We're pregnant.' The great surprise for me, when we first met, was that I liked him: it's difficult to get on with men in that everyday, intimate kind of a way. Andy refused to play most of the games, no posturing or point-scoring: he never engaged in (Ann again) that alpha shit and seemed hardly to notice it when a couple of silverbacks were grunting and wrestling on the floor in front of him. It's a curse to be a man with an ego these days, you've got to fight the war on so many fronts, and I've often been tempted to loosen my waistband and begin the slump into passive, feminised middle-age. But I am haunted by an essay of Orwell's in which he writes something like, most people feel like they are riding their own lives until they're about thirty, and then they give up, and succumb to the same predictable patterns of all the flabby no-hopers they've previously scorned. He puts it better than me, of course. But I'd managed to hit forty doing what I want or at least having the illusion that I did, and Orwell's theory has been the challenge that kept my courage to the sticking-place even when sweating over the lurid murder of another bloody co-ed virgin. Fuck him, I'm still hanging on.

★　★　★

Since Ann had confided in Tonia about my being given the flick I could legitimately see Andy for some sympathy beers without having to tell him myself. We met up in Hackney the next afternoon. Some kids hollered potential gaybashing abuse as we crossed the road towards the Lauriston, but Andy, a teacher, was used to brutal youth. I always felt safer around him. The pub was fairly empty; paranoid (unemployment will make you jumpy), I wondered whether the boys would follow us in. Without the usual drinkers you were able to see the big walls and the doorway, wide and ominous, but the place had a dress code — no baseball caps, no tracksuit tops — which was a comforting piece of paper. A beer calmed me down. After a brief exchange about the crappiness of the film world (tits-up, I told him) we didn't touch on my situation again. Andy likes to talk about the movies but only the ones he's seen. He is a Billy Wilder fan; he'd like life to be arranged like a Wilder film, tough and complicated but with the pure of heart winning through. It's one of his favourite words, heart, and things either have it or they don't. Tottenham are all heart; Chelsea have no heart. *Channel 4 News*, heart. *Newsnight*, heartless. Tennis, fishing, walking, all activities of the heart, in contrast to card playing, which is so devoid of heart it is an activity fit only for the dead. This caused the odd problem on our holidays, with me usually suggesting some four-handed 500 around evening two. Ann always cleaned up no matter who she was partnered with and that was OK because Ann had heart, she played with it, and Tonia too. On me the jury was — is — out.

He was tired, he said, and had a whiskey tic in one eye to prove it. A kid had come to school with a gun. A knife the year before had been bad enough; the gun was horrifying. The police were always there, people were keeping their kids home. Andy hated what he felt himself turning into: somebody who wanted to run away. He'd been like this before, his first couple of years in, gone to work shaking some days, waiting for the challenge he'd not be able to meet. But he had met them, all the different ways the kids had of fucking with your head, the silent treatment, the outright refusals, the laughter, the lies, he'd worked his way through and survived by staying the same. Consistency's the most important part of parenting, those infuriating, life-saving books say, though show me a parent who claims to be consistent and I'll show you a liar. Andy is, more than many people, ineffably himself, with his freckled beakiness and his heart. He should have gone into tertiary education but without ever saying so he felt drawn to teaching in crap schools. A Samaritan perhaps, or a masochist. There was one guy, he said, one fat fucker who was making life tough for him. Not a student, another teacher. Chippy as hell, convinced Andy talked down to him, always interfering, taking sides with the kids. He had nicknames for the nicely spoken teachers. Andy's was Lady Bountiful, so wrong it was brilliantly right. He's tall, with the unruly red cowlicks of a Norman Rockwell child, and massive hands and feet. If he were a woman he would have to be one of the incredibly posh and ugly sort. I, on the other hand, am bony and femme to start with, and it wouldn't take much to turn me into a purring minx straight out of Anaïs Nin. Sorry, not sure how I ended up here.

Andy seemed troubled by something more than the school complaints, but he wouldn't be drawn. Tonia was fine, his parents were fine, he was just tired. The beers felt good for us both. It wasn't long before we were on music and then Andy was rabbiting away to the soundtrack of obscure American college bands, those with heart and those who were nearly there but needed to evolve (I loved that phrase). He quoted lyrics, impersonated band members, delivered what seemed, since I didn't know the music, pithy and perfect analyses of song after song. It was a pleasure to bask in the glory of Andy's obsession, to be let off the hook of my life for a couple of hours.

When I got home the lights were on. I was a bit drunk, and knocked on the door instead of fumbling with my key. For what seemed a full minute I stood swaying slightly, staring at the chipped green paint, the brass knocker in the shape of a wolf's head, which we were meaning to replace; I knocked again, loudly. Footsteps sounded and Ann opened the door, hair wet, a towel clutched around her.

She looked at me — past me — and then

an odd thing happened. She shut the door. I was still outside. It took my fuggy brain a few seconds to register that she had slammed the door in my face. The wolf stared at me. I slowly blinked and like a cartoon character tried to shake the woolly feeling from my temples. I shoved around in my pockets for my key and jabbed it into the lock.

The house was warm after the cool autumn night. I called out for her. The unfinished, unpainted hallway was empty. There was a blur of motion as suddenly she rushed at me, pushing my shoulder.

'Bolt the door, bolt the door!'

'Why?'

Her fingers jabbed my shoulders, the towel slipping, her whole body white and shaking. 'It's him — didn't you see? Right behind you on the path.'

'Him? That guy?' I turned to open the door again to check.

She pulled me away, grabbing for the bolt chain. 'Don't do that!'

'Wasn't anyone behind me.' The path had been slippy with damp and leaves, the street yellowy dark in that London half-light way. There might have been someone behind me. I wasn't at all sure.

'I just saw him.' She was slightly calmer now the door was bolted.

I followed her into the front room, where she drew back the shutter, hiding behind it while she peeped out.

'Is anyone there?'

'No.' The shutter swung back into place. 'He's gone.'

Drinking during the day is never a good idea. I had drifted off on the bus back from the pub and now this hot panic from Ann made the ground drop away from under my feet. It was entirely possible I had been followed from the bus stop or the playground, I now thought, just as it was possible that Ann had seen nothing but a shadow and flipped out. Neither explained why she had shut the door in my face and left me out in the night, alone with the man.

After I'd gone round checking the locks on the windows I found Ann in her dressing gown, chopping onions at the bench in the kitchen. The room looked different. What had she done?

'Sorry about shutting the door,' she said before I could ask. 'That was stupid. I just freaked out.'

I hugged her. 'It's OK.'

'I feel so vulnerable,' she said, 'I think it's being pregnant. Fuck I want a cigarette.'

I coughed. 'You should have one.'

'No.'

We had agonised, when doing the place up, over what sort of kitchen to get. The cheapest was made by a company that had a long-running dispute with its workers — men had been on strike for years, families had cracked and fallen — and here we were with our food stored in their fitted cabinets, all in the name of a tight renovation budget and my inability to wield a hammer. Every time I put an expensive brand of pasta or extravagant bottle of wine in one of the cupboards I felt bad karma emanate from the shelves. Ann saw me looking around.

'I cleaned,' she said.

'I see.'

The doors were off the cupboards. Everything inside them was rearranged — glasses where flour and baking powder used to be, spices on the glasses shelf, stacks of tins in the wine rack and plates underneath the sink.

'It's better, don't you think?'

'Well — no, I don't get it.'

She slid the onions into a pan and stirred them around briskly. 'It's more practical.'

Ann thought she had left Australia long behind but she had that ruthless pragmatic streak and often managed to imply that we English were useless and effete, stuck blindly in pointless traditions such as doors on the kitchen cabinets and keeping pots and pans beneath the sink. The dismantled doors, apparently, were under the stairs, which seemed an appropriate place to keep my guilt. I went to look at them — I don't know why, to make sure they were there perhaps, still in harmless rectangle form, and hadn't arranged themselves into the shape of a pointing finger. Ann's hand had been on the cupboard here too: her toolkit was tidied, the coats hanging by colour, boxes of crap we had never unpacked stacked according to size. Something about all this order gave me a constricted feeling. I'd thought we were the types of people who didn't care about the neat edges of things, who understood mess and were not afraid of it.

'Are you sure you saw him?' I had to ask over dinner, a legitimate glass of wine in my hand. 'Are you really sure he was there?'

Ann sipped water. 'Yes.' Her expression was emphatic. 'Why would you doubt me? I don't understand why you would doubt me.'

'Sorry. You're right.' I felt terrible. Only some facts are known.

N.A.M.W. 03.07

They crash on to the large dark-wood bed, faces pale with travel against the crimson hibiscus-pattern cover. Ann feels weightless.

'I'm so tired,' she says.

'I want to fuck you,' says Tom. 'Take these off,' he says, tugging at her hot jeans, lifting the sticky shirt away from her stomach, his hand brushing her breasts. She peels off her jeans, her underwear, unbuttons the shirt, the creamy lei hanging over her naked body, and lies back down beside him, watching. He unbuttons his belt.

Her mind closes in on itself like a swarm of bees, warm, alive only to the humming friction, the heat, the thick grain of the linen underneath her bare legs, the smell of Tom. He pulls her up towards him, kissing her face before turning her over to fuck her from behind. 'Horny little bitch,' he says. She registers surprise at the pillow, as though it were a camera: the pornographic anonymity of the hotel room.

His eyes are closed; he pushes at her, lost, listening to the table fan, reaching to clutch at the thick auburn hair lying damp on the nape of her neck. A knock on the bure door. He pushes on in this foreign bedroom, eyes closed as he does it, one audible grunt escaping his throat before he rolls off her, rolls away, pads to the door. 'Yes?'

She lies watching him, her naked back exposed to the room, and stretches her arms above her head with satisfaction. Tom pulls a towel around his middle, opens the door and a porter stands there with their suitcase on a trolley beside him. The gesture of her nakedness feels like luxury. The door has not closed properly; a sliver of light. She loves Tom for bringing her with him.

Or not. Or, perhaps, this.

She lies watching him, her naked back exposed to the room. Wondering if he really didn't notice that she didn't come, wondering if it matters. Tom pulls a towel around his middle, opens the door and a porter stands there with their suitcase on a trolley beside him. In the shadow of the door it is hard to know whether the man has seen her. Tom scrapes the suitcase along the floor. Surely he will want to fuck her again, she is still here, smelling of crushed frangipani and sweat. The door has not closed properly; a sliver of light.

'It's the wrong kind of jack point,' he says, crouching down, looking at a skirting board, his voice tense. 'I've got to get an Internet link. Fuck!' he explodes, closing the bathroom door behind him. 'Always *something*.'

After a moment or two she exhales, gets up off the bed and walks slowly to the

unshut door, pushing at it until the snib
slides over, then locks, into the door frame
socket with a rattly click.

We decided there was no need to worry, we
promised each other in fact not to worry,
unless the man appeared to follow one of
us again. Ann agreed to phone me from
work if she was frightened and I would
come and pick her up. He was probably
harmless, we thought, just a care in the
community case who'd been out in the
weather too long.

With the second trimester hormones Ann's
mood soared. We fell into a honeymoon
dream, alive to our great luck, cherishing the
time together before the interloping child was
due. Although the meetings my agent had set
me up with had so far come to nothing, Ann
felt confident that a lucrative script-doctoring
job was just around the corner, and quite
happily ploughed through her wages to front
me. In the evenings I'd meet her at the
hospital after work and we'd take the bus into
town, go to a movie or to dinner, a late night
showing at the Tate, sometimes walking home
or taking gratuitous taxi rides along the river.
London that autumn was all red-and-yellow
neon signs in Chinatown, lacy rain, swirling
skies over the Thames, the pearl strings of

Embankment lights glowing through the night.

And sex, lots of sex. Not the dirty, fucked-up half-porn we were used to, I don't think either of us could have managed that while Ann was pregnant. We were self-conscious enough at the start. It had been over three months, the longest break' we had taken, and I know she'd discussed it with Tonia. For days, anyway, that was the last time either of us thought about the man or anyone else. At least I didn't; I can't speak for Ann obviously, only about her.

She looked more beautiful than ever in those weeks — wore her hair long and loose, instead of the usual falling-down knot at the back of her head. Her body lost its elbowy, gaunt aspect: even her lips took on a Pre-Raphaelite fullness, her eyes shone clear from drinking less alcohol, her skin was appley and sweet. But it wasn't as though she was morphing into a body-bound corn goddess with chaff in her head — her mind was sharp, quick — she could keep me up all night talking about sculpture, Jeff Koons or the Hepworth Museum or some other subject I had honestly no interest in whatsoever. Her fierce, almost feral, energy was too much to ignore. I'd wake in the morning to find another room reorganised, furniture shifted,

Ann on her knees behind the washing machine or scraping out the oven. The windows sparkled, the tiles in the fireplace shone. She was manic. She was fucking manic. I don't know why that word never occurred to me at the time.

And even as she became more vivid, more present, more her essential self (as I thought), she retreated from me too, the mystery of her core magnetically pulling everything into its dark unknowable space. How to describe it? She was, on the outside, larger than life — but inside she was shrinking.

Don't think I was analysing Ann's interior telescoping in any way as it happened. Why would I? We had our own house, we were in love, we were expecting a baby and this intoxicating surge of energy made us feel young. It was a golden time. Like all such times it didn't last. I'm a moron, OK? I didn't see it coming.

★   ★   ★

We had been to a play in Islington, something we would normally have run a mile from, a devised piece of physical drama with a lot of dry ice. I sat riveted, ideas for my otherwise stalled screenplay rushing towards me with arms outstretched. In the morning these would appear as ridiculous as the black-leotard performers we had thought so entrancing the night before, but we were still in the night before. Afterwards we found a Turkish place and sat at a low lamp-lit table eating mezze, a bottle of red wine between us. Ann was animated, one moment laughing about the earnest theatre buffs we had overheard during the interval, the next crying as she recalled a particular sequence from the play.

Just as suddenly, we were fighting. I had made a joke or a comment or something that was only meant as light teasing about her compatriots — look, we were in a café called Gallipoli, there were some backpacker types at the next table, I mean, come on. It was not a big deal. And she suddenly went nuts. She hissed in my face, called me a fucking English cunt, and stormed out. The connection line for the Switch payment broke down on the maître'd's first three attempts. Certain my card was about to be declined, I stormed back and forth between the cash desk and the street to look for Ann, inviting huffs about cold air from people sitting by the door I kept opening. By the time I had paid the bill and knocked back my wine and got into the street there was no sign of her. Some fat drunk bloke bellied into me and it was all I could do not to cuff his head. Instead I stood there twisting in the wind (come to think of it, exactly like a fucking English cunt), too embarrassed to call Ann's name. I walked a little way towards Highbury corner, then back towards Angel, increasingly annoyed. I rang her mobile phone before I remembered she still hadn't got it replaced after the derailment. And then — it still makes me shiver to remember it — just as I was thinking about the derailment, for the first time since it had happened, the man from the accident — Simon, *the television writer* — and his wife, the staring-eyed voodoo woman, crossed the street towards me. Perhaps it was the cast of the streetlights in the night but they looked unnaturally tall, lean and angled, like alien visitors alighting from a spacecraft. The first thing I felt, on seeing them, was dread.

They looked at me as though I was familiar but unknown. Stepping forwards I reminded them who I was, pretending to be shakier on their names than was the case. He found himself then and said, 'Of course, Tom *Stone*, of course, hi. How's the writing going?' I had to explain about having lost Ann, though didn't say we'd fought, stammering instead through some doubtless transparent story about money machines and different directions and neither of us having listened to the other. There was a moment when they both just stared in silence and I was glad of the darkness because I could feel myself blush. I never blush.

'Shall we wait with you?' Kate asked.

'No, God no. Please don't. Where are you off to?'

She nodded towards the tube station. Simon's phone trilled the theme tune from *EastEnders*.

'Sorry,' he said, looking at the caller ID then up to us both, no betrayal of smugness, master of his delight, 'LA.' He turned his back and wandered into the shelter of a doorway that I hoped might smell of wee, laughing Britishly and sounding conspiratorial, winning.

'How's all that going?' I asked, 'with your son? Is he all right, on the underground?'

She looked surprised. 'Oh yes. He never had any problems.'

I felt let down. 'Oh.'

'And Ann? How is she?'

'She's fine too. It wasn't that big a deal, I suppose.'

In the pause while I glanced again up and down the street for Ann, Simon began the ritual noises of signing off . . . did he really say 'old bean?' I looked sharply at Kate but her eyes were fixed on the ground. Her husband swaggered back to join us. 'Sorry about that.'

'I'd better get on,' I said, refusing him the pleasure of asking who that had been . . . Harvey? Ron? Steve?

'Jerry's people want me there for Monday,' he said in a low, serious voice to Kate that indicated the incredible fucking top-secretness, the cancer-curing aspects of his mission. 'I'm going to go pack. Maybe we should hail a taxi.' There he was, the jerk — super-English-guy for the Yanks, Mr America for us.

'But we've got our travelcards,' said Kate. She touched my arm, which had the entirely unexpected effect of making me want to touch hers. I restrained myself.

'Good luck,' she said. 'I hope you find her.'

'Nice to see you.'

They walked out of sight, arguing no doubt about her irrational need to save money. I looked back into the road for the black cab that miraculously appeared; Simon's black cab, I thought triumphantly as I threw myself right into the corner of the back seat, the pulse hard and fast in my throat. Lucky escape.

The sky got light after seven o'clock. I woke on the sofa, cold and sore. Around me the house felt dry and empty. In this place, so much bigger than our old flat, it was possible for someone to appear in a room without being heard. For the first time we had space, and solid walls. Out the door from the kitchen extension was a weed-covered garden, not deep but wide by London standards, like the house. Neither of us liked having anything to do with plants but we wanted the garden to look good; every evening Ann swore she would get out there, but so far she had not. We had only been here a few months. I loved the house on Daley Street with a passion that frightened me, an intensity I thought it was impossible to have for material things. It stood broad and square, rescued by us from dereliction, in a Hackney street of other houses similarly saved, or about to be saved. We were part of the generation that had decided not to care about crack dealers and gun crime in our neighbourhoods; it always seemed to happen to somebody else. Anything was worth putting up with for the sake of a piece of London, a postage stamp of earth, which was owned of course by the bank.

'Ann?' Nothing in the room had changed. I felt certain she was home. I walked up the stairs in my T-shirt and underpants and paused on the landing to rub pins and needles from my leg. I had no idea what I was going to say to her. Past the bathroom, my office, its closed door chiding me, *unproductive*, up the next flight to our bedroom at the top of the house. A chill draught blew over my skin — there was just time to register how cold it was up here — as I entered the room and saw that the four sash windows were wide open.

Ann lay on the bed, staring at the ceiling. In that second I remembered a comic book I'd been obsessed with as a boy. A devil spirit sucked out people's souls and left them lying in seedy Mexican pen-and-ink rooms, wearing not much and staring like this with their unblinking eyes straight ahead. The story went on in sinister fashion, involving a priest past his time and lots of long hair and crucifixes. I walked towards Ann. A shiny streak of tear ran down towards her hair. What on earth had we fought over? Where had she been?

A quick flash in my peripheral vision made me jump: my own reflection in the bedroom mirror. I crawled on to the bed and clutched her like a baby.

'I'm sorry,' she whispered.

'Me too,' I said.

We both fell back to sleep.

Downstairs later we made coffee and toast and talked too loudly and too laughingly in our relief. I told her about seeing Kate and

Ann confessed that she had spotted us, from the other side of the road, but been too ashamed to cross over. She'd felt sure I'd told them everything and couldn't face making up with me in their presence. 'There's something about that woman,' she said, 'that gives me the creeps.' I agreed. The peculiar amber of her eyes hadn't been as noticeable under the streetlights, but the taut skin of her face, almost like a mask surrounded by all that straight hair, left an uneasy impression. She seemed not like a real person but a carved icon. Perhaps this was how I had seen Ann at first, before I made her flesh and blood. No, Ann I had always been drawn to, had always wanted to touch — this other woman, Kate, frightened me, as though she were a primitive figure made of polished wood, hanging on the back of a door in a darkened room.

Ann had stood watching us from across the road and then lost sight of me — at the moment, I suppose, when I disappeared into a taxi. She thought she'd go to Tonia's in Borough, stay the night even, I could go fuck myself. So she walked down to the harsh fluorescent lights of Angel station and took a used travelcard from a guy wearing a filthy trench coat and with matted hair.

'Ann, Jesus.'

And on her way walking down the long,

long escalator somebody touched her shoulder and it was Simon.

'What do you mean?' I said. 'So you talked to them too?'

She nodded. 'I assumed they knew we'd fought so I said how embarrassed I was. They were confused. Then I realised you hadn't said anything, it was all a bit weird.'

'Great.' Exposed as a liar.

'They were going to King's Cross.'

So then they had stood in the halfway place between Ann's platform and theirs while Friday night types lurched past them to wait for trains. They'd talked about children in that way that people had started to do to us now. Simon, apparently, was very funny about childbirth and babies, and Kate was — as you could tell she would be just by looking at her — an enthusiastic advocate of natural birth. 'And I was still so *awake*, I felt like there was no sleep left in me ever. So when their train came first we were still talking about babies and childbirth and things, and we just kept talking.'

The milk had pooled in the centre of the coffee cup, a shrunken circle on the top. I swilled it out in the sink.

'It was odd, being underground with them, seeing as that's how Simon and I met. And oh, I realised then that their train had gone, I don't know how I let that happen, and I was mortified, so embarrassed, the next one wasn't for, like, fifteen minutes, and then mine came and he was in the middle of a sentence and I couldn't suddenly *go* right then, sorry you're talking now, bye!'

'You missed it.'

Ann giggled. 'Oh, Christ. Then I'm standing there, he's pausing like, are you going to? And I'm like, no, no, it's very interesting what you're saying . . . Oh. I've just remembered.'

'What?'

What they had been talking about. She had told Simon what had happened with Tranter. That I was looking for work.

'Ann, no.'

'He was lovely about it, he said you must call him, he gave me his card again . . . ' She left the kitchen while she was talking and stood in the hallway by the door, fishing in her shoulder bag . . . I let my head drop to the cool hard kitchen table, the thunk of which only slightly eased my humiliation . . . she was back in the room waggling his cards. 'Look, two! Really, darling, it was fine. Do you mind?'

'No. I'm just a loser.'

'Don't be ridiculous.'

One of the cards slid across the table into

my frame of view. 'Simon Wright'. A phone number. Nothing else, as though he hardly needed to outline his achievements, which naturally you would already know. He was shedding description and soon perhaps would reach the ranks of those known to the world only by a first name. *Simon. Simon.* His face on the cover of *GQ.* 'Simon says.' Ann interrupted my — what, obsessive thoughts?

'A train suddenly appeared, so I decided to take it with them to King's Cross, then get a cab from the rank.'

'OK . . . ' What did these people want? What was Ann doing?

They had had to stand — it was the last train of the night, packed and smelling nauseatingly of gin, tonic and fried food. It pulled into King's Cross station and Ann stood poised to get out, but the doors didn't open. There was a general groan. Through the scratched, greasy window Ann saw movement on the platform, figures pushing back and forwards. 'They're fighting,' she said.

Everyone within earshot craned to look. A loud crack as a man was pushed hard up against the carriage doors, facing the passengers inside. His attacker kept him pressed up there, holding his head to the door while he punched him in the kidneys from behind. Dull thuds came, sickeningly, through his body, through the door. Kate and Simon looked the other way, refusing to rubberneck. But Ann ducked her head beneath the crowded shoulders around her and watched.

She lowered her face to the kitchen table and said something muffled that I couldn't make out. When she came up for air she was laughing, like you do sometimes at bad news.

'It was him,' she said.

'Him?'

'The man, it was the man.'

'The guy from the playground?'

She nodded.

'But what did this guy look like?'

'I couldn't see clearly, the glass was so dirty, scratched.'

'Then how do you know? Ann, come on. A skinny guy in a hood? Identify him in a line-up?'

'I know,' she said. 'I know.'

'I mean, I can understand it wasn't a nice thing to see. But there is no way.'

She had stopped laughing. She nodded, and went to rinse her cup out at the sink. 'I know.'

The fighting men were dragged away out of sight and the carriage doors finally opened. Ann made hurried goodbyes to Simon and Kate and pushed her way through the oncoming passengers. Outside the station the queue for taxis was at least an hour long. She began the dark foul walk up Pentonville Road, steeling herself from street lamp to street lamp, trying hard not to keep looking behind. The mini-cab office smelled of stale cigarettes and musty carpet; she sat underneath the stark yellow light with nothing to read and wondered whether the man was the one who had been watching her or someone else.

'Why didn't you call me?'

Ann shook her head. She covered her eyes with her long pale fingers. In the loud, Saturday morning silence that followed, something smelled rank, sweet, like old fruit. A couple of softish apples sat in Ann's special blue and white earthenware bowl on the table. I tipped them into the bin at the end of the kitchen bench but even with the lid down, the smell stayed in the room.

* * *

Ann insisted she didn't mind doing blood tests alone, but I came along to the hospital for the diversion from my lack of a job. The nuchal fold test a few weeks earlier had been negative, or positive, or whatever it is when your baby has a decreased chance of Down's syndrome. This made us temporarily confident but she was still edgy because of being older, thirty-nine by the time the baby was due, even though she wasn't, pregnant at this age in these times, a circus freak. It was odd, she remarked, going to another hospital, the Homerton, all new brick oxblood and cream walls that gave an acidic feeling, so different from the rabbit warren dead-end lanes and grand stone of Barts. For the first few months in the radiation job she'd found it strange, voluntarily going to a hospital to work every day. It must have been how prison workers felt. Tonia had taken a job doing art therapy at Holloway, which she said was fulfilling though some of the women were so damaged it was like watching badly glued broken toys pull themselves around the place. Prison was murder but it was just as hard trying to imagine their survival on the outside. Nearly all of them, even the really hostile ones, came up at some point and asked her to help them. Help them with probation, help them once they were out. One girl was leaving soon and she was terrified, had nowhere to go, no place to sleep and they were trying to put her in a halfway house but she knew that would be the end of her. It was all Tonia could do not to invite her home. We wondered how she had managed it, to draw the line and stay on her side of it. Perhaps when you were doing something good it was easier to live with the stuff you didn't do as well. Christ, she walked into that place twice a week of her own volition.

'This is the thing,' Tonia emphasised. 'They've got stories to tell. Most of them pretty unbearable. You see the results. Personality disorders, self-harm, fire-setting. In *there*, for fuck's sake. Most of them shouldn't be.'

'Do you believe in prison?' Ann wondered.

'I don't know,' said Tonia. 'Maybe not.'

The hospital was a reminder of what women are expected to put up with once they're expectant mothers — like the pregnancy books that we scoffed at in bed, every sign, every brochure was geared for the retarded, accompanied by photographs of young women breastfeeding, imbecilic smiles plastered to their bovine faces. In the queue for reception we were eighth. The receptionist, tight blonde curls like wood shavings glued to her head, seemed slow on purpose. She disappeared behind a hessian screen. One heavy minute ticked by on the wall clock. Another. The woman at the front of the queue said loudly, 'I've been waiting an hour and three-quarters. I'm not used to being treated like this.' 'Go to the Portland then,' someone behind us muttered. Already there were three people behind us, no, four, we couldn't leave now, escape to the cafeteria, come back at a less busy time. There would never be a less busy time. In her hands Ann had the manila folder with her antenatal notes. She had read them in the car hoping for some revelation, an outsider's insight into herself, but they just contained a half page of ticks in boxes, meaningless groups of initials, 'FHH', 'no FMF', and the sentence, 'Mother in good health. Possible low blood pressure. Check again.' Mother? Was she a mother already? This was an exciting, legitimising thought. But she'd been pregnant before ... she wasn't a mother then. Five people ahead in the queue. Some of them enormous. Kids running up and down. Hospitals always felt dirty with the invisible spread of bacteria over handrails and doorknobs, the water-splattered toilets where they kept the bottles for urine samples, pale-blue paper hand-towels mulching away on the grimy floor. In this room, the antenatal waiting area, the carpet was striated with tidal marks of trodden-in street dirt. Where Ann had grown up it was scungy but not dirty. There was a distinction.

What did this scrawl mean? Ann looked at her file again. Yes. A note of past pregnancies.

The shorthand couldn't encapsulate the accident at fifteen, one week into her sex life, with a part-time boyfriend and a broken condom. Getting through the psychological questionnaire that would allow the abortion, worse than the hormone sickness, the anxiety about her father and step-mother finding out. The thudding loudness of her brothers playing basketball against the wall of the next-door room. Her part-time boyfriend scarpering and finally, after waiting five fearful and unhappy weeks from when she'd first figured it out, the procedure. Termination, procedure, operation — these were the words Ann chose, and who could blame her.

Three of them, she went through, in her free fall. And the third and final time she sat so alone with her troubles in that suburban Sydney room and there was I, at the same date down to the year and month, riding a train to my grandfather's deathbed and thinking I was seeing it all, becoming a man at last. What would I have done, had a magic mirror showed Ann lying on her candlewick bedspread, staring at the ceiling like the possessed woman in the comic strip, large tears sliding from the edges of her eyes down into the hair at her temples? I'd have flung open the door to her father's house, wouldn't have knocked, there he goes, there goes Tom, pushing through the open plan living room, television tuned to daytime soap, past the step-mother with a cup of instant coffee in her hand, her mouth a ridiculous O, into the room with the posters of American teen idols Blu-Tacked to the walls. Then what? Tom?

The woman taking her blood didn't look at Ann once, not at her face, just at the labels on the sample bottles and at her proffered arm. Maybe she looked at the raised zigzag that was Ann's lightning bolt scar, half visible under her pushed-up sleeve, the end of it lumpy and blurred as though a knife or whatever made the scar had slipped. The tourniquet went round Ann's bicep; she clenched her fist without being asked. The clinician ran a gentle finger over another, finer scar mark that ran up towards Ann's elbow.

'Hmn?' she said, not really requiring an answer.

'Yeah, I don't know what that's from,' said Ann. One, two, three tubes, the colour so rich and surprising, almost black, and back in the queue to make the next appointment, a white neat plaster in the crook of her elbow.

Next Ann arranged herself on the examination bed and the student midwife squeezed clear jelly on to the baby bump, then pushed some kind of microphone device around on it. The pop and crackle of a sound system firing up, then a pulse, thick and underwater-heavy, like listening to one of those whale sounds tapes, only good.

'Wow.' I gripped Ann's hand: she'd craned her neck forwards to see what the student was doing, and beamed at me over her double chin.

'No,' said the midwife in charge, 'that's *your* blood.' The student looked at her, uncertain. 'Keep going.'

My upper lip had gone cold at the word 'no'. Round and round Ann's belly swept the sensor device, pushing in at the sides, under the bump until she grunted with discomfort, collecting and transmitting no sound other than the swooshing, regular wave-break of Ann's own blood. Nothing else.

'How many weeks are you?' asked the senior midwife.

'Seventeen,' Ann whispered. The midwife hummed. The student's jaw was set with fear and her eyes were pebbly, rigid as she concentrated. One of those fair women whose skin blotches under stress. A large patch of red welled upwards from the collar of her shirt. Fiercely I hated this airless place, its potential for bad news. The older midwife was asking Ann when she had last felt the baby moving.

'I don't know.' Ann still could not speak above a whisper. She was trying, I knew, to keep her voice from breaking.

'Don't worry, baby's just hiding. Sorry, when did you last feel it move?'

Was she not listening? Ann's head rolled from side to side. 'I don't know, I don't remember.'

I fixed my eyes on the microphone, willing it to pick up the baby's heartbeat. Instead it stopped moving. The trainee looked at her superior and shook her head. 'Sorry,' she said.

As soon as the more experienced midwife took control of the thing we heard it: a fast little tick-a-tock sound, much lighter and quicker than the other. Ann laughed. 'There he is!' The midwife smiled expansively, as though she herself had conjured our baby into life. Afterwards, as Ann was queuing to make her next appointment, I pretended to have left some papers in the examination room and found that midwife in the small corridor, talking to an Asian man in a suit whom I presumed was a doctor. Waiting for them to finish I pretended to read the incomprehensible codes on a whiteboard, and skimmed the posters exhorting grown women to breastfeed, stop smoking, eat their greens, et cetera. The previous week I had been climbing the stairs at home when a paperback sailed out of our bedroom doorway and thwocked me in the side of the head. It was a best-seller on pregnancy and motherhood, and Ann had got to the reminder about the importance of washing hands before she'd had, in her words, just about fucking well enough. The midwife came free, and I stopped her as she began to walk away. Her face was so busy it had gone way beyond curiosity; perhaps news of a terrorist plane heading for the hospital would have mildly piqued her interest; anything less, including my gnat-like presence, was simply to be endured. In a way I rather fancied this manner — it reminded me of Bridget. Or my mother. Help.

'Excuse me,' I said, apologising for being about to lay into her, 'but was that really necessary, before?'

'Was what necessary?'

'Letting it go on so long, that palaver with the student midwife. I know they have to learn but couldn't you see we were very upset? That it seemed as if there was no heartbeat?'

She came into focus and looked at me, not without sympathy, and said, 'But we weren't waiting very long at all.'

I was nonplussed. 'We weren't?'

'It was a matter of seconds. I'm sorry if it felt too long. Even with an experienced midwife it can take some time, if the baby's in the wrong position.'

'Wrong?'

'Not wrong, just — lying quite far back, hard to get to.'

'Oh I see.'

'Was there anything else?' Now she gave the appearance of really studying me, as though there might be something else, something I wasn't aware of.

'No.'

* * *

My Switch card was finally declined at Tesco. We'd already booked and paid for a weekend break in Whitstable. That was how things were.

* * *

The Kent coast was rough, dark grey, and the Whitstable harbour creaked with salt and rust. The car had made the hourlong trip without dying, for which we were grateful. I was always surprised to see the car in one piece; it wouldn't be long before it sat battered in the street one morning in a glittering of windscreen, East End hail around the tyres. If it survived the Whitstable public car park I would give it a medal.

We walked and walked that day, round the coast path, along the sea wall, past fishing boats and gravel tractors and beach huts. The wind was too cold and loud for talking. This was a relief. Ann grew tired and we returned to the town for mugs of tea; I ate brown bread and oyster after oyster while she picked at cod and chips. Her energy levels, which had been so buoyant and vital of late, were back to normal again, or less than normal. She seemed reduced.

In the bed and breakfast that night we lay down, our hair thick and greased with salt, our lips chafed, on the soft patchwork bed. I reached for Ann but she rolled on to her side and said she was exhausted. 'Sorry,' she said, which I remember hating. 'Fuck sorry,' the old me would have answered, but I had already begun treating her with kid gloves. I lay listening to the insistent clank of a fishing boat's winch and to the sounds of Saturday diners having their night out downstairs, waves of laughter, occasional raised voices. The sea wind looped and groaned outside the building like the villain in a horror movie. Ann would never leave me, I thought. A simple unfinished sentence like that.

The first holiday we ever went on together was to Italy. London had laid on a particularly biting winter, and come late March the days of sleet and little money were wearing Ann down. Sculptures usually littered the floor of her Clerkenwell flat, cloth rabbits and whittled sticks, small creatures with blind eyes that multiplied until a swag of them were given away or exhibited in one of the thrown-together group shows Ann and her art school friends subsisted on. Now she had ceased production. The talismans dwindled in number until only a favoured few were left. It was because she was in love, she told me half jokingly, half angry, she had no spare time any more, no sexual frustration to work through in muslin and kapok and infuriatingly small black buttons. We lay in bed all weekend long until that tipped over from indulgent to depressing. Ann went silent. I took the money my parents had given me at Christmas time and booked us flights to Rome, where neither of us had been before.

It was difficult to believe that this balmy, happy world was only a couple of hours away from home. Dazed, we wandered under cartoon-like umbrella pines, sun loosening our shoulders, golden dust in the dirt paths that wound around the park towards the next gelato. All food, all drink tasted as though it had been spiked. This perhaps was heroin (Ann would know; I was embarrassed to ask her), colours washed to a vibrating brightness, wave after wave of perfumed air, each scent, coffee or garlic or car exhaust swooningly rich. The scale of Rome's buildings, the aggression of the scooters at your heels, the gobbledegook of the language which I had made no attempt to learn: all of these things floored me. Our room in the Campo dei Fiori overlooked the flower sellers by day and provided front-row seats to the bacchanalia of the local youth by night.

The first night we drank three bottles of red wine at dinner, the house Chianti because it was too hard to order anything else. I asked for what I thought was lamb and was served fish, or perhaps fishy lamb; my head was swimming, it was hard to be sure. The hotel, which we had found in a guide allegedly published for the cash-strapped but fearfully chic, was a pit with an orange candlewick bedspread, rough sheets and things sinister in the fuzzy bathroom grouting. There was no hook for the shower nozzle; you had to hold it with one hand while you washed, presumably to save on the hotel's water. Remembering Bridget's disdain for unthinking design ('it's greed, sheer greed') and the way it could taint an entire week abroad I braced myself ('*Yes* I want you to go down to reception and ask for another room'), but Ann was enchanted by the ivy outside the window that opened on to the Campo and effusive, even before the red wine, about everything she saw. How easy, how relaxed she was! I revelled in the comparison. ('Well don't *suggest* it if you don't want to do it. Oh, for God's *sake* I'll go.') After the fish-lamb dinner we passed out on to the cheap mattress, I don't remember even walking up the stairs. Then one of those jangly sleeps with too much tannin and sugar in my bloodstream, a running commentary of the day's new images flickering behind my eyes. My heart clenched, as with panic. In the morning Ann wanted to make love, but I was too ill. The next night she wanted to make love, but I was too tired. And the next night, and the next. By day we wandered like children in history and by night we lay in bed not touching each other, but not innocent; I was mortified and after a few days Ann, thank God, stopped being understanding. Perhaps I wasn't the first Englishman to be castrated by that city, but it was hard not to hate Rome. Ann looked exquisite, her hair shining auburn in the sunlight, her breasts beneath a fitted white blouse drawing frank stares of admiration from the local *garçons* or whatever they were called. What am I saying, of course I hated Rome, it was fucking my woman every time we stepped out the door and there was nothing I could do apart from shepherd her into another churchyard, tucking a cardigan modestly across her shoulders, making sure the hem of her skirt was demure. My jealousy rendered me impotent. Ann plied me with alcohol and walked round the small hotel room in nothing but her knickers, lounging in the brown speckled armchair swirling wine in bored come-on circles in her glass. I looked out the window. Paced. Cut myself shaving. Despaired, in the tawny light of another perfect Roman day, that I was so hidebound by my British fuckwittedness that I was going to lose Ann. That's right, I imagined her saying in years to come, that guy Tom Stone . . . fine till you get him on to foreign soil . . . Finally, on the last night of our holiday, we found a little bistro in Trastevere, a place with no concession to romance under the strip lights or on the menu. The old dwarfess who ran the place seemed instantly to glean that we were lovers in trouble. The menu offered only two dishes. Once we had chosen, the wizened *Señora* handed Ann the carafe of wine and indicated that she should pour me a glass. She was led up two steps into the small kitchen where she was handed a plate and given to understand that it was for me. She filled it from the high saucepan on the stove. The woman nodded again in my direction and Ann carried it carefully down the stairs. At the table she placed the dish gently in front of me and smiled. I smiled back, and felt an unexpected softening inside, a breath out, a surrender. The woman was at Ann's arm. She tugged her sleeve: and now you serve yourself. But I stood, despite protesting croaks in Italian that we didn't understand. I pulled Ann's chair out for her to sit in, took her plate to the kitchen and served her, and wish I was serving her now, still, bringing food for her, and drink, brushing out her long, long hair as I did that night in Rome, finally, the soft streams of it on our hotel room bed. The noise of boys and girls out in the dark square with their cigarettes, their night-time sunglasses, their crazy traditions and their youth was the background to our hot slow kissing, to the hum between my fingers and Ann's skin.

Ann's skin, Ann in Rome, in London, in Whitstable that last winter . . . Ann beside me in the bed and breakfast, sleeping. The lavender smell of her hand cream, the way her red hair looked dark in the darkness, the ripe curve of her hips, that yowling wind, so loud above the sound of her breathing. And I didn't know anything there, didn't know fuck, didn't even know just to stop and take it all in. My mind got busy on the problems with my script, the final, contract-ending draft of which I was meant to deliver to Rosemary the abortionist, as I had come to think of her, at the end of the week. 'We'll pay you for this draft,' Tranter had said, before letting me down, and it was the wretched hope that Rose could still be won over, decide to keep this fledgeling project, that made me determined to deliver her a knock-out. From these thoughts ballooned the money night-mare we were returning to in London, and the slow eliminations of possible sources of income. There were two people left I could beg for a job. Simon Wright was one of them, and I would rather have eaten off my hand before picking up the phone to make that call. The other one was Hallie. The Thames would have to be on fire before I would consider that.

* * *

Ann and I drove back from Whitstable in silence. We listened to music but didn't speak. I started a lot of conversations in my head but abandoned them one by one for being too confrontational in tone, and suspected Ann

95

was doing the same thing. Without knowing how, we'd arrived somewhere that was impossible to talk about. And, as the garish reindeer and holly lights strung around the shopping streets of East London reminded me, Christmas loomed. The combination — my empty bank account, Christmas and lengthy silences — sent me into a quiet panic.

My parents had invited us to join them in Wiltshire, where they retired to die several years ago. My father has long practice at filling holiday silences with his particular stream of consciousness. 'I'm going to make a cup of tea, who'd like a cup of tea, no don't get up, look there's a robin in the garden I said look Stella there's a robin in the garden, you wouldn't believe the bird-life we've had this year, global warming, monkeys and banana palms soon, now I'm just putting the kettle on and — oh — where were my — there they are — Ann would you like a biscuit there's nothing to you, are you sure?' The ease with which I embody him alarms me. My mother less so: she brings to mind the word imperious. If she had pince-nez she would peer over them. As she has aged, her body, her hair, even her features have thickened and settled, become emphatic. There is never a whisper of self-doubt. She suffers more than my father from being buried in the countryside. Where once he had been, if not a Londoner, at least a suburbanite (I grew up in Barnes), he has now become an Englishman. He has his birds, and a hitherto un-guessed-at talent for the rustic that bobbed up on his retirement: genuine pleasure in the changing weather, the mud and skies that instil in me nothing but agoraphobia. (Although I have, since that Christmas, had cause to be grateful for their isolation, and for the breadth of those skies, and the solitary places in the blessedly deaf woods.)

Some weeks earlier we had taken a deep breath and told them our baby news. They were delighted at getting any return on their measly investment of one child. Dad came over all quivery on the speakerphone. Then he made the mistake of asking Ann whether she was going to leave her job. 'I don't think so,' she'd laughed, and we could hear my mother in the background saying, 'John, you really are ridiculous,' in the same voice she uses to comment on him beyond his earshot, watching him, say, as he grunted with the effort of extracting their suitcases from the car boot that Christmas: 'Look at his bandy little legs. He walks extra fast to make them appear longer, but it doesn't make any difference.' She took the phone from him.

'Ann. Now listen. You too, Tom. You're not going to go in for one of these ludicrous home births. They're terribly dangerous.'

I began to back out of the room. I wanted the birth to be a sterile, white-sheeted affair if at all possible.

'No, Mum, I'm going to hospital.'

To me my mother was Stella, had been ever since I went to school, but Ann, in her colonial over-familiarity, called her Mum. We saw them maybe three times a year at most.

That winter I did not relish the thought of being snowbound in the middle of nowhere with Ann and her hormonal mood swings and my parents and my unemployment. If we went to Wiltshire would she begin shifting their furniture at midnight too? I had a vision of my parents' living room put together like an anagram of itself, dark rectangles on the wall where the watercolours had hung, the rugs pulled up, sofas pushed against the wall as though a space was cleared for dancing. Ann in the middle of the room alone, moving intently, rhythmically to silent music, to music only she could hear.

★ ★ ★

We stood on the down escalators, undergoing the long descent at Angel. Christmas shopping weighted our plastic carrier bags like platinum bricks, and it felt like I was carrying my flayed credit card just behind my eyes. Our free hands were clasped together in wordless acknowledgement of that last, stupid fight we'd had near here at the Turkish place, making our peace with it. A matted busker sat cross-legged at the foot of the escalator playing on one of those long pipe things, a didgeridoo or, to give it its correct name, a didgeridon't. The space filled with that objectionable low brewing sound, something rolling pointlessly round and round the bottom of a large bowl. A never-ending grumble from the bottom of the earth, maybe all right in the desert but not played by some smelly white boy here, it served the same purpose to my ears as the moan of bagpipes. I told Ann this theory — the revenge of the colonies, inflicting their music of complaint on the blameless English commuter. Her fingers grew stiff and tight in my hand and she began talking very loudly; I don't remember now what she was saying, only that it was from nowhere, irrelevant thoughts, punched out brightly like brass notes against the hot insistence of the Aboriginal pipe. She was trying to block the other sound out — I knew it then — she wanted to hear that menacing noise even less than I.

The question of Christmas had been solved, if you could call it a solution, by inviting my parents to stay with us. They were driving up on the twenty-fourth and had strict instructions to leave after Boxing Day. Perhaps it was because she was pregnant that Christmas suddenly meant more to Ann than usual. Traditionally we both merely tolerated the festive season; now she embraced it with a fever. The lassitude of only days before had left, her mood had spun right round, she was everywhere in the house at once, her voice piping higher than usual, dabbing away at things, busy. Fruit had been soaked, cakes baked, mince pies assembled. Decorations littered every conceivable surface, the house smelled of cloves and oranges, we were living in the window of a Dickensian department store. It wasn't until my mother arrived on Christmas Eve, bearing boxloads of presents for the unborn child, that I realised Ann's fervour even had a theme: 'A Victorian Christmas!' Stella exclaimed, eyes glowing with approval. 'Ann, how lovely.'

That night Ann and I sat up long after my parents had gone to bed. She had lit the fire and kneeled by it now, her long white hands smudged with soot, the velvet of her skirt spreading thick and crimson on the dark floorboards beneath her. It was the calmest moment we had shared in days. From where I sat on the sofa her pregnancy wasn't visible. She could have been the ghost of Janey Morris in a timeless London room. And then I saw Ann as she must once have been: sunburned, freckled, her hair starched with sea-salt, bare knees raw and chapped.

'Yeah?' she said, grinning. 'What do you know about it?'

'Did I say that out loud?' I was startled.

'Say what out loud?'

'What I was just thinking. You're fucking with me.'

'What were you just thinking?'

'Ah, nothing.' She was giving me a look, I knew what it was getting at, but the wine, the hour, the quite honestly castrating presence of my parents a floor away in the spare room, I don't know. I wanted to go to bed, but not in that way.

We were halfway through Christmas morning before anything went wrong. We'd all, under Stella's instructions, listened reverently to the latest adolescent opera sensation singing a few of the cheesier Anglican hymns: 'Jerusalem', 'Abide with Me' ('Feel like I'm at the FA cup final,' I whispered to Dad, who shouted, 'What?') and rounding off with 'Amazing Grace'. 'Once blind, but now I see . . . ' Ann closed her eyes

... was she nodding off? No, she was weeping, tears sliding out from her closed lids. Such sentimentality! I thought. But the hormones were doing that to her — these days she could cry at a television advertisement for loo roll. 'OK that's great,' I announced once the CD was finished, 'now I've got to make dinner.' Stella lounged on the sofa in the front room reading the novel I had given her; her short barking laugh of approval punctuated the air from time to time. My father and I were on KP duty, nubbling the ends off sprouts and peeling potatoes. Ann said she was tired and needed a rest, she hadn't been sleeping. Was there an accusation somewhere in this, I wondered, she had been kept awake not by sex but by frustration? She disappeared upstairs for some while; eventually I called to her, 'When do you want me to check the turkey?' which was English for, 'Get the fuck down here, I am drowning of boredom hearing about Dad's runner beans.' No response came. While I waited for one I checked the turkey anyway. Juice ran from its thigh, still pink with blood.

'What shall I start on now?' said Dad.

'Go and put your feet up, read a book.' Stella's 'hah!' came from the living room. 'If you can concentrate.'

The bandy-legged comment had predisposed me towards my father. We share a physique. My legs, doubtless, will go the same way.

He left, I sharpened the carving knife, and suddenly she was in the doorway. It felt like there had been a jump in time. I shivered.

She said, in her bright high voice of that Christmas, 'We don't need to set an extra place. He isn't coming down.'

'Who?'

'Him, I've asked him but he isn't coming down.' She spoke speedily, impatiently, as though I were an idiot.

A horrible streak of adrenalin shot through me. 'There's no one upstairs.'

'He's busy.' She met my eye. 'He's busy writing down everything we do and say.'

'Ann, you're freaking me out.' I reached behind her to shut the kitchen door. It seems terrible to admit but I was more worried about what my parents might think, in that vertiginous minute, than what was happening. Stella was likely to send us to the hospital. Accident and Emergency on Christmas Day. Was this an accident? An emergency? These were the thoughts that fired through me, badly aimed arrows, as Ann and I stood frozen. 'There's no one upstairs,' I said again. 'Have you been asleep?' Was she sleepwalking now?

Her eyes flickered. 'There's no one upstairs.'

I shook my head no. But was there? We slept with the bedroom window open, even in winter — had the man . . . ? Oh, for fuck's sake we were throwing madness back and forth between each other like a hot roast potato. Ann looked unconvinced. 'Let's go,' I said firmly, 'and see.' It was very important to break the spell, to confront Ann with the empty reality of upstairs; I steered her out of the kitchen by the elbow.

I pushed her up the stairs. No room here for creeping horror movie dread. She stumbled as I stomped and huffed behind her, overtaking her on the last flight of stairs to fling open the door to our bedroom. 'You see? Nothing there.' But she was not behind me. I found her back on the middle floor, staring at the closed door of my office, arms limply by her side.

'He was in there,' she said.

'Here?' The door swung halfway open, then hit something and juddered, stuck. I peered round it. 'There's no room.' Papers, computer, teetering, dust-stroked piles of books, the Perspex model of Ann's head, filing cabinet drawers stuffed open, boxes of film magazines — there was barely space to sit down.

'He was in the corner,' Ann said. 'With his back to the room. Taking notes.'

'In real life, or in your dream?'

She considered this, helpless. 'In my dream?' The upward inflection of Australian accents, everything an uncertainty, a question. We would not talk about this any more. It was ridiculous. I drew her back on to the landing and closed my study door.

'Now. Do you think this is a good enough excuse to send my parents packing?'

A note of relief sounded when she laughed. 'Don't say anything to them.' And quickly, 'I wish it was just us.' She clonked her head down on to my chest and gave a sort of self-directed growl. 'I wasn't going to say that.'

'You got the short straw on the in-laws.'

We kissed. The bump was pushing me further away every day. 'Should we make an appointment with the doctor? Get you a little electroshock therapy?'

She laughed and made a 'lunatic' face by sticking her bottom lip out with her tongue. 'I should get more sleep.'

We were better together after that, my parents the tangible common enemy. The sight of Ann across the Christmas table, the pink paper crown skew-whiff on her red hair, sent a swell of admiration rising in me. So what if she had acid flashbacks or low blood pressure or whatever might have caused this waking dream? She had chosen me, who for all my attempts at urbanity — here I went, collapsing time myself — was the child of this stolid respectable English couple, passing pickled walnuts around the table, so undoubting, so certain of the parameters of their universe, where normality began and ended. Anyone who lived outside of that zone was a freak, not that they would use that word. 'Different' was enough to imply distrust, contingency and doubt. I was different. Ann's love for me proved it.

The little episode was not mentioned again. We waved goodbye to the Citroën on Boxing Day afternoon with relief, leaning into a kiss as soon as the car disappeared, staying close, loving the comforting smell of each other, the emptiness of the street around us.

N.A.M.W. 04.07
She walks up the dusty street following the sound of a choir singing 'Amazing Grace'. Past a peacock-tiled mosque she comes to a white wooden church, small, its peaked roof unusual here. Ann stands outside the door in the sunlight, her hat in her hands, eyes straining to see inside the dark body of the church. Women stand in rows beneath its

ribs, singing. In front of them a man waves his arms. There are maybe a dozen women in there but it sounds like a cathedral-full.

Tom has spent the two days in Nadi doing research interviews. Everyone he speaks to — shopkeepers, hoteliers, police-men — has different opinions about the coup but it has made all of them poorer. Ann slept off her jet lag in the room with lizards on the ceiling. She swims in the hotel pool and walks the ramshackle shop-ping streets picking up souvenirs and putting them back again. Long-bodied dogs, some with only three legs or broken tails, trot down the middle of the street. On the edges of town chickens roam free.

'Hallie thinks there isn't any point,' Tom tells her, 'in getting into the human reaction. He wants goodies and baddies. Pow pow.' Tomorrow's resort is where, during the 2000 coup, some locals landed on the beach wielding machetes and took the guests and owner hostage for twenty-four hours. Every-one was rescued by a passing cruise ship; no blood was spilled on the sand.

But Hallie wants blood. He wants a visit-ing American hero trying to save his marriage with one last holiday, taking out the evil Fijian Indian businessmen (who are behind it all, in cahoots with evil British businessmen, masterminding the unknowing native pawns from their evil corporate head-quarters) with the help of a trusty Fijian guide who is to be DBTA. Ann has been with Tom for long enough now to know that that means Dead By the Third Act. It all seemed so hilariously pop and fun, this idea, in London. Now that they're here it is differ-ent. She shuts her eyes, her dress sticking under her arms in the humidity, listens to the women sing and wishes she and Tom had come alone, that they're not meeting up with this person Hallie on the island, that they had paid for this themselves.

The misty feeling of being in a fairy tale was palpable the night I called Simon Wright. In the limbo season between Christmas and New Year anything seems possible. It was certainly possible for the utility companies to keep billing us. Red letters from BT, Thames Water and EDF were magneted to the fridge. Although a constant stream of money out was required, money in was a dry spring. I'd delivered to Rosemary as promised and the final payment from Whirlwind had cleared my credit card. Ann was finishing work in April, when she would go on half-pay for six months. They'd hold the job open for another six. We were awed by our ignorance as we prepared to become parents. There was no way of knowing how Ann would feel about returning to work. Where would we want the baby to sleep? How long would she breastfeed for? Would we be groovy laid-back positively reinforcing parents, or nervous wrecks who lined our house with cotton wool? Who knew? That first pregnancy is a long sea journey to a country where you don't know the language, where land is in sight for such a long time that after a while it's just the horizon — and then one day birds wheel over that dark shape and it's suddenly close, and all you can do is hope like hell that you've had the right shots. Nothing was certain. Life was tight enough on Ann's income alone. Interest rates had been raised a quarter per cent, Happy Christmas from the Bank of England, and the mortgage had jumped. In December I had been to six meetings, delivered six pitches for each of my three ideas, toughed out as many humiliating Christmas parties as I could (no heart, office parties, Andy always said, but all right if you want to get laid), worked on plotting out the most commercial of the pitches. Surely someone would bite.

The stairs creaked as Ann descended. They were still unpainted. The hallway was mottled where we had torn down the wallpaper without replacing it. Here in the kitchen the cupboards bore marks of Ann's latest efforts, the doors refitted because she was sick of seeing the contents. Outside darkness gently concealed the cracked, weedy mess that was the tiny back garden.

'The cistern's leaking again.'

'That guy hasn't called me back.' A cheapo plumber, botched job, an unanswered mobile phone. London. In the window Ann was reflected on to the night, a white towel around her body and another towering on her head in a turban. Since the twenty-week scan she'd begun to look really pregnant, as though the magical visions of the ultrasound wand had drawn her belly forwards, changing its shape.

'What did you say to him?'

'Left a message for him to call me.'

'Did you say the cistern is leaking all over the floor?'

'I told him to call me.'

'Right.'

'Ann, what?' I twisted my neck to look at her in the flesh, not in reflection. A pillar of white. 'What do you want me to do?'

She exhaled and looked away. 'I'm going to bed.'

Simon's card was also on the fridge, half hidden beneath the final demand from BT. I steeled myself.

Kate answered the phone. Her voice was warm, woody, evoking that otherworldliness of hers, carved deep into the prosaic clog-wearing uprightness. If she was surprised to hear from me she didn't let on; she knew who I was immediately. Even as we mouthed clichés about Christmas I was tempted to abort the call. What did she think of me, this man phoning in the darkness at the loneliest time of the year?

'Do you have any plans for New Year's Eve?' The words came out of my mouth all wrong — it was meant to be a light time-passing question, greasing the wheels, keeping them spinning until the natural pause when I could ask to speak to Simon. It sounded desperate.

'Actually we're having a party.' The worst possible response. Silently I begged her not to invite us, to allow me the dignity of having plans.

'I just wondered if Simon was there,' I said.

'He's got some people here.'

'You've got people, I'm sorry.' My body kept tipping forwards, one of those nodding wooden birds, in my need to hang up. 'I'll call another time.'

'Well, what about New Year? Would you like to come?' Not, 'Are you free?' or, 'We'd love it if you and Ann could make it.' We're busy, I should have said, we've got *people*, we've got plans. Instead I fumbled churlishly through a series of ums and ahs, I don't knows and I'll have to checks. She cut across me. 'You could talk to Simon then.'

'No I don't think so, it's a work thing, look, yes thanks, we'd love to come to your party. If you're sure.'

Her laughter was light, relieved. This psycho conversation was coming to an end. 'Of course. I'll get Simon to call you before then.'

How sad were we, to see in the New Year with a bunch of people we didn't know. Andy and Tonia could not understand us and offered to break their rule of spending New Year alone together. But Ann liked the idea of revisiting Kate and Simon's house. Or maybe she just wanted to reinforce how pleased she was with me for having phoned Simon.

★ ★ ★

Their house was larger than I remembered, even with a hundred people in it. Kate and Simon were popular. Some of the guests were familiar to me — a director or two, a handful of television actors — a social coup, getting this lot on one of the biggest nights of the year. The rest had the feverish look of parents

112

who hadn't been out of the house for months. The cumulative babysitting fees from the kitchen alone probably ran to a thousand pounds. Simon had greeted us at the door. He hadn't phoned me back, and was all *mein Host* effusion and apologies. He'd call me tomorrow, he definitely would. No hurry, I said, looking him square in the eye. Whenever you're back at work. He took the proffered bottle of fizz and led us through the crowded hall and to that room the four of us had sat in nearly three months earlier when he made us coffee. Crushed in close behind him, I realised that the smell enmeshed with his hair and clothes, dull on the previous times we'd met, was cigarettes, chemicals and ash. Now it had a sharp, recent edge, as though the secret smoker had been dragging down a chain of final addicted puffs before the year turned. The urge for a cigarette stabbed me. He quickly palmed us off on a pale, sickly looking couple who were clearly at a loose end, grabbed a bottle of wine in each hand and topped up people's glasses as he moved towards the living room.

We were stuck with the boring couple for a good fifteen minutes and I began to worry that the stain of their inadequacy would rub off on us if enough people saw us with them. Ann abandoned ship first — she was adept at that — by claiming, pregnantly, that she needed to find the bathroom. We limped through another ninety seconds about the neighbourhood (the duration reported accurately here because I was studying the clock on the kitchen wall). Of course they were Kate's neighbours, these were not the sorts of people anyone had as friends. Blond wispy gluten-and-lactose intolerant angry non-voters. I asked about schools in the neighbourhood and wanted to slash my throat open with a cheese-knife. 'We're home-schoolers.' The boring man drained his glass and said as though he'd noticed a rare and fascinating insect on his shirt front that he was going to get more wine and his boring wife hastily said she would go too and I was left stranded, as if it was I who was the kiss of social death. The situation was all the more hopeless because I had just finished my drink and was gasping for a fresh one but couldn't run the risk of appearing to follow them to the bar and being shaken off again.

Which is how I ended up in Simon's study. I went looking for Ann. The loo under the stairs had a small queue and I waited until a man came out. No sign of her. A teenager who must have been hired for the purpose, with spotted cheeks and shaking hands, was pouring drinks in the doorway to the front room. I inserted myself in front of some-body's outstretched glass and got the refill I so badly needed, without making any new friends. Another aproned teen came towards me with a full bottle and I prised it from him, saying, 'Let me do that for you,' splashed meagre amounts into the glasses of two people sitting on the stairs and climbed over them towards sanctuary and Ann.

Only Ann was not about. There was a room off the landing that played host to a sewing machine and dressmaker's dummy. Of course Kate would make her own clothes, no matter how much wealth her husband accrued, and probably her children's too. I felt a rush of sympathy for Titus and Ruby-Lou, with their brown bread packed lunches and mental institution haircuts. The dummy was sinister (though armless, I weakly joked to myself) in the same way Ann's Perspex radiotherapy mask could be: the shell of a person waiting inside a room, always in the house, alive when you were out, helping itself to toast and making long distance calls. I continued. An enormous white-tiled bathroom at the top of this flight, nobody in it. Drinking all the while, almost wilfully because Ann was driving, I took the stairs three at a time to the next flight, peered into a dark spare bedroom, walked past another closed door — the mental patients, no doubt — and ended at the top floor front of the house, in the doorway to Kate and Simon's bedroom. So this is what television money buys you in Hampstead, I thought, and turned to go back downstairs to do something about Simon's terrible taste in music. I could not see in the New Year to the *Best of the Rolling Stones*.

There was a narrow stairway behind me going up. Another floor? An attic, surely. I ventured up, one hand shooting out to the wall to keep myself upright. The office opened to reveal itself the size of the bedroom below it. Light came in from the stairs I had just climbed and from the street outside, falling around two shadowy sofas and a bulky desk. Books lined the walls; at least a dozen more were stacked like a crooked man's chimney on the desk. The first one I picked up was a medical textbook, the next a guide to basic forensics. They were meaty numbers, on the way to rivalling one part of the *Shorter Oxford* for heft. He wouldn't fit these in his luggage on his trips to America. Perhaps he had another office there. He was a transatlantic asshole. And what was this? A copy of *Swann's Way* lying casually on a sofa cushion as though just put down at the sound of the doorbell? And above the sofa — oh ho ho — photographs. I switched on the wall lamp and the blurry blacks and whites of Simon's life pulled into focus. There he stood, on the steps of an anonymously grand neoclassical building, fluted columns behind and his arm around — could that be — Bono? Or just a random berk in dark glasses? Sweet pictures of the kids, one not very flattering one of Kate post-child-birth with a blob in her arms, and another of Simon and Kate all togged up in black tie, Simon holding a piece of sculpture about the size of a wine bottle in his hand. I raised my wine bottle to him in salute. There was the sculpture on the windowsill, clustered with more snapshots of the kids, the deprecating family man. It was of course a trophy of some kind, an award for Best All-Round Pronouncer of Foreign Words or Most Close-Together Eyes, a twisted piece of bronze that looked as though C-3PO had shat it. I peered at the wooden plaque the award was glued to: Best Drama Script from some backwater Central European festival in a country where the viewers were probably still gripped by Poldark. My head green and monstrous, I turned again to the wall . . . there was another photo, in the tawny colours of twenty or so years ago, of a girl standing in a doorway. White sunlight spilled on her shoulders, across her chest. She was wearing a blue cotton dress that gaped

117

slightly at the neck. Her face was beautiful and not quite formed, the nose a little too big, the cheeks soft and boneless — she can't have been more than fifteen. Her expression was as undefined as her features, soft, unreadable, that age when all you can do is absorb experience, walk through life as through a rain shower, unable yet to interpret what is happening to you. I had the slight impression of a timerush, that this was Ruby-Lou six years from now, that I had grown older standing still in this room while the world swirled about me. Of course, the girl in the photo was not Ruby-Lou. It was Kate.

My God, our women change when we marry them. They thicken up, on the inside if not out. Become pragmatists, wide-footed creatures with capable hips. The girl you fell for has a halo of frizz all over her hair now, she gives a grunt of resignation as she takes out the rubbish. In a cream silk camisole and with too much wisdom she handles you in bed. She knows secrets about life but you will never let her quite know yours. It's her sense of humour that shrivels you, the survivalist's wryness with which she copes. *I'm only teasing.* You never thought you'd miss the plate-smashing and weeping of women in their twenties but you do. Now she has the dread power of the life-giver: she has no end of puff, her love and occasionally her rage filling the bellows over and over again.

The light dimmed. I turned. Kate was there, silhouetted in the doorway. In that instant her strange impervious quality physically jolted me. Below her the stairwell light shone upwards, illuminating the grey in her bolt of black hair as though it was electric. She had been looking for me.

'Hi,' I said too loudly. 'Have you seen Ann?' It sounded like a cover. It was a cover. Really I had been searching for Kate's dirty underwear. 'I look like I'm snooping,' I said, and hiccuped. Hot wine regurgitated quickly in the back of my throat; I swallowed.

'Aren't you?'

'Yes.' I held up one of the books, pivoting my body to keep facing her as she walked past me into the room. 'Has he ever written a character that reminds you of you? A shrink decoding some nutbar patient?'

'Am I the shrink or the nutbar?'

'Good question.'

'I'm not a shrink.' She frowned at me. 'You know I'm not a shrink.'

'I thought . . . ' This was embarrassing. 'Aren't you a therapist?'

'Yes, I'm a naturopath.'

'Oh.' Ann had said therapist. Hadn't she?

119

You never listen, Tom. The image I had of her in an expensive chair, surrounded by medical textbooks, rich kilims and shelves of symbolic arcana from her travels, melted away. In its place appeared a shabby quack's office, cheap overhead lighting, everyone in the room egg-shaped, defeated.

She slid open a drawer. 'Ah.' A small velvet pouch on a tasselled rope dangled from her fingers. 'The wishes.'

'What are they?' I leaned too close into her. I could sense her holding her breath, so backed up to the doorway.

'For the New Year. It's a little ritual we have.'

'Like a witch.'

'I'm sorry?'

'A wish. For the New Year.'

You understand I had a sort of distant awareness of my idiocy. My reflection sloped in the angled mirror Simon had on a side table (a mirror in a study? Those eyes!) It was like catching a glimpse of myself on a film set monitor; I was horribly conscious of being a short drunk little fucker.

She peeled out from the bag a small rectangle of paper, the same size as for rolling cigarettes. I sniffed deeply, as though I could smell smoke, that longing again.

'These are wishes. Everyone writes down

what they want for the year. Then we burn them. They float, like amaretti papers, you know what I mean?'

It was easier to look at the floor than at her. For a frightening second I felt stirred by dread. Was it dread? Something spiked. I wanted to kiss her. No — much worse — I wanted to bite her neck, suck on her, leave a mark. Looking up unbalanced me and I swayed on my feet.

'Are you all right? Let's go down.'

I didn't want to explain it. I wanted her to know. (Know what? I was on a Möbius strip of repulsion and lust.) She lightly touched my elbow to indicate I should follow her downstairs. I waved her off, hiccuping grossly, it sounded like a sob. On the next level down the landing light had been switched off. The hallway was shadowy and I was grateful for the cool dark length of it in which to recover from my embarrassment. Just as I passed the children's bedroom a primitive cry came from within. Kate spun round and we performed a terrible little mutual shimmy as she tried to get past me to the bedroom door. 'Jazz hands!' I said, and demonstrated. She humphed in annoyance and disappeared through the door. I scuttled away as though it was I, Nosferatu, who had caused the nightmare.

Ann was deep in the back of the living room, talking to a man who was flirting with her. Since her pregnancy had become visible a particular sort of man found her even more attractive. Yuck, my inner eight-year-old said to that, but my inner thirty-year-old was flattered and smug about fathering a child and my forty-year-old self felt proprietorial in a way that Ann, had I ever mentioned it, would have objected to. The partygoers formed a dense crowd to sideshuffle through, but I felt more sober now. Between dancing bodies and laughing heads I had glimpses of her laughing, nodding, flicking her gaze around the room. A few feet away she became aware of my approach. We watched each other as I made my way closer. If Ann had not been my wife, if I had never met her before, the way she looked that night — sleepy, half-bored, amused by some private joke — would have devastated me all over again.

We were going to leave the party before midnight. I didn't want to run into Kate again and the house was big, but not that big. Drunken conversations, I remember, not the content but the diabetic rush off the wine, the sense of being fucking hilarious, of colluding with another couple in laughter over the orange skins of the TV actors amongst us.

Ann pulled me away. Together we filed through the busy rooms. Ann complained her shoes were pinching. I held my hand in the small of her back, supporting her. Two men deep in conversation blocked the way ahead. We paused in our path and Ann shifted her ass with almost imperceptible pressure back into my hand. I moved my mouth towards the curve where her neck met her shoulder and said in a low voice that I wanted to take her home. Her spine elongated as she arched her neck around to slide me a look that meant 'yes'. We were just in our coats when Simon appeared at the bottom of the stairs bearing a tray with the wishes, Kate's special little strips of paper on one side and a pyramid of sharpened red-and-black-striped pencils on the other. The two teenage staff followed with identical trays. One wrong move and those pencils would be everywhere.

'Surely you're not leaving?'

We pleaded pregnancy (I was beginning to see how useful a social tool this could be) and made our thank-yous and goodbyes to Simon. Ann supported me now as we walked up the black-and-white-chequered path to the street. We were in the car, buckling up, when Ann said, 'Oh, look.' I leaned over her from the passenger seat, tempted just to rest my head on her lovely pillowy breasts and fall asleep. Which house was I meant to be looking at? The lights in the wide double bay windows had gone out and the ground floor of Kate's house was in darkness. Ann breathed in audibly, her chest rising and falling as at first one — then more, then dozens — a hundred tiny orange flames lifted slowly in the air.

'We should have stayed,' she said. The moment was held, suspended briefly like the floating, glowing wishes. Then she started the car, shunted into reverse and forward, reverse and forward, to wriggle out of the parallel park, and quickly pulled away. Neither of us wanted to be there to see it when the electric lights came on again.

★　★　★

All over London car horns and firecrackers sounded in the New Year. Back in our neighbourhood after midnight, invisible boys threw bangers from dark doorways and low-rider cars doofed bass as they crawled along the streets. The house was warm; we'd left the heating on, but on the little two-stair drop close to the kitchen Ann paused to sniff the air.

'What are you doing?'

'Something stinks.' She backtracked, and

opened the front door again to inhale the outside air, then came back into the hall.

'I'm going to bed,' I said.

'No wait.' She opened the kitchen door. Her hand flew to cover her mouth and nose, and her body convulsed with a dry retch. 'Oh my God. Something's died in here.' All I wanted was sleep, but she gave me one of those marital looks, so I followed as she pressed on through the room to open the windows above the sink and the frustratingly stiff dead-bolt on the back door. It wouldn't budge, not even when she nearly tore the skin off her fingers with her grip. She sucked at her hand and hopped on the spot.

'I'll do it,' I offered unconvincingly, slumped on the top of the steps down into the kitchen. I couldn't smell anything. She waved her hands at me in an air traffic controller motion, holding her breath, then yanked open the cupboard under the sink, pulled on the yellow rubber gloves and tried the bolt again. This time it opened.

She exhaled with relief. 'Can you really not smell that?'

The outside light cast little visibility; it was like the lights in A & E toilets, tinged blue to prevent junkies finding their veins. There stood the wrought iron bulk of the garden table, a housewarming present from my parents and a piece of furniture that always looked as though it yearned for Wiltshire, where it belonged. We kept it covered with pots of herbs, tile samples for the bathroom we would one day decorate, and old silver Ann liked to pick up from Portobello and leave out there to tarnish. (She was convinced that Silvo would harm the baby, and I wasn't about to polish several dinner sets' worth of cutlery that we didn't need.) Beside the table were two plastic orange chairs I had rescued from the skip outside Tranter's office, hoping he would see me from the window and realise he ought to pay me more. Other than that, the back yard was empty.

It was freezing out there. I sniffed around but smelled nothing but my own boozy breath, which came in satisfying puffs from my mouth. Our Christian neighbours were up, and yellow light from their kitchen slatted through the fence on to the clutter in the passage down the side of our house. Ann picked up a long piece of dowelling and poked at the canvas, the paint cans, the skeleton of her bike. The only smell out there was the chill aftermath of rain on asphalt. I don't know what exactly is the hormonal trick that gives pregnant women a heightened sense of smell, but from the minute Ann conceived she hadn't entered the fishmonger's, or taken out the rubbish, or been able to 'gas up the car', as she put it, without wanting to gag.

'I can't smell anything.'

'I think it's inside.'

The back door creaked in a gust of wind and we both ran to catch it as it was about to slam shut. Ann tripped on the concrete step and hit the ground on the palms of her hands, hard enough to make her cry out loudly. I held her.

'Are you all right? We should go to bed.'

She shrugged me off. 'It's only going to be worse in the morning.'

So much for the promising way we left the party.

Nursing her left wrist, Ann poked around the kitchen for a minute or two, giving me a running commentary — first the smell was strongest in the corner by the oven, then high in the pantry, now under the sink. She was getting agitated, her voice was rising. I didn't like it.

'It's because you smoke, you've wrecked your nostrils.'

'Even if there is a dead rat there that only you can smell, what can we do about it?'

'There's no such thing as *a* rat.'

'OK. But you know what? There might be

dozens of undead rats in the walls,' I gave quite a good zombie rat impersonation, 'all arms outstretched and whiskery snouts, but the council are not going to pick up the phone for at least another five days. I'm going to bed.'

Three hours later I was still comatose in our bed from wine and fatigue, and Ann had removed every packet of dried spaghetti, jar of capers, can of flageolet beans, tuna, or crushed Italian tomatoes and stacked them up on the sink bench and kitchen table. She wiped down the surfaces as she went but there were no telltale rodent droppings, no gnawed corners on the paper bags of pumpkin seeds, linseed, Brazil nuts, all the various forms of trail mix she was taking for the baby. The stench wavered, now magnified, now receding; she crushed the ends of some lavender from the garden and left them lying around the room, where I found them, and the evidence of Ann's cleaning jag, in the morning.

I also found the hole she had smashed in the skirting boards.

★ ★ ★

The rat catcher, from the only private firm open at that time of year, looked pretty much like his prey. He clacked his teeth when he saw Ann's botch job on the skirting board and said, 'You'll be wanting a builder, love, not me.' He didn't do a lot more than Ann had in the way of looking, though he had a little torch that he shone under the stairs and into the bathroom cupboards. I felt self-conscious following him around, so joined Ann downstairs where she made tea. Once the rumbling of the kettle stopped we stood in silence and listened to his heavy footsteps, the joists creaking through the house. It was comforting to think that this man was here shining his light into all of the dim corners. Ann was pouring just-boiling water into the pot when the man gave a muffled yelp. Water splashed the sink and burned her fingers. I grabbed her hand. 'Quick, run them under the cold tap.' She shook me off and ran up the stairs. I followed close behind.

The rat man was on the landing, breathing hard. 'Jesus that gave me a fright.' He pointed towards my office: 'That head in there. I thought it was a person.'

Ann laughed. 'Skinny person,' she said.

'Creepy,' he said.

'Not as creepy as rats,' she said.

'Yeah, well, I can't see anything. That smell you mentioned, was it upstairs too?'

'No,' she told him, 'just down.'

'I'll be honest with you, love, I can't smell a thing.'

I watched Ann closely. She didn't flinch. 'Oh, no it's gone today. It comes and goes.'

'If it was rats, I don't know if it would come and go like that. Specially this time of year. They like to bed down. And I can't see anything but I'll leave some bait around anyway. Under the sink in the kitchen, in that gap beneath your bath and I'll put a bit out the back too. So mind fingers.'

The next day we went to Travis Perkins in Kingsland Road and bought a new plank for the skirting board. We walked through the timber yard, fingers intertwined, the picture of late capitalist home improvement bliss. The vast tracts of planks were covered with green tarpaulins against the weather, and loomed above us like sadly caped, elongated beggars. I gave the man the measurements and he came back with a strip of wood about twice the length of our kitchen. It occurred to me that I might have mixed up inches and centimetres, but I kept that quiet. We guessed how long a piece of wood we would need and returned home. It didn't quite reach across the splintered mess around the hole. We banged it in anyway, and after a few days became blind to the way it stuck out unpainted, like bad panel-beating, and the dark little gap on one side.

*   *   *

I told Kate and Simon the rat story, with embellishments, when they came for lunch with Tonia and Andy at the end of that week. In schoolboyish fashion my intention was to shock them; much the same motivation kept me going to the window to check the safety of their car. They owned a pale silver people mover. Despite her hippie appearance, she drove it. Simon looked the type of chap to have had his licence revoked. The children stomped up and down the stairs. We hadn't expected them but Kate had brought their lunch, brown paper bags filled with, I don't know, miso sandwiches. I settled them upstairs, left them transfixed by Japanese animation and ran back down towards our guests, afraid of what they might interpret from our living room ephemera when I wasn't there to monitor the scene.

A whole family of rats had decomposed here, I told them, after we heard them scrabbling in their death throes for days. Ann laughed, told me to shut up and come away from the window.

'Yes, why do you keep checking the window?' Simon asked. 'I feel as though I'm in a farce by Feydeau. Oh, open this,' he leaped up and pressed on me the bottle they had brought round, 'Don't cellar it, it's bloody good.'

'So is this,' I said smoothly, continuing to unplug the cork from my own bottle.

'Where were we, Kat,' Simon asked his wife using a nickname that disturbingly brought their bedroom into our living room, 'when we saw that something-or-other *je me'n fous*? Exquisitely constructed. The play I mean, the theatre was a bit run down.'

'The Comédie-Française,' she said, 'and now *you're* being insufferable,' her emphasis implying that previously it had been me behaving badly.

'I'm making sure your car doesn't get set on fire by the local youth. It's a bit flasher than the ones usually parked around here.'

'They don't burn cars,' said Ann.

'Those two look dodgy,' said Simon, who had taken over window duty.

'That's Tonia and Andy.'

Momentarily we left Kate and Simon alone in the living room and greeted our friends. 'How are you?' Tonia looked good. Women in London are thinner than women anywhere else and she was sometimes too thin, which didn't suit her now she was forty, even with that enviable West Indian skin ('Black don't crack,' she liked to tease Ann when they were moaning together about getting old). This day there was a warm glow in her face and an air of wellbeing clung to her. She was wearing her usual shabby effort. Most of the time she got around in jeans and some kind of boy's shirt. She shrugged off her French sailor's jacket and crumpled it over the banisters.

Simon stood with me in the kitchen while I cooked, and we managed to keep from an embarrassing work exchange or too sticky a silence by letting the conversation float around the property market, which was where my self-loathing really kicked in for the day. Gaily whistling up some risotto for a man I was all but on my knees before made the knife I was using for the onions quiver in my hand. Our phone conversation hung thick and silent in the room. I had let it be known, before Ann invited them to lunch, that I was on the hunt for any kind of writing work, that in fact, some long-running medical soap experience would be intensely artistically satisfying. If there weren't any openings I quite understood, but given that he'd mentioned, that time at his place . . . Oh, definitely, absolutely, in fact there might well be something coming up soon . . . he would be in touch. After this conversation I wanted to have a shower. Humiliation. No real likelihood of a paying job. Any money that might come in would be slow, a trickle. The mortgage fell due at the end of the week and that would clean us out until Ann was paid again next month. I'd paid the last lot of bills on my credit card. And still we hosted lunches! I was forty. Was this failure? Did it feel like this, like the need to stand under hot running water until the cylinder was drained?

Andy hovered in the doorway, offering drinks. I was sweating. On the bench next to the element the kitchen timer dinged, but too late, the risotto was gluggy and fucked, and I had forgotten to make the salad. When Simon offered to 'give me some space' I thanked him and topped up my wine. In the empty room I stamped on the bin pedal so hard that the metal spring popped out. The bin lid fell on my chopping board mid-scrape and vegetable debris scattered over the floor. A few liberal sloshes of Noilly Prat are very good for risotto and even better for chefs.

At the table my mind drifted up the stairs to my office and the parking fine that had already hit the double penalty date, the car insurance bill, the council tax bill, the Thames Water bill, the go-nowhere draft of the vampire script, Rosemary's lack of response, my decision to keep tinkering regardless and try to sell it somewhere else. It was shitty but it was over a year of work and I couldn't give up on it. Now I was the guy writing a cheesy genre film on spec, the sort of loser they make indie documentaries about, documentaries that are watched by people like my former, successful self in crowded screenings at film festivals. Ann served coffee. The others slowed down on the wine but I topped up my glass with mechanical regularity. Time to dive in.

'So how's work going, Simon?' Beneath the table Ann's foot pressed slowly but quite seriously down on mine.

'Great, yeah. Not here, bit of a dry hole here, isn't it?'

'Mn.'

'Had this American thing come up when we spoke on the phone?'

'No, I don't think so.' My voice almost wobbled with the effort of keeping it casual, it was like trying to look cool on a skateboard. Hadn't he been on the phone to America when we met in Islington that time?

'Yeah, I'm going to be out there for a while.'

I checked Kate. She was talking to Tonia, invisible blinkers keeping her eyes focused solely on her face, the stiffness of her neck betraying that she was listening to every word Simon said.

'What are you working on?' asked Ann.

'A new crime series. Filming out the back

of a Disney lot. They call it Mauschwitz.'

Everyone laughed. Kate and Tonia escaped their false bubble of conversation and turned to face the rest of us.

'What about your work here?' Ann again.

'Handing over to my second writer for a while. Be back and forth for a few months, it's going to be a busy time, but if it works out . . .'

'Your children will have American accents,' Tonia said to Kate, who looked stricken at the thought.

'Any stars?' Andy asked, which I loved him for.

Simon nodded. 'Some girl off a vampire show.' I HATE THIS MAN. 'Remember when vampires were the hot thing?' he laughed. HATE AND RAGE.

'The great thing about the undead,' I said before Ann could say, 'Oh, Tom's writing a vampire movie *right now*,' and everyone could think, isn't he behind the times! 'What I love about them, vampires, zombies, whatever, is that they know what they want.'

My wife made a scoffing sound and nodded between Simon and the almond friands, indicating he should help himself. He was busy performing an expert inspection of his cappuccino, which I happened to know had been frothed with an Aerolatte from

Argos and not the high-end steamer he was used to. After he hummed approvingly I tried to catch Ann's eye, but she wasn't interested in that game so I continued with my pet theory: 'All the undead want is to make more undead — they want to expand the group, they function like cancer cells or Jehovah's Witnesses.'

'Or pro-democracy hawks,' said Andy.

'Also undead.' This was Tonia.

'Exactly. Most sensible living people don't really want everyone to be the same as them. Except my mother. Most people don't even know if they want to be as they are or if they'd be better off being different. So we are far more equivocal than the undead, who at least have a simple, easily met want, and are therefore, in our terms, happy.'

Kate laughed. 'You equate simplicity with happiness.'

'Of course. We all want a log cabin.'

'Then I must be very unhappy,' laughed Simon. Ann mouthed the words 'big house' to Tonia, who frowned, confused.

'That life isn't any more simple than ours, it's complicated in other ways.' This was Kate.

'Do you really think so?'

'Yes. Anyway, don't you think there's something equivocal, to use your word, about

137

being undead? You're neither one thing nor the other. Like a bat.'

Ann shuddered. 'I hate bats. They stink.'

'Have you ever been to Sydney?' Simon asked. 'The flying foxes in the Botanic Gardens are extraordinary. They wheel around in massive flocks at dusk. And they absolutely pong.'

'Ann's from Sydney,' I said, as she didn't.

'Really? You don't sound it.'

'The thing about vampires is that you are technically not alive, even though you can move about and kill people.'

'You're undead!' said Tonia, 'that's why you're called undead.' She had kept pace with me on the wine front.

'Isn't it really limbo, or a kind of murderous purgatory, that you're in?'

'Purgatory to me,' said Andy, seizing the chance to get off genre, 'is last period Year 9 Geography. Bloody interminable.'

'Mine is when the children are ill,' Simon said, somewhat surprisingly. 'I hate that. And they whine.'

'Rewrites for Alan Tranter,' I said, 'thank Christ I've been spared that.'

'Not being able to help a client,' said Kate, smiling at me annoyingly. And then she said to Ann as if progressing naturally on, 'Whatever happened to that man who was following you? Did he go away?'

My chair trumpeted on the wooden floor as I stood to clear the plates. They had already been cleared. I sat back down again with a thud. Everyone was watching me.

'Sorry,' I said. 'Sorry. Ann?'

She just looked at me.

'Sorry, go ahead. Speak.'

Somebody else started talking, I don't remember who, only that the moment was saved and Ann muttered a sentence or two about it not really being an issue any more. Simon examined something in his coffee cup, dubbed it with a finger and discreetly wiped the finger on his napkin. Later I unfolded it and had a look. It was a small black smear, soft, unlike a coffee ground, which had once perhaps been an ant. I wondered how he had spotted it, so shiny and small and dark in the dark coffee. Perhaps he had felt it on his lip.

Rain slid silvery down the windows. Ann put on one of the classical CDs that only ever emerged when we had guests: dark and spare piano solos, full of mystery. I couldn't leave the earlier conversation alone. What can I say? In my defence, I am a berk.

'It might be more physically demanding but I just don't see how living on the land, in that pioneer delusion some people have, is complicated. There's nothing to negotiate apart from insects and malnutrition. In an overcrowded city, with dozens of different cultural and economic scales . . . ' God, Kate annoyed me then, her silence after I trailed off.

'Are you from London?' Tonia asked her.

'And all those hippies who think it's such a great idea to eat bread made from pea straw and sleep on sheep dung truly are ridiculous. Why ignore the industrial revolution, what earthly reason is there for living in those conditions if you don't have to? It's misogyny, nothing else.' Ann opened her mouth but I already knew what she was going to say. 'And don't give me that eco-bullshit, you can live carbon neutral without sacrificing technology.' She shut it again.

'I grew up on a commune,' said Kate. This statement was an opportunity for laughter that I managed to restrain. Of course, a commune.

'The damp Scotch kind?' (Orwell observes, rightly, that the Scots can't stand it if you refer to them as Scotch. Kate didn't flinch, and good for her.)

'Afraid so.' Did she have an accent? On the whole I thought not. London or Simon had knocked it out of her. Now even I could sense the discomfort around the table. What were the others thinking? Child abuse? Penury?

140

Rain falling on a neglected, rickets-ridden baby Kate, her black hair crawling with lice?

'Simple or complicated?'

'Those distinctions aren't really relevant.'

'You see, needlessly complicated! Sorry, but it seems to me absolutely typical of hippies to say one thing and do another, just like they're always crying poor and secretly amassing huge tracts of land to starve their sheep on.'

These weren't my exact words of course but that was the sentiment, and whatever I did say was no less charming. At the other end of the table Simon asked Andy for his expert opinion on the rugby. He had been treating him with embarrassing deference ever since learning that Andy had a 'real job'. Wait till he got hold of Tonia working at Holloway; she already had him laughing extra hard at her jokes.

'What was it like?' Ann asked Kate.

'Well, it was all I knew.' She looked at me. 'And yes, a lot of it was misguided. There was a fair amount of mandolin playing and too many collective meetings. It was hard work, my God! But no cynicism.'

I had been put in my place. 'Not for you now though.'

'It broke up.'

'But would you?'

A tiny shake of her head. 'No.'

'Kate, that's not strictly true.' Simon squeezed her hand.

'Simon rescued me. When I was fifteen. I'd snuck off with a mate to the pub down the road, we used to stand in the doorway to watch TV. When I was small I thought the soap operas, *Coronation Street* and things like that, were documentaries. There was a new manager, he didn't know about the commune and he pointed to the 'No Dogs, No Travellers' sign and tried to kick us out. My friend started shouting at him, and he called the police — '

'It was much more exciting than *Coronation Street*,' said Simon. I wasn't sure I liked this meet-cute anecdote, or him in his role of knight on white steed.

'Then my friend went berserk and smashed some glasses and Simon took her outside to calm her down.'

'What were you doing there?'

'Having a break from London, where I'd got my heart broken. Looking for truth in the Highland air. Day job,' he said, 'while writing the meaningful personal film of all time.' He laughed. 'We won't make that mistake again, will we, Tom? Older and wiser.'

My exhalation of acknowledgement was non-committal. Older! Was anybody going to comment on the fact that she was fifteen when they met? Was anybody else revolted by this? That photograph on his study wall . . . she was a child.

Kate laughed, 'And he saw my greasy hair and my jumper with bits of dirt clinging to it and thought, I'm in love.'

'That was before I took her home to the tepee. I reconsidered then but it was too late.'

'We moved to London together and never looked back.'

How old was Kate now? I wondered, but couldn't find a way to ask that wouldn't be obviously nosy. I had prodded enough. The stray grey hairs, her squaw-like bearing, the strange completeness of her, made her seem perhaps older than she was. Perhaps the poise had been developed to overcome nervousness, and inside she was an ever-unravelling ball of lanolin-coated homespun wool. After coffee we repaired to the sofas, where Ann quizzed Kate about baby inoculations or some such hoo-ha and Tonia sat quiet, on the outer. Titus and Ruby-Lou, bored from watching television up in my study, came down and began harassing their parents. 'When can we go home?' 'I'm bored.' 'I'm hungry.' 'Is there any juice?' Tonia's eyes saucered: this was the future?

Ann stared at her friend while Kate and

Simon performed the 'we really must be going' ritual: her look meant 'stick around'. It was hard not to compare the three women. I'm sure Simon and Andy did it too — skinny Tonia with her soft cloud of black hair, Ann's tall, curved profile as she and Kate had a whispered conversation in the doorway, the pale orange light catching in Kate's tawny eyes. One goodbye was enough — I can't bear that faffing in doorways that goes on — and I banished myself to the kitchen and the dishes. Andy sat at the table flicking companionably through the Sunday supplements. When the front door closed I felt palpable relief.

'Oh my God you're so right!' Ann said from the hallway. They came in. 'Tonia reckons Kate looks like Bridget.'

'Bridget who?'

'Your ex.' The idea amused Ann. Like all women she loved a pop psychology conspiracy.

'Kate? She looks nothing like her.'

'There's something in her manner.'

'She's got a sort of watchful energy.' Tonia picked up a random red wine glass that was waiting to be washed, and gestured with it. Her eyes were drifting. 'And the way she says certain words.'

'Really?' This was a subtle, probably

unconscious move by Tonia to establish Kate as the enemy and herself as Ann's closest friend.

Suddenly Ann banged the chopping board down on the bench. We all jumped. 'God *why* did you talk such shit about hippies, Tom? To sabotage the chances of him giving you a job.'

'Good of you to ask the question if you already knew the answer.'

Apparently I was scuppering my shot at a regular writing gig because I thought I was too good for it (untrue) and, worse, I had directed the blow not at myself but at the Devil's (yes) innocent (maybe) wife.

'Guys, guys, can it.'

'I'm sorry, but what is up with those children's names?'

'Of course the key to good risotto is the *parmigiano reggiano*.'

Tonia rolled her 'r's in the exaggerated Italian way that Simon spoke. This was a direct quote from him and I laughed along cruelly, despite having my own opinions about the key to good risotto, which doubtless would sound equally wanky if aired.

'How old do you think she is?' I asked, feeling it was safe.

'Impossible to tell. A good deal younger than him clearly — cradle-snatcher.'

'Yes, that is weird. I mean, what is it with fifteen-year-old girls? I was a nightmare at fifteen. Andy always says they're terrifying, I mean, you can't imagine finding one of your students attractive can you?'

'Absolutely not.'

'He must have been one of those men who couldn't get a girlfriend his own age.'

'What's his writing like?'

'Exquisitely constructed.'

'Oh shut up, Tom. Just shut up.'

It had been a mistake, the whole stupid lunch. She should never have tried to put these people together. Ann went into the bathroom and emerged some minutes later with red eyes.

I felt lonely at the thought of Tonia and Andy leaving and was flooded with gratitude, all over again, towards Ann for being pregnant, for filling our home with new life. We loved to lie in bed feeling the baby move under our hands, underneath Ann's warm skin. That cliché — I can't imagine my life without you — is bullshit. Of course you can imagine it. A poor, grey rag of a thing. Silence at the breakfast table and nobody to share the joke. Hollowness on waking. Sleeping at the wrong times. Uncoupled from the regular swing and tick of time. Doubled over in the supermarket, choking for breath by the freezer section, waving offers of help away, unable to meet their eyes. The shopping list in your hand not because there's so much to buy but because you can't hold anything in your brain. Buying her favourite biscuits. Six packets of them unopened in the cupboard at home. I could go on.

We drank more coffee, the four of us, and sat in familial silence with the papers. The day darkened, and Ann put on the lamps. I was nodding off when three sharp raps sounded at the front door — the wolf's-head knocker announcing something from another world, a call from a police inspector or death in a comedy shroud. My neck was stiff; I opened the door on to a beautifully damp rush of evening air. There was nothing on the path but the steadily falling rain.

'Did I dream that,' I asked the others back in the living room, 'or did someone knock?'

'Yes,' said Andy, 'I heard it.'

'Kids,' murmured Tonia, 'knock down Ginger.'

'Dream on,' Andy said, 'more likely coming to rob you.'

Ann shivered. 'Did you shut the door?'

Instead I wandered a little way along the rain-glimmered street until my shoes were wet and water slid ticklishly from my hairline down my face. Across the road, by the badly lit playground, central-locking lights flashed yellow on a car and a young white guy ran towards it, his puffer jacket slick and shiny in the rain. The car gunned off, its noise a fuckyou to the street. I was awake. Back in the house the first thing I noticed in the hallway was the smell. The bitter, flat stink of alcohol — where were the wine bottles? Where was the recycling bin? — the smell of cigarettes and of stale sweat on clothes, the scent released by the rain. Was this what Ann had smelled, what she had thought was an animal decaying behind the walls? I imagined the man then in front of me — his hooded sweatshirt, the split ends of his fingernails, the punched-up, wet-brain look on his face. All this was fleeting. When I walked back into the living room, the door closed on the street behind me, everybody I loved was still there and the smell and the man were gone.

N. A. M. W. 04. 07

The island accommodates just a dozen guests, and three couples are already at dinner when Tom and Ann step into the restaurant, a building modelled on the traditional style: thatch roof, glassless windows and the seaward wall missing. The tables are decorated with a single hibiscus flower. 'Very restrained,' says Tom, and Ann can tell by his tone that the surfeit of good taste is getting on his nerves.

She follows the young Indian woman with a long black plait to their table. The waitress is wearing a plain white shift dress identical to Ann's. It glows against her dark skin. Ann is pale, freckled, red haired. She feels like a hospital patient in this pillow-slip dress. Someone is looking at her. Tom. The waitress. She sits down. 'A vodka please,' she says, hoping it is the right answer. 'With lime.'

Sunset is long past. Outside, over the sea, streaks of pearly cloud underline the unfamiliar stars. A breeze licks through the restaurant.

Vincent Desjardin, the resort owner, enters some time after the marinated fish and shrimp sambal have been served, at first unnoticed in the doorway, then greeted with coos and light applause from his paying guests. Tom looks round, alarmed.

'It's not for you.' Ann bursts into quiet laughter. 'Don't panic.'

Desjardin's hand is suddenly on Ann's shoulder. 'Ann. Tom. This is Jimmy, our ace fisherman.' A Fijian man shakes her hand, then leans across the table to shake Tom's. Ann feels Desjardin's fingers, papery and cool, slowly leave her shoulder.

'The fish is delicious,' she offers.

'Jimmy really knows these waters,' says Desjardin. 'Of course, Reverie Island was uninhabited when I bought it,' he laughs, 'this is not Diego Garcia — but Jimmy's tribe have been around this chain of islands for a pretty long time now.'

Jimmy nods as though putting up with the spiel is part of the job. 'I'm fishing for *maki* tomorrow,' he says, 'judging by the weather.'

As he leaves, Ann notices a tattoo on his arm that looks like lettering. It is mostly hidden by his pale-blue sleeve: she can't quite make it out. A small rectangle of words, like a page from a miniature book.

The other diners have gone. They are alone under the thatched roof, the warm wind coming in from the sea, the white tablecloth smooth between them, rum in their glasses, their heads thick from the drink and the frangipani and the sea, distances swinging. Ann feels drugged, she should go back to the bure, go to sleep, but she is too heavy and humming to move. This is their last night alone together before the producer, Halliburton, arrives. She's never met him before and she isn't looking forward to it. But for now it is the two of them perfectly alone. She is smiling at Tom and he is smiling at her, reaching across the oceans of white linen for her hands.

She knows what it is before she unfurls her fingers to look at it. Tom has slid his arms back, he is hugging himself with them, looking out at the darkness where the invisible sea lies, not looking at her. The ring is small and sharp in her palm. She holds it against the light of the glass lamp on the table top. The protected candle flame reflects and gleams in the gold of the ring.

'Is this,' she says, 'is this . . . ?'

He meets her eye. 'If you like,' he says, and she thinks he has never been so vulnerable, the knowing of it and half laughing at it not making him any less so. 'Yes it is.'

She smiles at him. She has been smiling at him for some time. 'Yes.'

When Stella calls, even the ring of the telephone sounds commanding. She was coming up to town for a little light shopping and intended to take me to lunch. This meant a linen tablecloth establishment in South Ken. where she had once seen Sean Connery. She will no longer consider eating anywhere else. 'He was looking at me,' she tells me every time, 'most definitely *at* me. A *very* direct gaze.' It was a bus to Liverpool Street and then the achingly slow Circle line — I left home an hour and a half before we were due to meet and arrived just in time, which is to say a minute after Stella had arrived and already requested another table from the one she had been shown to (a habit of Bridget's too, hence my trick of arriving late to avoid the embarrassment of traversing the restaurant, wine glass in hand, jacket over my arm, and the I'll-take-it-no-I'll-take-it tussle with the waiter over the menu). She shook the new scarf she had bought from its tissue paper and passed it over for me to admire.

'How is Ann? When will she stop work? She seemed pressured at Christmas time, though perhaps that was having guests, as you know I cannot stand to have people to stay and avoid it wherever possible. Of course I will make an exception for my grandchild. Or grandchildren, if Ann takes to motherhood she might well have another quite quickly, plenty of older women are having babies these days though it must be hard to find the energy, perhaps that's where all the young Romanian nannies come in. Better than prostitution. Poor young Romanian women. We're terribly lucky Tom, we must *appreciate* our good fortune, there's only random chance to thank for our freedom. Oh, I must tell you there has been the most enormous fuss in our area about a gypsy camp.'

All this slid from her uninterrupted as I chewed a grissini. Grissino, grissina? Simon would know.

'Brought out the most unattractive aspect in people. We left a drinks party because of the way Willy Handforth — you know Willy — had been talking. Most provocative. And there is his daughter, a lesbian, not that that's the same thing at all, but there she is pregnant by her sperm donor,' the voice did not pause, did not drop at this: at a neighbouring table a man in an expensive suit glanced my mother's way, 'and Willy of all people is talking about the decay of the moral fabric! It isn't the poor gypsies' fault they've got no money, they're dreadfully oppressed all through Europe, education is the key. If they are going to settle in communities, which is far more likely to help them achieve than all this — roaming — what's the word . . . ?'

She was still partially trying it on for size, old age, but this was Stella as she would become, increasingly emphatic and brassed-off by the failings of her memory.

'Nomadic,' I supplied.

'Nomadic. Well it doesn't work any more, does it, in this day and age, but that's no reason to lose their culture, their traditions. They should be supported, helped into housing, into education. Especially the

153

women who are themselves oppressed by the men.'

'Hmn.'

'You know sometimes I think the temperance movement should be revived.'

I waggled my glass at hers.

She laughed. 'I know, but truly, Stanley Marriott — you know Stanley, Justice Marriott — ninety per cent of the terrible cases he sees are alcohol related. They talk about a cocaine epidemic,' again, nicely enunciated for the suits at the next table, I swear she got a sexual thrill from this, although that is the last time I want to think about my mother in that way, 'but booze is far, far worse.'

By pudding I had been reminded of a good half-dozen people my mother knew — most of them terribly influential, having 'the ear of all sorts of people' and given a whistle-stop tour of her politics. She is liberal in her own lunchtime, my mother, and believes she could tell the Home Secretary a thing or two thank you very much, while retaining the unshakeable baseline opinion that her brand of English tolerance 'with limits' is the only right way of living in the world. The oxymoronic aspects of this core belief do not give her any trouble.

'So tell me about work,' she said. One of

her great and good acquaintances had a son who was doing rather well in writing for the cinema, as she put it. The name, mercifully, escaped her. But he was in Los Angeles now, having meetings. Somebody important had bought his last film after it was in a festival. Had I ever heard of — she pronounced it — *Meeramax?*

I nodded. 'That's great for him, fantastic,' and smiled to show at least I was making an effort.

'How is the new draft coming along?'

I hadn't had the heart, or the guts, to tell her. 'Fine.'

'Now.' She had twiddled her fingers in the air for the bill. Her long, rectangular Smythson clutch was suddenly on the table. She placed her credit card in the waiter's proffered black folder. A chequebook emerged. I took a sip of water. Over the years she had often flicked me the odd hundred quid, but I just felt sick at continuing to take her money even though we needed it badly. We had long given up euphemising these handouts as loans. Pocketing the cheques I felt cold, like a worm; banking them made me elated. On the way here I had sworn to myself it would stop.

'Did you drive up?' I asked.

Finally she lowered her voice. 'Now. How

are you and Ann off for money at the moment?'

The feeling was like a caffeine surge on an empty stomach, and I almost thought I would vomit. She had already started writing my name. Two hundred pounds would tide us over, if we were careful, until Ann got paid. Put food in the fridge. Pay the interest on the credit card. Halt the escalating traffic fines.

'We're great, Mum, it's kind of you to ask but you can put your purse away. Thank you for lunch.'

She shot me a look over her invisible pince-nez. 'You sure?'

'Absolutely. Things are great.'

'Good.' She gave a half-nod, and a quick proud inhalation in the direction of the suits. You see? They might be corporate lions on expense accounts but here, lying to her and keeping the extent of the disaster even from his wife, was her magnificent son!

★ ★ ★

Ann began to sculpt again. She hadn't for a long time — probably, if I thought about it, since we were married. They began to appear, those odd little clay figures that had always slightly given me the shivers. One of them was waiting for me when I came down to breakfast on a Monday morning. I had watched DVDs late into the night before and when I woke up Ann had already left for work. The house was softly full with that intoxicating hush of someone's recent departure. In my robe and slippers I padded down the stairs, looking at the hallway floor for any envelopes. In winter, sunlight from the living room didn't reach the hall, and the space was dark and church-like. After scooping up the various bills and mini-cab flyers I paused in the doorway to the living room, thinking about putting music on, but the neighbourhood was quiet at this time of day and I enjoyed that. If I didn't open the door or look through the windows I could be anywhere — my cage was not Hackney, East London, but rather this cool, dim, airy structure of grey-white walls, rough wooden stairs and paint-splattered floorboards. With my eyes shut to outside it might as well be Notting Hill, and this house, I mused as I flicked through the windowed envelopes whose brightly coloured corporate initials spelled looming destitution, would be worth a bomb in Notting Hill. Even Islington, it might be Islington out there with, OK, its share of street crime, but the cafés! The fishmongers! The Screen on the Green! Better still the house might stand high and alone in the mountains somewhere, a Victorian folly erected by a madman. No jumped-up food shops, no cinemas, just the purple hills rolling out far into the distance, outlined in black. Such were my thoughts as I paused in the hallway. My mind was still murky with sleep when I entered the kitchen and saw a blackened homunculus staring at me from its perch on the bench. The letters fell from my hand and hit the floor with a slithery sound. The man was made of clay, and rubbed with soot — my fingertip came away smeared with charcoal. Its body was the size of a coffee mug and it had one sort of fused leg massed into a seated posture so it could balance on the bench edge. A thumb had been pressed in where its face used to be, giving it a spoon-like aspect, but then two eyeholes had been scratched in too so that out of its inverted face it seemed to be capable of a squint. My instinct was to throw a tea towel over it but past experience with the fragility of Ann's objects prevented me. Was it a joke? A little message? Or had she just been noodling around and not considered that it would look as though the man were meant for me? This was the problem with Ann, you never knew when to take it personally. Whatever was behind it I didn't want to have the damn thing sitting down here all day, staring into the middle distance like some parody of me, a floor above it in my office, staring into my computer screen. It did look kind of like me, even with the spoon face and conjoined legs — a sort of slouch in the shoulders. Perhaps while I was working it would hop up, hip-wiggle around to make a cup of tea, have a flick through the *Independent*. I swore out loud with frustration.

When I finally got through the hospital phone system and reached Ann, I made sure to remove all trace of disgust from my voice. 'Is he for me?' I asked, in the hopeful, dare-I-dream way a child might enquire of a puppy.

'Not really,' said Ann, 'It's for the house. A sort of guardian. I don't know, I got itchy fingers.'

'I thought I was the guardian of the house.'

She laughed. 'Another one.'

'Do you think he's very fragile?'

'No.'

'Good. I'd hate to knock him over while I'm wiping the bench.'

'You can move him if you like.' I loved her for saying that. It was impossible not to hear the trace of reluctance in her voice.

'No no. He's good there.'

And so there he sat, covered with a prisoner art tea towel that had been a house-warming present from Tonia. It was, I told myself, glancing over my shoulder as I left the room to check that it hadn't moved, just like having a budgerigar asleep in a cage. I was very pleased Ann was working again. But still, as I shrugged off my robe to step into the shower, a shudder passed down my back. I locked the bathroom door. Even then an unwanted thought buzzed inside me, wouldn't leave me alone. Not a thought, a knowledge, something existing below the solar plexus. A known fact. The last time Ann made these figures was when we came back early from Fiji.

N. A. M. W. 05. 07
The resort workers have decorated a little pavilion between two palm trees on the south side of their small island. Tom stands beneath the sweeping bellies of pinned silk. Tentacles of frangipani and bougainvillaea trail around him. The hibiscus blooms, hot crimsons gathered in each corner of the canopy, are already closing into wrinkled flutes against the dense air. He wilts in the heat, in his long-sleeved white shirt and the charcoal trousers he flew in. He looks like a waiter. His feet are bare on the shaded sand. It is late in the afternoon and the day's heat has intensified, doubled in on itself to exude

from every grain of sand, every leaf, a thick throbbing heat that makes Tom, pinprick aware and woozy all at once, feel he must be in a dream.

Around the corner of the bay, out of sight of Tom and the pavilion, is a canoe strung with white flowers, manned by three of the fishermen with blue-inked scrolls along their backs. Ann's own mark, her scar, is visible; she wears a white linen shift dress from the resort boutique. Panic comes in a peristaltic wave. All sound is indistinct, the swishing of the surf the only frequency her ear can pick up, its small grey noise determined and soft. The men push off from the shore, paddle efficiently through the gentle water.

A group of women from the nearby island sit cross-legged on special cloths laid over the sand, their smock-dresses bright, bell-like. Ann sees the pavilion, Desjardin in his coloniser's cream suit. The night before he tried to deflect Tom's questions about the coup with his little shrug. 'I blame you British, right? You give them God, penicillin, tourism — of course they're mad at you.' After he'd gone Tom made a small exploding noise under his breath. 'Nuclear arsehole,' he said. 'Typical French prick.'

And there is Tom, the man she is marrying for real this time, no fingers crossed,

Tom who must be sweltering in crow-like black trousers, that damp shirt. Is it too late? Ann thinks of the coral garden she saw from the glass-bottomed boat tour she took while Tom was working. One by one, they had tipped over the edge to snorkel in the tepid water over the reef. She had lain suspended with her arms out like a starfish, no sound but the in and out of her breathing rasping loudly all around her. Can she dive down into the water, disappear into the coral kingdom, never come back? The choir of women roll out 'Amazing Grace', drowning the sound of the sea.

Ann bursts into tears in the middle of her vows and crying, laughing, opens her face towards Tom — he doesn't know what to do with the moment, giddy with heat and luck. Desjardin softly touches Ann's arm, sympathetic, giving her a moment to compose herself. The ceremony is brief, or maybe time is running fast. The official language brings her back into herself. This is a contract, a legal agreement, and that sharpness, the scratch of Desjardin's Montblanc pen on the register, comes as a lifeline amidst all the fruity perfume and foliage. Surely that frangipani stem, so waxily perfect, cannot be real.

But that flowing-over feeling from the

wedding — the world shiny and new —
stays with Ann through the guitar-strumm-
ing night, the bitter druggy burn of the
kava, her tongue too numbed to properly
talk, the whump in her chest of the drums
as a group of islanders fire-walk under the
thick velvet sky.

Tom scrambles to his feet. Red-faced,
muttering. His voice more English than ever,
'Hello John, hello.' He is embarrassed, she
divines it instantly, that he has spent the
afternoon getting married instead of working.

John Halliburton is a monster, a colossus
in shorts and a patterned shirt, he booms
and thwacks and grabs her wrists so hard
they might break, twists her hand to see the
ring. 'Married on my dime, eh!' he shouts
over the drumming. The night sky clings at
her, the palm fronds, the fire, the oily surface of the pool. She has to leave.

This is the wrong bure. She apologises to
the guest she has woken. Desjardin is somehow there. Can't ask him for help. Knows
his type. The water smells like all the water
here, slightly sulphurous. Soft in her mouth.
The bed-sheets are soft and she presses her
face into them. Gets up again to check she
has locked the cabin door. It all ends indefi-
nitely and not as anyone means it to, this

wedding day, Ann curled in sleep beneath the pristine white sheets in their cabin, Tom rolling in the sand with a rum bottle sticky and empty between his knees, Halliburton somewhere behind them in the back of the dunes, howling with laughter.

I don't know. We got married in Fiji. Hallie arrived that night. We drank too much kava. Ann locked the door of the bure. The rest is only a guess.

★　★　★

It's quite an experiment, if you're a middle-class urbanite, to have to live without buying any new produce until everything in the pantry is gone. I'd banned myself from bookshops until I had read all of the books on my shelves; now Ann imposed a similar restriction on food. For the first week it was no hardship. We had enough packets of pasta, cans of borlotti beans, tinned tomatoes and jars of pesto to survive a small Tuscan apocalypse. Tuna, you may remember from your student days, can be rendered interesting in multiple ways if you don't think about cat food. Brown rice bestows moral superiority for at least an hour. All of those wacky jars — Indonesian pickles from a trip to

Amsterdam, pitted cherries, jalapeño peppers, salsa, olives, Christmas mince — that had been transported, dusty-lidded, from one house to another over the years, at last came into their own. In the second week, wakame and arame from Ann's dried seaweed phase, amaranth and millet from the obscure grains period, and that lingering can of sauerkraut provided us with some much-needed nutrients. By week three my gums were bleeding. While Ann was at work I raided the back of the sofa for enough pennies to buy a softish apple or ten Silk Cut from the corner shop.

Ann was getting healthier as the pregnancy wore on, drinking nothing but loony tea and doing yoga though she could no longer touch her toes. The fridge was practically bare but for her mysterious tinctures and herbal supplements. Where had these come from? Vile though they smelled, something in them worked: the pale moony cream of her skin and warm glowing hair almost became light sources. Her eyes shone like polished glass. We could have saved on electricity, I joked, and just had Ann standing lamp-like in the corner of every room. Heat pumped from her, although her hands and feet were always icy. This newly poor circulation, the gloves and socks in bed at night, the stinging fingers checking the bath temperature each morning, gave her pleasure because it meant the blood was thumping around the baby instead. Martyrdom begins.

★ ★ ★

Andy and I had begun a new running circuit, meeting at the rose gardens in Victoria Park. They still hadn't found the murderer of a young woman jogger who had been killed there about a year earlier. There'd been similar attacks in two North London parks since, and the killer was thought to be a teenage boy. I don't know why we still used Victoria Park. There was, I suppose, nowhere else to go, except maybe the canals, where a suitcase containing a dismembered young woman had recently been opened up by some kids. No wonder we practised our running. Sometimes I asked myself what I would do if such a suitcase should bob along the water past my feet — any suitcase, in fact. Fish it out or keep on walking? Did I secretly yearn to save a woman from a hooded teenage knife-wielder? Did I seriously think I could?

The park smelled of wet earth; our trainers skidded now and again on the paths. Andy took tiny steps, running at an almost stationary shuffle, his elbows winging out as though he was doing the chicken dance.

Although the shortest day had passed the night closed in quickly. When we reached the gates, juicy with sweat, breathing hard, they were locked. My hands closed around the cold iron bars; I leaned my slippery head against their coolness, breath clouding in front of my face. The spikes at the top were enough to put us off trying to climb over, even if we hadn't been wheezing like a couple of old men. I tried the council on my mobile phone while Andy jogged off, clutching a stitch in his side, to find the park keeper. As the phone rang and rang into an empty office I wondered if this was the moment when I would see the man, whether now he would lumber up to me, perhaps even on the other side of the gate's bars, look hard at the ground with his ratty face under the hood and deliver me a message.

The little monitor on the side of my phone flared and died: out of battery. I was starting to get properly cold, and did some jogging on the spot. I called out for Andy, not very loud, self-conscious because a small gang of boys was watching me from across the road and I didn't want to look afraid or make them laugh. A couple of them sat on the bonnet of a car, smoking, while one wheeled around them on a stripped-down scooter that was undoubtedly stolen and another just leaned against the passenger door, glaring at the world as though he dared it to come any closer.

'You stuck, man?' one of the boys on the car called, and they laughed.

'Yeah.' The streetlights were on but it was not entirely dark yet. During a break in our run, Andy had told me a brief staff-room anecdote about one of the other teachers, a man I'd met round at theirs, a white South African guy who had to do daily battle with the children who mocked his accent. The clock was ticking for this fellow, Andy said, London was slowly getting to him, it was only a matter of time.

The boys had sauntered over the road to stand directly on the other side of the gate. I willed myself not to back away. The one who'd called out to me proffered a pack of B&H Gold through the railings; I smiled and shook my head.

'Thanks, no. Trying to get fit, you know?' I despised myself for the nervous middle-class granddad routine, getting down with the kids, but was aware of having no alternative. This was me; this was all I could do. For at least the last decade I'd been under the illusion that I was invisible to male aggressors, whether they were my own age or younger. It was the one decent thing about getting older:

guys with something to prove didn't give a shit about you any more. Unless, like now, you were trapped on the other side of some bars like a monkey in a zoo, an early evening entertainment.

Casually, not at all in a panicky where-the-fuck-is-he way, I looked around for any sign of Andy. Surely he had found the park keeper by now. It occurred to me to go and look for him, but without my mobile I was as lost as a child, and — I only realised it in that moment, with a hot flush of shame — in the back of my mind I was convinced that the man, Ann's stalker, lived in the park. Here he appeared in my imagination fully fleshed, a boogeyman bush-dweller, ready to stumble from the undergrowth, his breath reeking, to mark me with a contaminated paw. Mean-while the hooded spiders, who probably had an average age of twelve but posed a far more tangible threat than my unmaterialised man, were climbing the gates.

When Andy finally showed up, in response to my now unrestrained cries for help, the kids were gone and I had been well and truly mugged. I had not explained to the boys about the phone having died, but let them take it without complaint. Of course even in my sad old tracksuit pants pocket I had brought my credit card, planning to stop at the wine shop on the way home, so they had that too. It was so odd standing there, waiting, my insides boiling as the boys levered themselves over the spikes at the top of the gates: the leader looked as though he'd done it a hundred times and knew just how to place his hands, like a Russian gymnast, supporting himself on his wrists to hoist himself over the top. The efficiency of movement made it clear there was no point trying to run. We could have been different species then, those boys and I.

The shuddering wouldn't stop, even at home, even in bed through that cold, cold night. I don't remember getting home, only lying on the sofa while above my head Andy joked to Ann about the credit card getting used less by the muggers than by me. Every time I saw her she was on the phone, getting through to the bank, or the police, or Orange to report the mobile lost. She thought I was in shock but the scabby doctor, next morning, diagnosed bronchitis and a lung infection. Ann took the day off work to look after me, and the next. Two rounds of tetracycline had no effect other than to give me stomach cramps and make me sweat, which I did in bed, slipping in and out of sleep, Ann's blue Ventolin inhaler in my fist. My meagre productivity slowed to a trickle, nothing more than surrounding myself with pages of redrafts and spending hallucinatory afternoons watching the telly at the foot of the bed.

Ann returned to her days at Barts, heading out wrapped in enormous blanket clothes like an Inuit woman. Before she left she would bring me lemon and honey drinks, toast on a tray, and the latest example of her sculpting. The little people accumulated fast. It was like being Gulliver in your own home. Soon I recognised familiar faces. My mother rendered in salt-shaker-sized clay, the pleased and proud set of her jaw, a quick firm line of mouth Ann had pressed in with a thumbnail, so she looked at once utterly herself and also the self-appointed Mayor of Toytown. Costcutter's slipper lady made an appearance, doomed even in miniature, her standards as well as her stoop somehow appreciably lower than those of her clay compatriots. There were Andy and Tonia, sweetly, if blindly, embracing, faces buried in one another's shoulders. All these were three-dimensional sketches, work Ann did quickly, intuitively, late at night or early in the morning — sometimes all night, moulding the people by hand, a brief squeeze here, a smudge of thumb and fingers, a slow careful twist. The oven timer was constantly on, these soulless little creatures forging on a low heat. Maybe it would have been nice to have a wife who baked biscuits, but through my illness I was proud of Ann's productivity. A couple of workmates grew overnight, the dumpy receptionist and a hulking orderly. Kids from the estate with foetal alcohol syndrome. The moon-faced man always standing outside the off-licence. One by one the neighbourhood crept indoors. She refused to do me: 'You'll hate it,' she laughed, 'people always do.' I knew she was right, though I longed to see myself reflected through her hands. She was magnificent then, the apron stretched over her belly smeared with clay dust, high from lack of sleep, from the sheer output she was forming, the incremental covering of every surface — mantelpiece, stereo speakers, between the newel posts on the stairs — in her work. The one figure she returned to, over and over again in different forms, was the slipper lady. Even when the body changed, became twig-like or pear-shaped, the air of craziness hung around her, of being askew in the world. Ann couldn't say why she was so fascinating, just that, 'She knows something we don't.'

'Yes,' I said, reaching to turn out the bedside light and knocking some homunculus or other to the floor. 'What food from a

172

rubbish bin tastes like.'

'Don't be mean. She doesn't eat out of bins. She's got dignity.'

'Oh my God,' I laughed, 'that is the one thing she hasn't got. She goes outdoors in her nightie.'

'Her slippers. I think that thing she wears is actually a dress. I like the way she doesn't care whether she's in public or not. That's the point.'

'Don't you think it's a bit sad clown to be romanticising this tragic old bat?'

'Oh, fuck off.'

A coughing fit overtook me. Ann passed me a glass of water, which I drank before saying, 'You're telling me to fuck off an awful lot lately.'

'I wonder why.'

'Come and have a cuddle.'

'I want to work. Populate our house with more pathetic ladies.'

'Please. I'm ill.'

'Poor baby.'

She slid into bed with me, and we held each other. I drifted off to sleep like a king. In the middle of the night I woke to find her side of the bed empty. My clever wife, working. The air above me was cool, but under the blankets I was cosseted, snug. Soon it would be Ann's birthday. We would have a big party, and she could display her figurines on the night — a kind of joke on our expanding family. Ann's friends would be impressed, and if the right people came — who these might be I had no idea, about the art world I am clueless — she might be offered a show. She would work while the baby rocked in a Moses basket, I would clear out the tiny shed in the back garden and build her a proper studio. No more cancer patients. I couldn't believe I hadn't thought of this simple and brilliant plan earlier. Despite the hour, despite the cold, I swung out of bed to go downstairs and tell her. As soon as I stood my empty papier-mâché head bobbed forwards and I nearly fell, but steadied myself on the armchair. The dizziness was not unpleasant. My knee joints were weak and filled with sugar syrup. There was my jumper. I could see it draped over the armchair. It took me three reaches to pick it up. My shoulders aching, I pulled it on, rallying to its daytime feel. Tomorrow I would shower and dress, no matter how bad my chest. The soles of my feet sparked with cold, recoiling from the hard chill floorboards. The bedroom door opened like a deep freeze, into a wall of cold vapour. The landing was misty, grey, as though we lived in a dolls' house with the wall lifted away, our miniature lives open to the night, and I quickly started down the stairs, my mind on the slippers by the front door. Ann must have a window open, I thought, was she trying to kill me? And then I stopped thinking, as you do when it's numbingly cold. Quick, quick, through the silent middle floor to the hall downstairs — ah, the slippers, their red-and-green tartan muted to grey checks in the half-light. I had just slid them on when my body stopped moving. Slowly my brain worked out it had frozen at the sound of talking. From the kitchen, down the length of the hallway, a line of bright light shone under the door. Ann's voice. Not the burble of talking to oneself. The straight road sound of telling somebody something. A silence. Then, unmistakably, the deep, urgent timbre of a man. 'ARGID BLEDDIN LOGEL MUD.' The voice cut off abruptly. My own breath was loud, mouth open.

Then Ann again, louder: 'Tom? Is that you?'

She opened the kitchen door, an oblong blaze of light surrounding her silhouette.

'Who's there?' I called.

'It's me.'

'Who's with you?'

'Nobody.' She began to walk towards me. 'You're shaking.' From a long, long distance her thin fingers touched my face. Her thin fingers touched my face. 'For Christ's sake, Tom, you're burning up.'

'I heard talking.'

She shook her head. Ann, dear Ann, she looked so familiar then, so reassuring and concerned. 'The radio. I'm listening to the radio.'

I started to walk towards the kitchen. She stood in my way. 'You should go back to bed.'

'I'd like a drink of water.'

'I'll get it.'

All of a sudden it was too hard to stand up any more. Blackness swam on the edges, my nose and hands were cold. I pulled myself along to the bottom of the stairs and thudded down, then carefully dropped my hot, swollen head between my knees and shut my eyes. Projected on to my closed lids was a memory vision, the sickly green rectangle of light, the centre obscured by the blackness of Ann's shape.

She helped me take the stairs back up to bed, slowly, pausing on the landing for me to cough. 'I'll go back to the doctor tomorrow,' I said once I had lain down and Ann had pulled the covers over me. Though she said I had a fever, I was frozen to my core and the piles of winter duvets didn't feel weighty enough. We had a little tussle over me not wanting to remove my jumper.

'Don't go back to that horrible place,' she said, 'I think that waiting room made you worse anyway.'

It was hard to argue with that. The stained carpet, the dozens of people waiting on broken plastic chairs, the *People's Friend* magazines with their cheap soft paper, the children with slugs of snot making glacial progress towards their mouths, it all screamed infection, infection. What would we do when the baby was born? Could we inflict this Petri dish environment on our own child? There were whole supplements every week in my newspaper, *family* supplements full of headlines about immunisation and school holidays, that I had thus far been able to avoid. Soon we, too, would madly seek the best, only the best even in darkest Hackney, no food that was not organic, no man-made fibres, no microwaves, the pure tonal shifts of Bach mathematically bouncing off every surface. We would join the ranks of middle-class hopefuls attempting to create a master race in their own Ikea kitchens. Could we become the wankers I'd read about in the *Guardian* that take their kids to Harley Street for cranial osteopathy? I shut my eyes. I would put nothing past us.

Two or three days followed in a dream.

Ann took more time off work to keep an eye on me. The thought of giving her the virus, whatever it was, worried me but she insisted she'd never felt stronger. She brought me soup on a tray, turned the radio off when I fell asleep, read me the paper, changed the sheets. My temperature rose and fell and rose again.

'Ann. Ann.'

The blinds were down, the room nearly dark. It must have been late afternoon. Twilight is when you feel lost, the day washed away taking with it everything you know.

'Ann.' I had thought she was in here, but maybe not. The jug beside the bed was empty.

'Ann.' A fear seized me that perhaps she had gone out. I was afraid without her. And as though the force of my need summoned her, the bedroom door opened and there she stood.

'Darling. I'll get you some water.'

'Ann. I keep thinking there's someone in the house.' My sleep was full of a shadowy figure sitting on the end of the bed, or a man downstairs who wouldn't give his name.

'Kate's here.'

'Oh.'

'Shall I bring her up to say hello? I didn't think you'd feel like seeing anyone.'

'No. I hope she doesn't think I'm rude.'

'Of course not.'

I drank my water and strained to hear the conversation far below. Not even a distinguishable murmur. Fevered as I was, I imagined Kate and Ann as just-frozen statues outside the bedroom door, breathing as silently as possible, listening to me trying to listen to them. This was nuts. I rose dizzily from the bed and creaked over to the bedroom mirror. Ah, Christ. Not the pale, drawn invalid of fantasy, but an unshaved, puffy and red-nosed self. My beard grew in alopecic, testosterone-deficient patches. If Kate could see me she would be revolted, put off. Put off from what? Did I want her to like me? I scraped a longish fingernail against the white crust that had gathered in the corners of my lips. The days away from running had left the skin over my ribs slack already. The door opened too quickly for me to leap out of sight.

'Jesus, Ann.' I dived for my robe and the bed at the same time. The door slammed.

'Sorry!' Ann called from the hallway. 'I thought you were asleep.'

Silence. After a few seconds the landing floor creaked and I knew they had gone away. Under the duvet I clutched my robe tight around me. The dreams that followed were short, prosaic, peppered with sudden physical jolts. And then I was aware of people in the room. Kate and Ann stood at the window, having a whispered conversation. Sleep wrapped its soft grey hands around my eyes, and I succumbed.

'Sometimes in the night I've thought of going out there with a brick and taking out the light.' Ann said that. Kate laughing. Another, lighter sound, of metal rattling, which I couldn't identify. Maybe I spoke in my sleep. A hand pressed firmly down on my forehead. Kate. I knew it before I flicked my eyes open, briefly, to see her tawny stare pouring directly down upon me. Her fingers were warm and dry. They would come away greasy. This thought left me as I let sleep take over again, under her hand, the pressure of it oddly lightening, helping me float away.

Later that night Ann gave me a spoonful of herbal medicine, a concoction that was as hard to keep down as a mouthful of barky mud, was of much the same consistency and had a powerful burn. No sooner had it guttered down my throat than I was seized by a deep coughing, a cold hand reaching inside my chest and wringing out the lungs. The air I gasped in was sickly with eucalyptus. Calmly she passed me a bowl, as though she had been expecting the retching that followed. Everything inside my head fell away. Whiteness swamped in from the periphery and I passed out.

I was out for two days.

I woke to Ann's profile next to me in bed. She was white, carved of wax, deeply asleep. In a rush I sat up. Kate was in a chair in a corner, her face just revealed between the thick black curtains of her hair.

'Tom.'

'What are you doing here?'

'Ann needed to rest. The remedy made you sleep.'

Remedy. I breathed in and tried to cough. Nothing. She stood up and stretched.

'I'll make some tea.'

While she was downstairs I snatched clothes from the drawer, ran down a floor to the bathroom, scrubbed myself under the shower and dressed. We met on the stairs.

'I'll come down,' I said.

In the kitchen she passed me a mug of licorice and mint. 'How are you feeling?'

'Great,' I said, 'like I've been hoovered out by a particularly strong Serbian cleaning lady. I think there's a Magic Tree hanging where my sinuses used to be.'

'Good.'

'Should I thank you? Is this your natural remedy juju at work?'

She smiled. 'It's all right.'

We studied each other for a moment. I felt remarkably clear and sort of high. 'I'm worried about Ann,' I said.

'I know.'

'She's quite hyper.'

'It could be the hormones.'

'Yes, I know.'

'But you think something else?'

' . . . No.' Kate waited. 'Well she's so busy, you see, as though she's trying not to listen to something.' I couldn't bring myself to mention the abortions, wondering whether they might have inspired some kind of guilt fit now she was having a baby. It would have been like trying to speak Tagalog suddenly and finding out Kate was fluent. 'Her mother died when Ann was little. She never talks about her childhood, it's as though life started when she came here.' Whoa, this was a flume train of indiscretion. I had no judgement, in so many years I'd never talked to anyone about Ann and now I'd tipped myself over the slope it was hard to know how to stop. Kate asked whether Ann or I had ever been to 'see someone'.

'No. And I wouldn't. I can't bear therapists. Ann can't either. No offence.'

'None taken. I can give you some herbs.'

'She's already taking loads.' Suddenly I

realised — Tom, you retard — Kate was giving her those. Of course. 'Maybe. I don't know.'

'The other thing, Tom, is that she's under a lot of pressure. All women feel intense about having a baby, whether they've been pregnant before or not. And she's working' — this was her way around saying *she's worried about money* — 'and she's been very frightened about that man.'

'Has she seen him again? Has she told you?' Revealing my distrust. I was hopeless at this. Time to shut the door.

'Just more about that day of the derailment. Seeing him at her work.'

'Kate.' I was bracing myself to say, 'Do you think there is any chance Simon might have some work for me,' when the stairs above me creaked and Ann called out, 'Hello?'

* * *

On the doorstep we stopped dead. Light bounced off the snow that lay draped in swathes over the street like so many abandoned evening gloves; the lowering grot of litter lay hidden beneath these rivulets of heart-lifting, purifying white. The plane tree outside our house — the lucky tree, Ann called it, the one that had made us buy the place — cast witch finger shadows across our path and we walked in the direction they pointed, away from the bus stop and the Costcutter, towards the swelling sky in the east. The glare was dizzying; the pavement rose and fell without warning.

'Look at you,' Ann laughed, 'you're a newborn foal. You all right to do this?'

'Post-convalescent high.' Even the air seemed clear — an illusion brought on by the cold thinness of it, as though we were in the Alps.

'You know Andy is beating himself up.'

'He could have got those boys to do it and saved himself the bother.'

'Was it his fault?'

'Not at all. He's mad to feel it was.'

'He'd seen them there before he ran off, he said.'

'So had I. I could have gone with him. They did it, they're responsible.'

'Why didn't you go with him?'

A sports field opened up on the other side of the road, puddled with patches of snow. We were near one of the motorway onramps; you could hear traffic. A lone jogger chugged along the side of the field, his breath visible.

'I don't know.' There was no reason why I shouldn't have joined Andy in search of the park keeper. Was it my fault I had been mugged? Had I, having lived in London all these years, learned nothing?

Ann looked across at me, then away. 'Not that I think you brought it on yourself.'

The phrase popped from her mouth with the force of relieved pressure, a ping-pong ball of thought she had been dying to get rid of. Of course that's what she thought. Inside she was screaming at me, 'You brought it on yourself!'

I wanted a cigarette, and knew there was a Londis on the next street. A quick drag was needed to settle my lungs again, settle my nerves. I coughed in anticipation. We rounded the corner and a squirt of acid shot through my bowels. Three boys in hoods stood in front of the Londis right in our path, one leaning against the railing, the others bulking out the footpath in full harassment mode. I grabbed Ann's elbow and spun her around, back around the corner, walking quickly in the direction from which we had come. All the way down that road my spine twanged with the sense of them coming after us, their footfalls soft in trainers, the shushing of their shell suits, the laughing whisper of their threats. 'Look at him, he's fucking bricking it,' one of the muggers had said that night a week ago. 'Why'n't you run now?' They'd all laughed. 'Run, old man, you going to run?'

The one who'd been first over the fence made a vooshing sound and mocked up a slow-motion action hero run towards me, stopping inches from my face.

'Tom, it's all right, they're not following.'

Ann had stopped walking. She was calling to my back. I took a moment before turning around and returning to her. The empty street felt an unexpected luxury.

'Sorry,' I said. 'That was silly.'

'No.'

'They weren't even the same guys.' We walked on together, her arm hooked through mine. The baby bump protruded sideways these days too; walking like this with Ann was reassuring in the same way that it slows your heart rate down to stroke a cow. So to speak.

'They didn't need to be the same guys. They're a type.'

'I don't know how people tell them apart. They all look alike.' She laughed.

'Do you ever think — ?' I was going to ask her about the man that had been following her, if she'd somehow conflated more than one homeless guy to produce a pattern of stalking. But I wasn't quite ready to question the man's existence. Not ready for the question it would really be asking of Ann. 'Kate's pretty impressive.'

Ann smiled to herself. 'Yes.'

My head hurt and the muscles around my ribs still ached from coughing. A low-slung car with blacked-out windows prowled down the street. We were nearly home.

'Do you believe in ghosts?' Ann said.

Oh my God. 'No. No. Do you?'

She shrugged. 'I don't know.'

Such are the differences between men and women. Ann read her horoscope most days. She and Tonia talked about people in terms of their 'energy' and 'spirit', this gateway language that led straight to hardcore, A-class beliefs in ESP, visions and their own spooky powers. They had coincidental dreams, which they bothered to repeat. They paid for massage from practitioners who didn't even touch them, and claimed to feel the benefits. In their language, the universe was less a space-time continuum than a cosmic deity that bestowed favours or withdrew pleasures according to whether or not you had been a good girl. I had actually heard this from both of them: 'The universe is trying to teach me something.' 'Do you believe in ghosts?' comes from the same English-New Age translation phrase book. That's why I didn't bother to go into it. Excuses, excuses.

N.A.M.W. 05. 07
The horror of his bigness, his redness, he

couldn't be more Ocker if he tried. He
clearly likes it this way, it must unnerve the
money guys. Slaps himself fatly.

'Married on my dime!'

Tom leans over, tipping on to her, laughing, kissing her — she pushes him, *not
now* — pulling back to say, 'Ann's been
married before. I'm her second husband.' He's proud of it, the dickhead.
Why does she feel so hostile? The kava
— the long hot day — something is
making her sick.

Hallie glances at her sideways. 'You Australian?'

Tom looks impressed. 'You clocked it. Set
a thief to catch a thief.'

'You told me, mate.'

Some seconds tock by while Hallie looks
at Ann's upper arm. She raises her other
hand to cover it, catches his gaze. Drops her
hand and looks away. She will not look at
him. Time is opening. She needs to leave. In
the space between them his bulk swells and
inverts, becomes silence.

Tom tips his head back and the edges of
his vision flare and bleed in the torch light.
Cones of fire against the black sky. You can't
get it back. This is your wedding night,
you've drunk too much you've fallen you're
under the spell under the toad and you can

never get this night back.

Ann is standing in the doorway of the wrong bure, apologising to another guest, someone she has woken by mistake. She is in her bathroom splashing water into her mouth. She is alone in bed. Someone is knocking on the door.

The bure is at the north end of the island, near a hill with a white wooden cross. Tom gets the words 'wedding' and 'funeral' mixed up. The day before Ann had sat swinging her legs over the edge of the balcony, her feet golden underwater, their edges wobbling in and out in the refracted light. An orange dove flapped past her and back towards the trees behind. In exchange, a pair of seabirds swooped out over the sea, lifting and falling, joyously firing forwards.

I woke to the sound of a person moving furniture around. The long stretch of bed beside me was empty. Ann's energy dazzled me, even in my sleep-dampened state; I pushed my head deeper into the mattress, in contrast to Ann's busyness, conscious only of the duvet's exquisite touch against my skin, and quietly chased back the narrative of my dream. Hours or minutes later — or maybe only seconds, who knows the time-collapsing power of REM sleep? — I became aware that

Ann was standing over me, beside me, by the bed. The scouring smell of ammonia filled the air, burning my nostrils and throat.

'Ants.'

'What?'

'We've got ants. Everywhere. All over the ceiling downstairs. Rivers of them.'

'You're kidding.'

I didn't want to go downstairs and see snake trails of ants winding out of light sockets and over the walls. I didn't want to get the step-ladder and wipe them up, constantly rinsing the cloth of ant bodies, picking them off, sticky and dark like chocolate hail. I must have groaned, because Ann said, 'Don't worry, I've done it.'

'Really?'

'I was awake.'

I pushed myself up in the bed. The ammonia was waking me up and knocking me out all at once. 'Can you open a window?'

She did. A finger of cold air came through the room. I asked Ann whether she wasn't tired now. She was, she said, but she didn't get back into bed, or even sit down. Creakily, my knees sore from the evening's run with Andy, I swung out of bed — ah, wincing as my right knee took my weight for a second — and limped across the landing to run her a bath.

'You're the loveliest boyfriend I ever had,' she said as the bathroom filled with steam.

I liked being called boyfriend, not husband: it nicely balanced out that middle-aged knee. 'You're no slouch yourself,' I said, taking the yellow rubber gloves from her hands. 'You shouldn't be climbing ladders. You probably shouldn't use that cleaner either.'

She lowered herself carefully into the hot water. I stared at her round belly, the thick blue veins running down her breasts, the enlarged, darkened nipples. What must it feel like to have your body play host to an alien force? Of course she had wanted the baby, it wasn't as though she had been invaded. But nevertheless — how odd to feel the growth and movement inside you of a creature that feeds off your body, that is about to rule every aspect of your life but at this moment in time doesn't really exist.

I was about to go back to bed when Ann started to tell me about the ants. She had got up for a drink of water and remembered that she had to take one of her herbal remedies, the hippie stuff she had for the pregnancy, so went downstairs. She knew something was wrong as soon as she turned on the kitchen light. It was the feeling, she said, of being on a boat waiting to leave dock, and the boat alongside pulls out so you have the uncanny sensation that you're moving backwards when you should be moving forwards, yet you're really not moving at all. A sort of peripheral crawl. Slowly, she looked up. There were cracks in the ceiling, fresh black cracks scored diagonally through the plaster. Repair work: she felt the familiar lurch of money worry in her heart, then ducked her head, so dizzy from craning her neck it seemed the cracks were wriggling. A deep breath and another look confirmed it. They were on the move.

She had done a brilliant job. The ceiling gleamed in streaks with the swipe of her cloth and downstairs smelled of bleach and artificial pine, which made me gag, but there was not the smeared trace of a single ant. I carried the stepladder back outside. The air was sharp against my thin T-shirt, the courtyard full of familiar shadows. I breathed deeply. Ants inside for the winter, a rat decomposing in the walls, the wrong kinds of creatures seeking haven in our house. Tomorrow I would set bait, lay traps, scour out sink pipes. On the way back inside my hands brushed against the rough leaves of the potted lemon geranium, and it was that verbena-tea scent, sweet and clean, that I took with me back upstairs. Ann had fallen asleep in the bath.

We found some clever plug-in devices to

keep rodents away. They emit a high-pitched sound, too high a frequency for the human ear, but just right to send little rats and mice running mad. Ann laughed at the vision of them packing their suitcases and huffing down the street, paws over their ears, to a quieter neighbourhood. We did worry that the constant tone of a sound we couldn't hear might drive us unknowingly insane. And what about the baby? Ann wondered, but I reminded her what the midwife had said about the blood rushing round the womb being as loud as a vacuum cleaner. This didn't stop her trying to brainwash the baby with Mozart, prematurely turn him into a giggling twerp in a periwig and breeches. She drifted further and further down the yew-hedge maze of witchery, brewing up vile-smelling pots of what looked like moss, making faces like a disgusted three-year-old between each bitter sip.

'Why do you do it?' I asked her, 'can't you just take a vitamin?'

She shook her head, her chin puckered. 'Better this way,' she said.

Kate had prescribed drops of this and that to go under her tongue, oils to rub into her skin and different fruited incense cones to burn at various times of the day. The dreamcatcher was the last straw. Ann hung it in our bedroom window, a manky little feather thing with shells and beads hanging off it. I found her downstairs, cross-legged on the living room floor, the stereo headphones clamped either side of her belly, and dangled it like a dead canary in her face. It was, she told me, for keeping out bad spirits.

'Jesus Christ, it's like living with Stevie bloody Nicks,' I said, 'only without the cocaine, which would be more fun.'

'All right,' she said, 'I'll keep it in the bathroom. You're only worried about what the neighbours think.'

'That is so untrue,' I laughed, 'I despise our neighbours, it's what Andy and Tonia will think that worries me.'

Then, as though she was a picture focusing and revealing itself, I saw her, really *saw* her there with the Mickey Mouse-size headphones over the baby bump, and asked her what on earth she was doing.

'I knew you'd freak out,' she said, 'I'm playing the baby some Debussy.'

I didn't know we even owned any Debussy. Debussy, apparently, was the thing these days. She had gone out and bought it specially. For the baby, which probably didn't yet have ears. I did, at least, have the wit to know that most of our bickering on baby-related topics was a way of dealing with fear. In my case, the entirely rational and prescient fear that once the baby was born, Ann and I, as we knew each other, would cease to exist. We didn't know then that it was a boy but Ann always, perhaps with some premonition (to use her New Age language), called the baby 'he'. He would come between us, be the primary man in Ann's life, a defenceless, even smaller, version of me, on whom Ann could practise all her powers of loving and control. It would be the baby she lay next to, the baby who took her breast, the baby in whose ear she whispered.

★　★　★

Bridget was already there, sitting at a table for two by the wall, when I got to the bar in Exmouth Market. I kissed her hello on both cheeks and ordered a glass of red wine from the waitress. On the bus in I'd had no idea why she'd wanted to see me, but now it was clear it wasn't to have a laugh over old times.

'You look well.'

'Thank you. So do you.' She looked down at the table, leaking tears. 'Sorry.'

'It's OK.'

We waited for her to compose herself. She shook her head a little and smiled brightly up at me. 'I heard you're having a baby.' The end of the sentence tailed off; she just mouthed the word, like 'cancer' or 'herpes'; it would have been funny if she hadn't been trying so hard to keep her tears under control.

I nodded, but she had looked away again. 'Yes.' I stood to intercept the waitress and take our wine glasses before she got too close to the table. Bridget was rummaging in her bag for a tissue. 'Are you all right?'

She laughed. ' 'You look well,' that means fat, doesn't it, means I've put on weight.'

'Oh Jesus, Bridge, I thought we'd broken up. I don't have to walk into these gin traps any more.' It was reflex, flirting with her, involuntary.

'Don't worry. I have gained weight, I don't care.'

'You're beautiful.'

'So bloody masochistic. Oh fuck, I shouldn't have called you. I just have' — she wobbled again, everything wavering — 'such regrets, such terrible regrets.'

'Bridget.' I reached across the table for her hands but she drew them away into her lap. 'You were happy.'

'I am, I have been — why didn't you call me? I had to hear it from Sam.' Dead Martin's partner. Ann must have bumped into him; he'd have raced to the phone to tell Bridget, he was cruel that way.

'Well, it's been so long since we saw each other.'

Her words ran over mine. 'I had that abortion.' Oh, fuck. Here it was. 'You agreed.'

One for the road after we broke up, just before I met Ann. Bridget had been pregnant at Martin's funeral and told me in a stony phone conversation the next day, after I had woken with my mind filled with Ann. Had I been too hasty, to ready to encourage her to have the termination? Now she was telling me she would have to have a hysterectomy, that she had endometriosis, one of the only treatments for which was to see a pregnancy through to term. I thought of Ann and the persistent fibroid that showed up on that early scan, but which the baby had, as promised, eclipsed in size. This wasn't my domain, these fleshy inner workings. Even the wine had a bloody aftertaste. How to say to her, I'm sorry? What difference would sorry make? At the next table a group of young women burst into laughter.

'What about John?' They lived together, I knew; we had exchanged change of address emails.

But now he had moved out. 'Every month, the pressure.'

I rubbed my eyes. Had she really expected to get pregnant with John? She had always, it seemed, been old, and now she must be pushing fifty. Sexy still, but old, and if she were to have a baby she'd just about qualify for a *Sun* headline, like those wrinkled long-haired Italian crones whom doctors were always impregnating.

'I'm so sorry.' This was easier. Sorry about, not sorry for. She let me take her hand. Bridget, so tough and raw. Looking at her there, older, her chic haircut more grey than blonde, lines running between her nose and mouth, I wondered whether we could have made it work if I hadn't been so stupid as to be scared of her. Whatever inadequacies she made me conscious of I had forgotten. Others, of course, had taken their place.

I rang Ann. She answered from my study, my computer, trying to source some cheap wax and clay, she told me; she was out of materials and had plans for more figure work.

'I thought you were coming home to watch that new drama of Simon's.'

A one-off play he had made before returning to *Casualty*. What a guy. 'Can you tape it?'

'It finished an hour ago. Where are you?'

'Just going to see Bridget into a cab.'

'I'll probably be asleep.'

We stood on Rosebery Ave. for a long time, talking sporadically. In the silences I inched closer towards her. At the bar, beneath the table, our legs had pressed against the other's, neither of us acknowledging the touch, a couple of people sitting in a cauldron and pretending the fire underneath it is not lit, whistling while behind the bushes cannibals sharpen their knives. She was shocked to hear about the mugging, though had her own robbery story to counter with. Her architecture practice had been burgled twice in the past year, mostly for computers. She'd taken to carrying her work around with her all the time. It was going well, she told me, while we waited on the street, in the tone of someone who had arrived at success and discovered it wasn't what she cared about. She'd won an award.

'Bridget, that's wonderful.'

'Thank you.'

She held my gaze. Everything unsaid ran between us, a current I badly wanted to give in to. My coat was around her shoulders. I felt deeply connected to her; we had been through something painful together, though admittedly the pain had been all hers. The night was still and quiet, and the few taxis that cruised past had passengers already. We decided to walk towards Angel. As we were about to cross St John Street Bridget slid her arm through mine. My right foot was out in the road — I had mentally already crossed it.

I stepped back to the kerb and pressed against her. Both her arms were around my waist now. Her face was hidden against my chest. I lifted her chin to see her in the tawny London light that passed for darkness. She stared at me and blinked slowly. We were drunk. I half laughed and blew out a small gust of breath. 'My God,' I remember saying before I kissed her. 'I can't believe I'm going to do this.' Her mouth was waiting for me but first I pushed her collar aside, put my mouth to her neck, felt the beautiful hot pulse beneath the skin. 'Ah,' she breathed, just as she had always done.

On kissing Bridget I was swept with relief. Yes, the weaselly line that as she was my ex this didn't really count as cheating slipped into my mind, but was quickly flicked away. There was nothing to excuse this, nothing to justify it. It had been years since I'd given Bridget any real thought; after meeting Ann I'd never yearned for her. An enormous weight, the burden of fidelity, lifted from me.

'You were such a hopeless *boy*,' she said to me. 'Such a boy, broke all the time and always trying to get another job and now you own a house, you're going to be a father.' Her hands were in my hair.

'I'm no different, Bridge. Nothing real has changed.'

Unbalanced together we staggered backwards, away from the road, to the display window of a posh butcher's shop. Crazily the liberation of kissing Bridget was all tied up in euphoria at being out of fucking cunting Hackney, away from nasty streets and smelly shops and hateful littering people. There was more of the same everywhere in London, this I knew, but had forgotten how necessary it was to go regularly to the cleaner places, where there was no dog shit and people spat less. The tiles on the butcher's shop were smooth and clean under my hand as I pressed my body right into hers. God it was familiar, it had been eight years since I'd kissed her, she must be forty-seven, poor Bridge, she would never have a baby and yet here she was entirely womanly, her soft waist curving in, her hips lifting up towards me. Her neck led unimpeded to that hollow at the base of her skull, no mass of hair to negotiate, only Bridget's beautiful, queenly head. I had turned her around and had my hands on her ribcage, I was kissing her neck and my fingers made out the curved wire of her bra. One of my legs was pinned between hers. If there'd been a hotel room — a bed — the back seat of a car . . . My hand pushed her skirt up her legs, shifted the fabric aside, felt the heat between her legs. In the close reflection of the shop window I watched the side of her face, her closed eyes above the square shoulder of my winter coat. She twisted again to face me, her breath coming quickly, and our glazed eyes locked together.

'We have to stop,' I said.

The last thing she said to me as she was getting into the taxi was, 'You see who this has made me become? I never would have done this before.'

'It's all right,' I told her. 'Don't feel bad.'

She sank back into the seat and I lost sight of her.

★　★　★

As I unlocked the front door of my house, the elation of betrayal dispersed like steam. I stood for a long time under the shower before climbing into the bed where Ann was sleeping. The wine and tiredness blanketed my shame but it was all waiting there for me in the morning. Ann was dressed and ready for work when I woke. She must have smelled the booze, and looked at me with amusement.

'How was your ex?'

'Oh, she's not in very good shape.' Ann pulled the blinds. Light came into the room like oxygen. 'She's got to have an operation.'

'Poor her.'

Non-committal. She knew I didn't want to start pleading Bridget's case, but it was genuinely painful and I wanted Ann to understand this, to bring it into focus: 'A hysterectomy.'

'She doesn't have any children?'

'No.'

'That's awful.'

Yes it was. But then I wondered, after Ann had kissed me goodbye and chucked a packet of Nurofen on the bed, whether it wasn't somehow Bridget's fault. She had had years in which to have children, especially with that guy she lived with before we met. She just hadn't wanted them. And now, although it had probably been too late for some time, she could view her life through the lens of mine and even make me feel subtly guilty about her problems, as though I had put the disease in her womb. I couldn't believe that just hours before I had felt like the executioner myself of that unwanted pregnancy, a pregnancy she only told me about once she'd decided to end it, in a procedure she didn't even want me coming along to. She had rejected my offer to hold her hand, my offer to pay for her to go private (she knew I didn't have the money but I'd have found it somewhere, I would, I would). I had kept the news from Ann, who had that minute walked into my life. And now it was my fault all over again. Well I would not take the blame.

Ann had left the computer on all night, and its sick starter-motor hum contributed to the buzzing in my head. The screen displayed a web page, black with green text and a heading in the style of dripping blood. Clicking back through Google revealed that she had typed in the search words 'ghost house Hackney'. Fuck's sake. I stabbed the off button without saving anything. A ticklish, erotic shiver ran through me. If Bridget was here now . . . Oh, you fucking fucking fuckwit, Tom, you lightweight fucking idiot. Without even meaning to I had crossed a line that could not be uncrossed. The promise of total faithfulness I made to Ann on our wedding day was broken, and so lightly. This was the behaviour of a careless twenty-four-year-old, not a man soon to be a father, a man who loved his wife.

'Ghost house Hackney': those three words had begun to sum up where we lived. Asked to confirm my address on the phone to BT or the gas company I felt tempted to utter them: 'Ghost house Hackney, down the lane from Hangman's Alley, opposite Bluebeard's Cave, E9.' You'll notice that ghosts generally appear in East London, where the locals are more credible. Ooh, apples and pears I seen the headless lady — or the sinister dead after-hours drinkers, howling Blitz victims, any number of murdered infants. The East Enders are forever choking their babies and hiffing them out of windows. And famous people never get any rest in the afterlife. Churchill, Pope, Anne Boleyn and assorted reputable vicars are kept eternally busy gliding over the uneven footpaths of London, along with Dr Crippen and a couple of whores murdered by Jack the Ripper. Not Jack himself though, probably because he was in fact the Marquess of Salisbury disguised as Queen Victoria, or whatever is the current wisdom. Ghosts crawl over this landscape like termites on a rock.

London as a restless cemetery: it's this kind of sentimentality that reduces great cities to theme parks, politics to jingoism, and every girl in a nightgown to a victim on a flight of stairs. It was hard to believe that Ann, who had a finely honed sense of the ridiculous, was even interested in this stuff, website after website devoted to superstition and gossip. I tackled her about it that night, the night after I kissed Bridget. Once my hangover had lifted my mood that day was triumphant. As though pheromones were in the air, Cheryl had phoned me with the news that Rosemary wanted to see the vampire script again, once I had finished this current pass at it. If the universe, in Tonia's parlance, was teaching me anything, it was that illicit snogging is good for your mojo. Ann raced home and dropped her bag heavily on the hall floor, flourished a bottle of champagne.

'You're going to make it work, Tom, she's going to be all over this script, she's going to want to fuck it.' How radiant she looked, how unsuspecting!

'She's only said she'll look at it. You can look at a dog turd on the street.'

'You can look at the fucking Taj Mahal.'

I followed her peachy body up the stairs, we barely made it to the bed. Afterwards we opened the bottle, drank out of the bathroom mug, naked in the unlit room. When you're drinking with a pregnant woman you've got to pull more than your weight — life is full of these hardships. I felt all-powerful, in on a cosmic joke.

'What's this about ghost house Hackney, Ann? You can't be serious.'

'Why not?'

I laughed, and reached for her ass again.

'I mean it,' she said, pulling the sheets up, shifting away. 'Why shouldn't there be forces we can't see? Why restrict yourself?'

206

'It's all so clichéd — slime down the walls, glowing balls of fire, I mean, come on, most people on those websites who claim to have haunted homes just want to be rehoused by the council.'

'You're such a fucking snob.'

'OK. It's true. But for good reasons.'

'Like what you should do with your serviette after you've eaten? Your fucking napkin?'

'How did we get on to this? I don't care about that stuff. That's my mother's shit. So what if you call the living room the lounge, I don't care!'

'You notice. You do care. You cringe inside.'

'I do not! Why are we talking about this?'

'Because you are so closed off. Your world is tiny, this tiny little garden gnome world.'

'Ann, stop it . . . ' I tried to laugh.

'Only you can be right, you and all those — ' She spat a frustrated growl.

'All those who?'

'You thin men.'

There was hate in her voice. The room, the glow of sex, everything was turned inside out. This had somehow to be about last night. I scrambled for my bearings. Bridget must have phoned Ann. She knew where she worked. But why wasn't Ann asking me head on? 'Look. Maybe I am a snob. There are worse things to be. Are you seriously telling me you believe in ghosts?'

'Don't you? You're the one who writes vampire-slasher films.'

'For. Idiots.' My voice was loud. I turned the light on. She looked ugly.

'That is your problem, Tom, you think everyone else is a moron.'

'Only when they are! Have you read any of those so-called sightings? The ghost of a bear? The smiling red-haired man? You've even got a ghost of your monk, Rahere, the guy your bloody chemo ward's named after. Or,' I remembered a good one, and hunched over, running a finger across my neck, 'a small man with a slit throat?' I laughed. 'People who think they see *kangaroo footprints* in Hyde Park! The ghost kangaroo of London, you seen it lately? Hear it boinging in the night?'

'You know what, fuck you.'

It took me little time to apologise. When hurtful things were said we were quick to clear the air, each truly sorry to wound the other and neither of us wanting to sulk. Apologies and forgiveness came easily, and the mood that followed was always light, pure, as though a window had been opened. Perhaps we brushed aside our conflicts faster than we should have, aware of a gap between us too appallingly large to peer down into.

That's hindsight, which is not always the most generous lens through which to remember love. Kinder to say we were not grudge bearers, we were not children; fallible, of course, but gentle on the whole.

The champagne bottle was empty. Silently we dressed and went downstairs. I talked about God knows what, as if nothing was the matter, made us dinner and behaved in a generally saintly fashion ('controlling', my remorseful present self cries out, 'wilfully blind and controlling'); we watched a little *Newsnight* and then I went up to bed.

I was almost asleep when I felt Ann slide in beside me. At this stage in the pregnancy she had taken to sleeping in a fortress of pillows: under the bump, between her knees, under her ankles — it was like being in bed with the Michelin man and about as sexy. I heard the pillows gently thudding one by one to the floor. Ann's body felt velvety and generously curved without the frightening visuals of the swollen belly. Her thighs were squishier than before. I scratched the backs of her calves with the top of my fingernails. She wore a bra, a satin cantilevered thing that thrust her breasts up into pornographic handfuls. I pulled at them so they spilled over the bra cup, rubbing my thumbs along the nipples which were silky as water, lightly and then

209

harder until she made a sound. In the pitch dark of our room behind the blackout blinds, we slowly fucked. I bit her earlobe. She put my fingers in her mouth.

When I got out of the shower in the morning she was standing there wearing a creamy-gold slip in the steam, examining the smudged finger marks on her chest and thighs, the red spots on her bony knees. I kissed the side of her throat. If I could have stayed there for ever I would have, my mouth lying against the damp skin, the pure line of her collarbone, her hair falling over me, protecting me. All manner of secrets could have been whispered into the brave, delicate column of her neck. Ann's pulse throbbed.

'I love you,' I said.

We looked at each other through a porthole I rubbed in the mirror; she began to brush her hair, a mermaid, siren from another world.

'Brute,' she said, with some satisfaction.

'Talentless brute,' I reminded her.

She laughed. 'Yes. Although you're not a bad fuck.'

'Watch it, while you're holding that hairbrush.'

'Get out.' She pushed me. I left the door open a crack and perched on the stairs, not wanting to be too far from her. 'Oh God, I'm so old to have a baby,' Ann moaned from the bathroom in that half talking to herself, half talking to me voice that married people use. Without spying through the gap in the door I could tell by that voice that she was attacking her grey hairs with the tweezers. There were hardly any — it was a vain gesture that mattered only to Ann. I loved that voice, I loved hearing Ann's inner thoughts as they rose gently to the surface, a ribbon of intimate words floating out of her mouth on the bathroom steam and through the door to me, where I opportunistically sat, ostensibly waiting to clean my teeth but really living for this moment.

★ ★ ★

We all needed to get away. I finished the draft of the vampire script and forwarded it to Rosemary. The last push of the rewrite left me gasping for a break, some seaside air. Things were very bad between Tonia and Andy. I knew this through no conversation with Andy, but from Ann. To use that horrible phrase, the emotional housework was done almost exclusively by the women in our friendship. Andy — who was, I knew, under great pressure at work — and I had met up with some of his old college friends to play football. It was a way to get the tension out; Ann and I couldn't have bruising hot sex every night. Once upon a time of course I could have, he says with a spluttering cough, but the pregnancy was a convenient excuse. As Andy and I thudded over the hard winter ground of some South London sports field, our throats burning, our women were busy cleaning out the Augean stables behind us. We men were free — to mask our wine addictions behind pretending to be connoisseurs, to try to keep up with new music, to banter about foreign, not domestic, policy, and to kick a ball around. Except all of the old college friends had families now, and Andy didn't want to socialise afterwards while they proudly knocked a few casual kicks back and forth with their kids. We'd be the ones sloping off first, past their mixed-message wives (pressed blouses: pray with me; jeans tucked into boots: pray for me) as they bliddle-ipped the remote control locking function on the four-wheel drives. Even football didn't improve Andy's mood.

From the start that trip was different. In the old days we'd bag some cheap flights to Pisa or Barcelona or Malmö, hire a car, zip along empty continental motorways towards our rented villa with pool, if it was summer, or boutique hotel if it was not. This long, pregnant winter we rented a cottage in Cornwall. The girls were in charge and Ann had decided that fat as she was, she wasn't up for the cud-chewing shame of economy travel. We arrived late on Friday night, in our separate cars. Poor Andy had some meeting with the head teacher that he couldn't get out of so they were late leaving London. It fell to Ann and I to warm up the old stone house, light candles, light the fire, open wine, all of these things she loved to do and was so good at. As she switched the kitchen light on it burst with a second of brightness then went out, dead. By the steady circle of her torch light Ann found a spare bulb, found the master power switch, cut the current, steadied the rocky kitchen chair with a square of newspaper, climbed up on it, swapped the tinkling darkened bulb for the new one, and gave us light. I was not such a fuckwit as to have been standing there watching while all this went on — in fact I had been shaking woodlice from the firewood before bringing it indoors — but I saw the chair beneath the bulb and worked it out through my brilliant powers of deduction. Either that or she was planning to hang herself from the light fitting and it didn't look as though it would hold her newly bulked-up weight. Oh, this is a new one, gallows humour. I can make jokes about Ann's death. Not funny ones — that would be too much to expect. Perhaps this is one of the stages of grief that eluded Kübler-Ross. Maybe it goes anger, denial, bargaining, bad taste.

The walls inside the cottage were painted a creamy white over the bricks, and in the living room the candlelight bounced off them casting Ann into rich pools of yellow. I tinkered with the ancient stereo, looking up every few seconds to watch her move around the room, practising her new galleon way of walking, leaning with that awkward stateliness over an ottoman to find bedding. Watching her gave me a pleasure that echoed through my whole body, the vibrations of a copper bell. My wife.

It was our tradition that whoever arrived last was given the choice of bedrooms. Together Ann and I made up the beds, and she filled me in on the troubles between Tonia and Andy — more conviction on Tonia's part that he was seeing someone else, another teacher at the school, and his increasingly indignant denials.

'Can you ask him,' she said. She rubbed the small of her back, panting slightly as I tossed the pillows on to the bed in the attic room.

'It's dusty in here,' I said. 'Are you getting asthma?'

'Maybe some chimney dust. But Tom, can you? Tonia would really be grateful.'

'Well, no.' I explained: Andy was hardly likely to confide in me something he was denying to his wife. He would likely be furious. I couldn't understand why Tonia, on this holiday, would want to force a confrontation.

'Safety in numbers?' Ann guessed.

The lights of Andy's ancient Saab swung past the window, over the crunching rise in the driveway. One, then another, the car doors banged. I followed Ann as she negotiated the slippy wooden stairs.

'Hello?' called Tonia's voice.

We could feel the cold night air even from the landing and I did not have a chance to respond when Ann murmured, 'Not everyone's like you, Tom. Sometimes people want to know.'

Later, it didn't seem worth prodding her further. The battles we choose to avoid, in marriage, are crucial to what keeps us together, but now those victories of silence are bone-cold, hollow ice caves. So you kept the peace, well done, well done. Congratulations on all those clichés you failed to open, the cans of worms, the floodgates, the boxes fumbled at by Pandora. It takes a special skill to lean whistling against the cupboard door while inside the skeleton lolls, beating at the handle with its ineffectual rattly hand, trying its hardest to get out. Around Ann it was easy to live in the present tense because she made life seem naturally lifted. In this way she was very English, attentive to the surface, reluctant to, in the language of Americans, get heavy. That long weekend her grace flowed in clear contrast to the tense civility that passed between our friends. Tonia and Andy were at odds over everything, starting with which bedroom they wanted. The attic room was the nicer but rather than a double it had two single beds. Ann and I were happy to push these together, although I worried about her asthma up there, but we let them decide. To break protocol now over choosing a room would somehow be to disrespect the family-ness of us four, and Ann was not about to pull rank because of being pregnant. Back and forth Andy and Tonia went, and it was clear to any fool that Andy was pushing for the twin beds while Tonia was determined they would share the double. Ann and I pretended to rummage in the kitchen looking for wine glasses. Both couples hissed at each other in different rooms.

We took off for a drive before the others

woke the next morning. Tonia had won the battle with Andy so we'd slept in the twin beds in the attic, and Ann was a little wheezy. It was ridiculous, putting her friends' sex life before her health, but she'd insisted on supporting their choice of room and now we were driving to St Ives in search of a Saturday morning pharmacy. Neither of us minded the mundanity of the errand. Last night we had pushed the beds together and held hands in the perfect country darkness, tucked in chaste as children under single sheets. Strange children, I suppose, pregnant and neurotic, but happy ones. For a while we whispered about our friends. Their troubles made us feel close. Ann fell asleep first and I lay listening to the shallow neediness of her breath, never quite enough getting in or getting out. She sat beside me now, her shoulders slightly worked with asthma, face pale, as we drove at crawling pace through a sea-mist that muffled the world in white. That day we drove all over the Lizard and saw nothing but the road a little way in front of us. St Ives was a long search for a car parking space and after that to find a pharmacy that would fill Ann's out-of-date script for Ventolin, a soft rag of paper found that morning in the bottom of her handbag. That was typical Ann, to carry a prescription but not the medicine she needed.

The all-hours pharmacy owners were not as suspicious as their London counterparts and did not believe an inhaler was a mysterious but necessary ingredient for homemade crystal meth; they handed the magical device over and Ann was instantly opened up, she bloomed again like a paper flower dropped in water. There was a monstrous crowd at the Tate, so we walked for a while in the Barbara Hepworth gardens before returning to brave the cottage. I don't know what we talked about. Really there are few conversations that are easy to remember, and even fewer actual statements. When I put words into Ann's mouth, on these pages, it's made up, of course, another way to get her to speak again. The way she talked, I can be faithful to that, and the occasional line. But mostly Ann and I, like everybody else, just asked each other to please pass the salt, and what we really meant was, 'please pass the salt.' Maybe, at the Hepworth Museum, amongst those dark plants and curved lines, we were silent, wrapped still in the invisible fog that held us together and obscured everything. The real fog lingered on the roads back towards the cottage. Tall Cornish wild flowers poked holes through its wisps, rising out of the low clumps of long grass that remained in shadow. We got through the night by playing

Ex Libris with the cottage's supply of old paperbacks. The next day, after breakfast, we went out again with Tonia and Andy and drove along the same roads as though they belonged to another planet. All trace of mist was gone. Sharp sunlight brought the green and yellow world right up to our faces. Hard on our right was the vanished drop of cliff, and beyond it, stretched tight as far as the horizon, the surprising turquoise sheet of sea.

Ann and I had begun to behave like parents or nurses, making dinner, taking charge of the wine, suggesting plans for the last day of our break. The silent understanding between us all hummed like the golden stroke of a violin, it was restful and sustaining. In line with the quantity theory of happy relationships she and I were tightly, telepathically as one, while in the back seat of the car Andy and Tonia fell away from each other, vertiginously, into their dark individual thoughts. It was better, perhaps, that they didn't try to cover up, put on a show for us — that would have been pretty unbearable, taut smiles fixed over their hollowed-out skulls — but all the same I found myself thinking, after hours of sympathy, oh please go and be miserable somewhere else. The day had clouded over and it was as though Tonia had made it happen, she was all barking laughs and hate for everything: the crab lunch at Mousehole was out of a tin, of course she'd walk to St Michael's Mount if the rest of us wanted to but it was definitely going to rain, did we know that Sally, a mutual friend, was dating a drug dealer and this would end badly for her but that was typical Sally, she had a self-destruct setting, blah blah blah. She was right, at least, about the rain, which arrived suddenly and thunderingly from the sea as though a series of giant waves were spraying over us. Yes, Ann said to the slushing windscreen wipers as I negotiated the search of another bloody car park near — what town was it, I don't remember — and Andy sat silent in the back. Yes, Ann had spoken to Sally about this guy and she seemed very much in love. Well how could she be, Tonia demanded, she doesn't even know the fellow. He's a drug dealer. Scum. Surely Ann had told her to get out of the whole thing?

'No,' Ann said. 'it's not my business to tell her that.'

'Yes it is, you're her friend.'

'But she didn't come to me for advice. She's happy.'

'Well it's fucked. It's going nowhere.'

Through the blur of the street a red-painted CAFÉ sign shone faintly. If you squinted you might think it looked welcoming. As soon as I braked the car, Tonia opened the door into the rain and went skipping off across the parade. Literally skipping, like a child unprotected, towards the beach wall. The rest of us stood under the rain-bashed café awning, huddling into our ugly orange waterproofs while she flung herself up and down the liquid sand, black corkscrews of hair lashing.

'Sorry about this.' Andy had to shout over the drumming rain although we were right next to him.

Ann said, 'I'll go.'

We left her to talk down the nervous horse (the friend whisperer: perhaps I could work this into a premise for a comedy, call Simon Wright in LA) and agreed to meet in the coffee shop. Andy said when I asked that he was all right, but he would rather not talk about it. This improved my mood. We read the *Cornishman* of the day before: 'SCANDAL OF BULGARIAN WORK TEAMS'. It was a good twenty minutes later when Ann came into the café, drenched, and announced that she and Tonia were just going to look around the shops for a bit — this being code for 'the job is not yet finished,' which pissed me off. More annoying still was Tonia's mood when an hour after that they did return, bearing anonymous plastic bags of junk-shopped trinkets: her step was light, her cheeks shining, her voice infuriatingly care-free. She had stolen my wife and she carried Ann's loyalty like a trophy. Fuck it. Right. I stood.

'Are we ready? Let's go.'

'Oh — we were just going to get some afternoon tea.'

'Can you grab a sandwich? I want to get out of here.'

But Tonia was already at the counter ordering a cappuccino. Ann tried, Andy tried, attempted jokes were wheeled out and unwittingly patronising questions asked of me ('So how is the work going?': Andy. 'Are you sure you don't need me to look at the map?': Ann) but the afternoon was ruined.

Andy offered to drive back. Only one of us was talking — Tonia, about some new CD or other she promised to inflict on us later that night. There would be no later that night, is what I decided. I do not mean I planned to go postal, as our American friends say, and send us all to our doom with the cottage cleaning bill unpaid. I just planned to get away, with Ann. Getting away with Ann was one of the best things about my life. God, I have known what it is to stand on the cliff top looking down at the Whirlpool of Self-Pity.

My toes have gripped the crumbling earth, loneliness bending me at the waist, arms windmilling to stay upright, stay on the edge, just watch that loose stone tumble down into the sucking water, see how quick it disappears from view. Self-pity must be resisted, not out of moral fortitude but as a means to survive. Quick, I would say to myself in those gashed-out early months after Ann had died, quick, think of someone worse off than you — think of Alan Tranter who laughs nervously to make you like him even as he is chiselling away every penny he can behind your back, even as he abandons ship. His desperate people-pleasing hair. His penis car. And think of Bridget, no child to drive her crazy, all of those empty weekend possibilities. Don't, for God's sake, think of your incredibly fortunate parents who in forty-five years of marriage have suffered nothing more than the odd gallstone and a dodgy prostate (dad's, just to be clear). Or all the friends you know who have each other still, who do not bear this black mark of *bottomless pit*, the frighteningly unknowable brand of *loss*. You'll turn into one of those sad protagonists from a feel-good film, strolling down the street alone at Christmas time, all around you mistletoe couples and shoulder-riding families rosily bouncing past, until you reach a park bench and have a meaningful conversation with a wise, gnarled old homeless man, and so set forth on your path of reform, towards true love with the shop girl who twenty minutes ago in movie-time you treated like shit. Oh, Tom, I would say, parked outside my house and howling in the car, Arlo bewildered in his baby seat in the back, especially do not think of bad successful movies because you only remind yourself that you never even delivered to the penis car driver a bad unsuccessful screenplay and anyway you're only harsh because everything else looks or reads like shit when you're working on something, you know that to be true. You're harsh because you lost your wife. You're harsh because, like Tonia that day in the sand and the storm, you have been RIPPED OFF and everything is your barking laugh and hate.

Andy was driving. He remembered, no doubt thinking to neck a bottle of Pinot Noir as soon as we reached the cottage, that we had drunk all the wine last night, and swung back towards the small row of beachfront shops, where there'd been an offie. As he indicated to pull into a diagonal parking space there was a quick flash of a yellow indicator light in my peripheral vision and the complaint of a car horn.

'Hey, I think you've just stolen that guy's space.'

'You know what?' he said. 'Too fucking bad.'

Andy recalled it for us later, though he could only remember clearly the moments up to the attack, before the gaps opened up in his mind like pages of black ink. It was an effort to open the umbrella; the handle shook beneath the driving rain. The world between the car and the off licence was doused in grey. He slammed the car door shut behind him and we were encased again in quiet. Andy couldn't see anything in the rain. Suddenly his left hand was wrenched from his back pocket — the wine money sprang from his fingers — and that arm was forced right up into his shoulder blades in a sickening twist. The umbrella arm flailed at the relentlessly wet air behind him as he was pushed into the deep doorway next to the shop — the handle easily tugged from his hand, the umbrella kicked away. He felt the brush of nylon, then pressure at the back of his head and thunk face first into the rough concrete wall.

We sat in the car cocooned by the drumming rain, but Ann saw the umbrella spinning down the street. When she opened her door to get it she heard Andy. At the same time we all saw the white boy-racer car parked on a diagonal, its doors flung open. Andy's arms were cradled over his head when we reached him. A woman was shrieking the name Gary and pulling on the arm of Andy's attacker. Gary was bald, his neck bursting with spider web tattoos. Rain bounced off his head and his soaked nylon jacket clung to his heaving chest. He spat at Andy, which was easily the worst part of the whole thing. Andy began to move. I flinched. He drew a hand from his forehead and examined the speckled grit and blood streaked on his palm. Gary looked slowly around at the rest of us — his eyes fixed on Tonia, who'd run to Andy, was holding his face — and he said something I didn't catch. She drew a sharp breath. A voice I'd never heard before exploded in my ear, ragged and pointy, shouting obscenities. Ann. She screamed, her face vacuum sucked towards the strangers, white flecks at her lips. Gary's woman clung to him, blonde rats' tails straggled down her face in the rain, she screamed back at Ann and in a tunnel somewhere Andy was saying, 'It's just a fucking parking space mate, what are you, a fucking nutter?' Tonia had the police on her phone — she waved the handset at Gary as if it had magic powers — but it was obvious that, yes, Gary was a fucking nutter, there would be no point calling in the law. The blonde came closer, her thin little face shoved right into Ann's. 'She's pregnant,' I said, reaching forwards, but she gasped, the blonde, as though she was going to be sick. Ann had punched her hard in the breast. The woman swung back again towards Ann with a clawed hand. I got a grip on her wrist just as she grabbed Ann's hair — she yanked Ann's head and my arm with it down towards the ground.

Ann had punched her. In the breast. There was a pungent smell on top of the woman's alcoholic skin and sugary perfume. Her hand was locked into a mass of Ann's hair like iron. Andy and Gary said words to each other very loud and slow. I prised at the purply cold fingers. The lizard feel of them, the torn edges round the nails made me want to retch. Ann cursed the woman in a low Australian litany — 'fuck you ya cunt ya dirty fucken little mole ya skank whore' — and I was thinking, get rid of her, get this woman away from us somehow, without bringing down more Gary, more nylon shell suit pain. We were going to get knifed. Our baby stabbed, kicked, hurt.

Ann twisted her neck round and bit hard on the woman's wrist. 'Fucking hell' and the blonde released her, ran clutching her forearm back to Gary. It all depended now on what he did. The woman got in the passenger seat of their car and screamed at Gary from behind the windscreen. He turned to look at her and back again. He was still between us and the road, us and our car.

'I've called the police,' said Tonia. 'The police are on their way.'

Please don't come for us again, I was thinking. Please don't have a knife.

'You're a fucking idiot,' Gary said to Andy, and to all of us, 'People like you make me sick.' He stuck his middle finger up at us as he drove away.

'Was she bleeding?' I asked Ann. 'Did you break the skin?'

She turned her head and spat on the ground. I turned away. 'I don't think so,' she said.

The horrible smell was still there.

Tonia said, 'I saw him about to pull into that parking space.' This sentence tumbled like concrete to the ground.

'So did I,' Andy said. 'Sorry.'

Ann pulled me to one side. 'I don't want to go to the police,' she said.

I didn't either but it seemed to be something we would have to endure. 'Why not?'

She burst into tears and looked down. 'I've wet myself,' she said.

The cops told us that I couldn't take Ann home before we had to go and give a statement. Andy wanted to drive us but his hand shook so he couldn't make the key go into the ignition. Ann sat in the back on her Windbreaker, her head in her hands. 'It's not that bad,' Tonia said. I concentrated on following the squad car to the small local hospital, where Andy was seen straight away. Ann found a bathroom and cleaned up as best she could. In a beige hallway we sat on office chairs. The officers looked self-conscious, the way cops always do outside a police station, as though the uniforms they wore were stolen from their big brothers and they were waiting to be found out.

The assault report was basic. Andy, a white rectangle of plaster on his scraped cheek, told them Gary was wearing jeans.

'I'm pretty sure it was tracksuit pants,' I said. There was an awkward pause, in which Andy looked at his gauzed hand.

'Yes,' said Ann, 'it was a light-blue tracksuit.'

None of us could agree on the details. Tonia said the girlfriend had brown hair, when it had definitely been blonde but darkened by the rain. Were they driving a Citroën AX? No, it was a Ford of some kind, perhaps a Laser. It was white, a white car, a three-door. Or not. Maybe a five-door hatchback. Tonia had written down the number plate; one thing at least was beyond doubt. They agreed to discharge Andy as long as he promised he'd come to the station if they needed him to identify the man. Frankly, the older officer said while his colleague was checking through the paperwork, that's unlikely.

A nurse told us we were free to go. 'But what about you?' I said to Ann, 'We should get you checked out.'

'I'm sorry,' said the nurse, 'is there another patient?'

'No,' said Ann, 'we're fine.' To me she said, 'Let's just get out of here.'

Back in the attic room I sat on the edge of the bed while Ann, freshly showered and changed, cleaned her teeth in the small basin.

'You're sure you didn't break that woman's skin,' I said, 'when you — you know.'

'I didn't.' Ann laughed softly. 'It takes a lot to break someone's skin.'

I hesitated. 'You looked like you would know.'

'Sorry. I lost it.'

'You freaked me out.'

'I freaked myself out.' She stroked down the side of her belly in a newly habitual way. 'I guess it's being pregnant.'

'Yes.'

After she'd finished at the basin she sat beside me and held my hand. 'Are you OK?'

'Are you?'

Andy was like a sculpture in the armchair and Tonia sat on the sofa on the other side of the room. She swung her legs off it when we entered, drew Ann down beside her. I poured everyone a glass of wine.

'Did I start that,' said Andy, 'what I did?'

'No,' said Ann. 'Nothing justifies that violence. You can't think of him in that way.'

'What way?'

'The same as you. Someone who might be reasonable.'

'I don't feel very reasonable.'

'You heard what he called me,' Tonia said.

'What did he call you?' I'd missed it.

Nobody wanted to say.

'Never mind,' I said.

After a while the room was dark. Ann rose to turn on the yellow lamp. I cooked pasta. When we were scraping the bowls in the kitchen I whispered to Ann, 'Would you mind if we went back to London tonight?'

'I'd love to. But what about the others?'

'Let's see what Andy wants.' There was a current, a rip, pulling me out of that place, and resisting it was hard work. Like Ann in the hospital, I just wanted to go.

The others had dug out the dusty old television set from behind the sofa and were watching a new comedy show. We flung ourselves into it; no one mentioned the TV ban that was another one of our holiday regulations. On the tiny greenish screen people said horrible things about each other. Ann gripped my arm and laughed till it came from her in short high whimpers, tears pouring from her eyes. In the commercial breaks normal conversation trickled back in, a note of kindness. 'God, Andy,' Tonia said, 'poor you, darling.' She slid off the sofa to sit on the floor, leaned against his knees. It was all right to leave after that.

Ann slept, surrounded front and back by her oddly shaped pillows, for most of the journey home. We should, I knew, be driving straight to the Homerton A & E department for blood tests, maybe a tetanus shot if pregnant women were allowed tetanus shots. I had been watching the woman, watching Gary, not Ann — perhaps she had wiped her mouth, perhaps there had been streaks of red in her spit. Why had we not already seen a doctor? What could she be tested for? Yes hello, my wife bit someone, can you check her for rabies please? Ann pissed herself and *bit* someone, she bared her teeth and put her mouth on that disgusting woman and bit her.

That, and the ease with which she cursed her, the voice that came out like it had always been there. Waiting inside. My back hurt from driving, there was sandpaper behind my eyes. The only CD in the car was *Blood on the Tracks*, which I was sick to death of but let play on repeat. 'If you see her, say hello . . . ' I drove past the first signs telling me how far we had to go to London. Red tail lights blurred through the rain. The wheels clicked over the road as we passed under tall highway lights, marking off distance with the relentless progress of a metronome. Dylan sang. We had been to see him at the Brixton Academy, before Ann was pregnant, a world ago. We stood at the back with Andy and Tonia and tried not to mind that we couldn't understand the words. Ann I don't think did mind, she was there for the atmosphere, being in the presence. But Dylan was about the lyrics and without them I was cheated, sore legs and bad beer in a joint full of men in leather waistcoats who looked like they were fresh from jail. With a lurch I woke up floating across the lane lines . . . the blare of a car horn trailing in the night. Quickly I righted the car. A people mover hooshed past on my left, jabbing its horn. Ann jerked awake.

'What's happening?'

'Sorry.'

'Jesus, Tom.'

'Sorry, sorry, lost focus there for a second.'

'Were you asleep?'

Adrenaline squirted through me. Lights flickered and burned, flickered and burned, there was no way off this motorway and I'd just nearly crashed us. It seemed a miracle that the car was still going forwards intact, that we weren't a hundred yards back there in a mangle of smoke and flesh. Half of me believed we were. There was no way to slow down, no way to stop and all I wanted to do was pull over, park on the side of the road, in a ditch, I didn't care, to turn off the shuddering horrible thing and unbuckle myself and walk out into the freezing fresh night. Instead of that freedom we were trapped in the car, the delicate circle of the steering wheel and my control of it the only thing between us and death. No choice but to keep going, to rely on my paper-thin ability to keep us aligned, to not swerve into the barrier, to not let go.

'There's a lay-by. Pull over.'

I swerved into it. My hands were shaking. Ann leaned over the seats, pulled our coats and a travel blanket into the front and arranged them around the two of us. 'Five minutes' kip,' she said. 'It's all you'll need.' It was hard to get comfortable but bliss to not be driving. Ann ducked behind the open passenger door and had a wee quickly, shamefully, on the gravel, in the dark. Perhaps ordinarily I'd not have minded. The smoky smell of her urine stained the night air. 'Quick, shut the door,' I said, 'it's bloody Arctic.' I didn't know when I would want to kiss Ann again. She'd need to wash her mouth. I shut my mind to it all, let the random images of sleep eat me up. We clutched at each other's hands and rested our heads together, eyes closed. It was like being in an aeroplane, on a long-distance flight.

N.A.M.W. 05. 07

The aluminium frame of a doorway is sharp along her upper arm as she leans into it, there's the light pressure of a screen door on a hinge against her back. This cabin looks like hers but the person in front of her is not Tom, this is a young woman whose smooth body Ann has watched as she delicately walks the beach in her bikini. The girl clutches a sarong to her nakedness like a sheet. She is angry. 'You're in the wrong place.'

'I'm so sorry.' Ann sniffs and wipes her nose with one upward sweep of her hand.

She's been crying for a few minutes. 'I have to go.'

This is the second bure she has tried. The one before held the girl's parents. Shells pricked beneath her bare feet on the path between the cabins.

'Who is it?' Vincent Desjardin comes out of the bedroom, a towel around his slithery hairless body. He scowls at Ann. 'You are in the next bure on your right.'

'Thank you.'

She is in her bathroom splashing water into her open mouth and spitting, spitting into the sink. Her veins are drained of blood, her body shaking. Sand showers from her when she moves.

The bookshelves of the Camden flat. Tom is out. Ann stands frozen, still. A man's voice. Nonsense words. She is afraid that it might have been her who spoke them. Snatches her keys from the hook and runs down the steep stairs, heels skidding on the carpet, out into the hot and fume-filled street, particles of dirt coating her skin, comfort in strange faces.

She presses the machine down on a face mould.

She lies under the mosquito net in Fiji and at the same time on the thin aluminium bed of the mould room. H. lays the plasters over her upper arm, her cancer. 'This will feel a bit cold.' Somebody else said that.

Maybe Ann dreamed this. Maybe I did. When I woke up in the lay-by it was one in the morning and Ann was snoring lightly, jaw open. I pulled the car out on to the much emptier motorway and drove us back to London, letting her sleep. She floated slowly up the path, eyes still nearly closed, as at last I unlocked our front door with its beautiful dents and flaking paint and grimy door knocker. I nearly kissed the wolf's head. We kicked aside the new bills, hauled our bags up to the bedroom, cranked up the radiators and slid between our blissful sheets. Ann quickly slipped into sleep again. I got out of bed to check the phone messages. Nothing from Rosemary. She must be out of town, I thought.

★　★　★

The baby was very active now. Ann loved the feeling of it pushing inside her, the rolling over of a foot across the front of her belly, the dream speed at which it twisted around. Small, slow, below-the-surface eruptions rose and fell into her hands as she held the bump, the baby seemingly feeling her touch and kicking towards it. Her skin burned with the stretching until she began to use the special oil Kate gave her, which left grease smudges on the sheets. It was unperfumed; the very nothingness of its smell had a certain grey aspect. She slathered herself morning and night after her increasingly long baths. What had her own mother felt, she wondered aloud, pregnant with her, so much younger than she is now? The bath was the place where she cried. She tried to describe to me the fear she felt in having to do this blind. Tears splashed into the bath-water, drowning world, I rinsed her hair with the jug and told her everything would be all right. She spoke of being swallowed — not from any loss of self but from the engulfing crash of love that broke over her even now, even when the baby was still only a burgeoning idea. Books warned her, the doom merchant receptionist at work warned her, anything can happen, take each day as it comes. But Ann knew this baby was going to be perfect, to arrive whole, perfect and alive. Steam billowed through the bathroom and slid into a slick of moisture on the walls. Very hot baths were warned against, but Ann couldn't resist. She liked the sting of the water, the feeling the pressing heat gave her of being held. She climbed out into the waiting towel I unfolded for her and I held her too.

Kate had had both of her children at home. I thought this was a bloody stupid idea and to my relief so did Ann. 'I spend all my time in a hospital,' she said, 'I don't care if it's another few days of my life.'

The Saturday after Cornwall we trekked to the baby section at a massive department store up west to elbow our way through the confusing welter of Moses baskets and buggies. For the first time Ann, who had appeared so blithe about our financial peril, panicked. Here was reality: the saleswoman in her blue polyester looking through us while counting the minutes to her lunch break, the pairs of much younger parents ordering two-way strollers and step-ladder highchairs, the stacks of bed linen in half a dozen different sizes, the hold-your-breath cost of this new pastel world and its insistence on its own necessity. Ann gripped my elbow. 'The baby can sleep in a shoe box, we can use a drawer from the dresser, he can wear, I don't know, customised socks or something, I'm going to breastfeed so who needs bottles, who needs to pay fifty quid for a steriliser?' Now, on the fourth floor above a heaving, grimy Oxford Street, all pear-shaped girls and mullet-faced shop-zombies, we were looking at car seats that came in colours from pistachio to dusk, averaged one hundred and fifty pounds, and would not last the baby much more than nine months. 'Didn't we all just bounce around in the back? Or have a basket or something you could wedge in?' She was laughing but it didn't mask her desperation.

'The law requires you have to have a car seat, you won't be permitted to leave hospital without one.' The saleswoman had the black lower-eye smears of dairy intolerance and low blood pressure. It was all our fault. 'Of course you could look at this three-in-one travel system. The infant car seat comes as part of it.' She gestured towards a contraption that might have been designed by NASA.

'Oh, that looks nice. How much is it?'

'Five hundred and thirty pounds. The specially tailored fabric is only sixty-nine.'

'But I can't have just the fabric. That wouldn't meet safety regulations.'

A blank stare. You're not funny. I want my sandwich. 'No, madam. You would have to purchase the whole item.'

'Right, well I'll have to think about it.'

Time waster. 'I advise you to order your purchase well in advance.'

'Thank you.'

'You know what?' I said just before the woman was out of earshot, 'I bet we don't need one this flash.'

Ann took a deep breath. This was the best though, the best car seat for our baby. It wasn't just a car seat, it was a travel system! We would be depriving our child if we didn't have it. Likewise the orthopaedic cot mattress and the cashmere-mix blankets. These remarks were only half mocking. Other people had these things. Why couldn't we?

'Listen,' I said, pulling my wallet from my jeans pocket, drawing out a credit card. 'You know what? I'm going to get this.' The travel system in my arms, I marched over to the queue to pay, dumped half the stuff we'd gathered on the counter, let some of it slide around by my legs. The woman in front of me looked down at her ankles where the box of bottles was impinging on her personal space. I glared at her: 'What?'

Ann joined me. 'Tom. We can't afford it.' A couple of baby-faced expectant parents by the cloth books stand looked in our direction. I ignored everyone. This was what credit cards were for. Ann hissed. 'Just put them back. We'll come back later.'

'Ann. Relax.'

'Don't tell me to relax!' She picked up a pile of the cashmere blankets. I snatched them and plonked them back in front of the cashier. One of them tipped over the edge into her navy Crimplene lap. Without looking at us she returned it to the bench. Ann tried to grab the car seat off me. I clung to the handle. The woman in front ostentatiously moved out of our way. We tugged it back forth, back, forth, mine, *mine*, and eventually I managed to wrench it out of her hand. 'Ouch!' Ann rubbed at her wrist.

'I. Am. Getting. This,' I said.

Her cheeks mottled red, she quickly walked away without giving me another glance. Beep, beep, beep, our new baby items passed through the red barcode light and disappeared into giant rustling plastic bags. My hands itched to snatch the car seat back, dash round the corner where they were stacked and replace it with a cheaper version, but I gritted my teeth and toughed it out. Beep.

'Sign or PIN?' the cashier smiled.

★   ★   ★

Ann took the phone into the bath and had a lengthy conversation with Kate. I watched telly in bed and when the sound was muted in between programmes I could hear the endless murmuring loop, devolving into helpless laughter. The next day neither of us referred to or touched the pile of department store bags that were still in the front room

242

where I'd slung them, Ann pretending quite convincingly that neither they, nor I, existed. That afternoon Kate turned up with Titus Groan, Ruby Tuesday and a carload of baby kit. I helped her unload, both of us struggling not to slip on the icy ground. It had sleeted in the night and the sky was dark; spring would never come. Our hall floor disappeared beneath a checked holdall full of baby clothes, another bulging with bedding, a wooden highchair, a car seat and the three-wheeler buggy it clicked into, as well as a bottle steriliser that looked suspiciously new.

'Oh my goodness.' Ann couldn't thank Kate enough. 'I don't know what to say.'

'You're doing us a favour. We're never going to have another baby and it's so nice to be able to pass these things on. You've given us our hall cupboard back.'

This was laying it on slightly thick, I thought, but in the face of such generosity who was I to criticise the way it was delivered? I joined the gratitude parade.

'Please,' said Ann, 'stay for a cup of tea.'

'Oh, I'd love to but Titus has a lesson over at Lea Valley in twenty minutes.'

'At the riding school? That'll be a bit chilly!'

'They're doing stable work today.'

Titus scowled. He was an all right kid.

'Just some plastic plates, stuff like that.' Kate laid the last of the boxes on the floor in the kitchen. More shopping bags sat fatly in the corner, bulging with the brand new. She clocked them but said nothing.

'Right,' I announced after they'd gone. 'I suppose this is it.'

I had been avoiding clearing out the former spare room that was to be the nursery, which would need a thorough scrub and coat of paint before the arrival of Baby A. Damn. We both stood in the hallway, locked up by our mutual reluctance to begin the hard graft of cleaning.

'You should take the other stuff back.'

'What do you mean?'

'To the shop. We don't need it now.'

'Oh bloody HELL.' Another weekend day consumed by that soulless world!

'We can't afford it! You can't just go on racking up your credit card. It's not real money.'

The anger that had simmered since the day before, that I'd nurtured overnight, rose darkly behind my eyes. 'I am really sick of the way you're talking to me. I am not a child.'

'Oh, fuck off.' This was new, this dismissiveness. It hurt.

244

'You think you're so fucking right. You're cold.'

'That's a horrible thing to say.'

I didn't follow it up with anything else. Cold bitch. She tried to help me carry the bags out to the car but I wouldn't let her. Things go wrong and you realise you're completely alone. That person who lives in the house with you is a stranger. You see the crust in their eyes, step back from their rank breath.

I stopped off at a place in Bethnal Green and bought the paint for the baby's room, pretending I knew enough about brushes, rollers, types of enamel or eggshell or whatever it was called . . . we had decided, after nights poring over the colour charts, on off-white. Ann had plans to make the curtains herself, in a typical swing between wanting to source obscure hand-printed fabric from Japan at whatever the cost, and deciding to run up a few squares of gingham on the kitchen table after midnight. All of these choices came with value judgements. Nothing was free.

At the department store they wouldn't give me the money back, of course. I came away from the venture with a credit note and a parking ticket. Keeping my temper through the exchange with the pissy customer services officer gave me a perverse pleasure. The fifty-pound fine that waited for me under the windscreen wiper confirmed bitterly the tax on life that this city exacted. There was a laughable, shameful pride in my shrunken meanness. I drove home via Marylebone to really rub in to myself the world I was missing, the tapas bars and bookshops and Scandinavian interior stores where you could buy wallpaper from an eight-foot blonde, not some balding, ash-dripping East End troll.

As I waited for a young mother to cross the road the tight grip on my heart relaxed a little. I would bring Ann down here, we would barter our department store dollars for an eight-pound glass of wine and some exorbitant cure-all from the beauty products shop . . . Suddenly a familiar shape in a green coat caught my eye — was that Rosemary stepping out of a restaurant? I searched the rear-view mirror, twisted my head to see past the four-wheel drive behind me. Was she with *Hallie*?

The SUV tooted. I thrust my middle finger up over my shoulder at it and began to drive slowly on. It was right up my ass. I dropped my speed to a worm-crawl. The SUV horn blared without stopping. The other side of the road ahead was clear and it pulled out to pass me, its giant blackness a hair away from scraping my car right down its side. 'Wanker!' the blonde at the wheel shouted. I pulled over to a loading zone and tried to control my trembling, tried to push back the creeping grey edges of my fear. Rosemary was not out of town. Rosemary hadn't called me. There was only one way to read between those lines. I didn't know what to do. The promise of something working out with the vampire script blew away like a scrap of newsprint in the wind. I thought I might be sick, then realised I had forgotten to eat anything that day. A silver-and-black-jacketed parking warden, invisible behind the uniform and dark glasses, tapped sharply on the driver's window. Move.

A strong draught blew up the hallway and blew the front door shut with a slam. I started.

'Hello?' I called. 'Ann?'

The hallway was clear. Everything Kate had dropped off was gone except the buggy, empty at the bottom of the stairs, its triangled front pointing like an arrow towards the open living room door. I followed its directions but none of the baby stuff was there and neither was my wife.

'Ann!'

I thudded up the stairs. My office was empty and the bathroom was too. At the top of the house the door to the baby's room was open, Kate's boxes crowded in the entrance. Across the upstairs hall our bedroom door was wide open. The house was a living thing with eyes and ears, portals for its breath. I stood at the top of the landing, breathing hard. She must have gone out. Our long-burning fight, which I had forgotten in the overwhelming tide of hardware shopping and traffic abuse, resurfaced. Fuck. Well, I would work. I'd clear out the baby's room and clean it and paint it and then from the mountain-top of the moral high ground I would peer down and see whether Ann, scurrying ant-like down there, was ready to make up with me. Without a script to throw myself into I needed some physical activity, some exercise.

A crashing sound splintered from all the way downstairs, like a drawer full of cutlery hitting the floor. 'Ann?'

Suddenly I was in the kitchen, my hand hot from skimming the banister on the fast run down the stairs, looking at the open back door. A smashed fruit bowl and the shardy remains of a wine glass lay on the tiles. Cold fresh wind blew all around me. A gust must have knocked the things over. I stepped over the broken pieces to close the back door and then I saw Ann in the corner of our garden, her long red hair hanging down her back. I walked slowly towards her and a dreadful image appeared before me: both sides of her head covered in that blanketing hair, a full circle of Ann revealing no face, no front, only the back of her head, the back of her head. She raised a hand and pointed to the fence. I came alongside her and saw her dead white cheek.

'He was there.'

Instantly I knew who she meant. Hood. Spider body. I yanked a kitchen chair out into the yard, banging it clumsily against the door frame, cursing, and stood on it to peer as far over the fence as I could. Of course nothing was in the alley but the chair was too low for me to see right down to the ground behind the fence. He still could be crouching there. From the return, the passage down the side of the house crowded with paint cans and Ann's rusting pushbike, unused since the pregnancy, I hauled the step-ladder. More useless pulling at things, a tarpaulin, the bike pedal scraping my leg as I tried to bend over all the fucking crap to reach the ladder and haul it up, my back threatening to seize at any moment. Ann put her hands over her ears at the scraping noise the step-ladder made along the paving stones as I dragged it to the fence. Shakily I climbed its flippy steps and with a surge of adrenaline hoisted myself on to the flat top rung, bent double, as though to touch my toes, to grip the corrugated iron fence top. My knees were in danger of buckling. Not for me the graceful gymnastics of a Hackney mugger. Ann called a warning about the fence, which was painted with creosote or something toxic that she said would give me a rash. I did get a rash, tiny raised spots burning up the inside of my forearms. She put E45 Cream on it that night in Andy and Tonia's bathroom. Later, we lay on their living room floor, Ann with her head in my lap, my hands in her liquidy hair. Our friends gave us wine and camomile tea and consoled us, reassured us we were not idiots, promised us our child would be safe.

I looked left and right along the alleyway. Saw nothing but the giant council rubbish bins at the end.

⋆ ⋆ ⋆

I was sick of calling him 'the man'. He needed a name, Bob or Bill or Randy or something. I imagined snow in Hackney, dusting the crowds at Columbia Road, a soft unsettling early December snow, not really meaning it. His feet are cracked but he doesn't feel the cold, not any more. James, he

250

might be, Arthur or Dexter or Sam. He has to have a name, but maybe even he has forgotten it. Maybe, if somebody were to hold out a blanket at the Embankment shelter — extra volunteers at Christmas time, people feel guilty at that time of year — and if that person were to say, 'Here, Carl, take a rest under this,' he wouldn't lift his hands, wouldn't gather the blanket into him and add it to the bulk of his matted clothes and matted hair for warmth. He doesn't know who Carl is. Who is this Carl? Is he a boy who loved spaghetti and snow fights, who every year helped decorate the Christmas tree and once his older brother left home had the special task of placing the tinsel star on the top? Is he a young man hearing voices in his bedroom, frightened by some, comforted by one or two, unable to tell anybody the things that they say? Is he this guy outside the front of the tower block waiting for his dealer to come home, waiting to get the thing that's going to make it all quiet again, enable him to sleep? The man who hasn't slept properly, hasn't slept in a bed without nightmares and visions, hasn't shaved his beard or cut his hair in years? This guy, sitting in a damp stink on the hospital bed, a ward nurse approaching him and willing herself not to gag as she prepares to cut the boots off his feet and see to his toenails? Who is Carl and where is his father? His mother? The brother who left home long before him and who works as a travel agent in Leeds? 'A brother, I had a brother but we've lost contact now,' he says to the woman he's dating at the nice Italian restaurant, the spaghetti on his plate a tangled mess he can't quite eat. 'He wasn't right in the head, cut himself off.' 'Poor you,' says the woman, thinking, if I married him I'd find his brother, I'd take him with me and we'd find him together, put them back together, and thinking too, why did he let his brother go, how does somebody just disappear from their family, there can't have been love, or not enough of it, or not the right kind.

⋆　⋆　⋆

The boy the police sent round, PC Cordwell, was twelve. Bank tellers, travel agents, cops — puppies these days. Fairlashed and pale-eyed, a salamander in a blue uniform, he sat at our kitchen table drinking our tea ('two sugars, please' — it took an age to find the sugar, there could have been five old-lady bashings and three car-jacks while I banged and crashed around Ann's newly rearranged pantry), taking notes. As we spooled out the story of the man from Ann's very first sighting, through the growing sense that she was being followed, into our self-doubt and uncertainty, what seemed strangest about it was that we hadn't contacted the police before. It's a big city, we explained, trying to appeal to his worldliness, if he had any; calling the police would have been an overreaction. Cordwell appeared to take the whole thing very seriously. He lectured us about care in the community cases, schizo-phrenics and crack addicts, and warned that we must never approach the man.

'What do you do?' he asked, almost as an afterthought. Was it my imagination that he paused when I told him I was a writer? A fantasist, was he thinking, a citizen of the twilight zone, makes up stories for a living?

'Oh,' he said, 'written anything I would've read? Tom Stone . . . sorry . . . don't think I know your name.' He was clearly disap-pointed not to be processing a complaint about the stalker of Terry Pratchett.

'I write screenplays.' This cheered him up.

'Don't suppose you could get me a meeting with Keira Knightley.'

'No.'

He blushed. 'And you,' he said to Ann, whose description of the man he had taken down word for word, 'What do you do?'

'I work at St Bartholomew's Hospital. In the radiation department.'

'Right. Very sad, cancer.' He gave the impression of only recently being bold enough to say these words. *Cancer. Care in the community. Crack addict.*

'Yes.' Ann slowly stood down on my foot.

'And this man has ah, followed you there as well, has he?'

Ann paused. 'Yes.'

'You're sure it's the same man, madam.'

' . . . Yes.'

His pen paused. Then he wrote it: 'Uncertain.'

Cordwell, I could see, was going to stuff the entire notebook into a rubbish bin on his way back to the station.

'Well of course it's the same man,' I said, 'it's not as though you're blind, you recognized him clearly each time.'

The googly eyes rounded quizzically. 'You really can be certain?'

'No. Yes.'

'And at the time you were convinced this man was stalking you.'

'Yes.'

'Any reason why he might be stalking you? It's important to say, a lot of these cases are quite random. But any connection, any link he might have had with you?'

'No.'

'And you, sir,' the moony beam directed at me now, 'I realise you didn't see him today. But you can verify you've seen this same man before? Around the property, before today? Seen him in the playground over the road, is it? You can individually identify him?'

It doesn't even take a second, a decision like the one I made then. 'Yes,' I said. Ann squeezed my hand. Of course I would lie for her. 'Yes, I've seen him too.'

I showed Cordwell to the door. 'I have met David Thewlis,' I offered by way of compensation.

'Sir?'

'Never mind.'

'You are lovely,' Ann said once the door was safely closed, her arms wrapping warmly round my chest, her belly pressing into my back. 'My saviour,' she said.

'Fuck, Ann. I don't want to leave you here alone.'

'Where are you going?'

'I mean in general.'

'We'll get good locks.' She reached into a cupboard for the local phone directory. 'Here. We'll get someone to come right now.'

'Maybe we should move.'

'No.'

'He's coming closer every time. He wants

something here. Maybe you. That isn't going to stop.' I covered her hands with mine, stopped them flicking through the Hackney white pages. 'I am really, really scared,' I said.

'That man is not going to lever us off our land.' She wriggled the phone book out from under my grip. 'He is just not.'

N.A.M.W. 06.07

She is in bed. Someone is knocking on the door and calling her name. She curls tighter into herself. On the other side of the cabin, behind the mesh screen, the round aluminium door handle turns, back and forth, the sound travels over to Ann like the noise of a cork being slowly squeaked out of a bottle. She twists the new wedding ring round and round on her finger.

'Ann!' It's Tom.

She stands, naked, leans against the window frame. The sky is white. At some point morning happened. A hard wind buffets the palm trees to her right. She closes her eyes and grips the wall.

'Ann!'

She starts towards the door to open it.

'Mate. Come and wash up back at mine. They're doing breakfast. We need to get working.'

Ann walks into the bathroom of her

256

locked cabin and locks the bathroom door.

In Hallie's bathroom, Tom shaves. This should be a marital moment. He feels queasy, unmanned, unsure whether Ann has locked him out or is simply in a drunken stupor. Perhaps he has trapped her and she wants to get away. He has failed to get close to her, just as he has failed to get close to the real lives here, lives of those who gain and lose, the military, the leaders they so frequently depose. Some people call it corruption and some people call it the way things are. He has not learned anything from people with homes and decisions to make, it is closed to him, this world of chiefs, the workers, the unemployed, the healers, the sick, the spirits, the landowners and foreigners and the people who aren't allowed to own land. And here he is in resortworld, the new world that tries to look old with its wood-beamed bar, the thatched roofs and traditional tapa cloths on the walls. Timeless décor and modern convenience, created for people who demand Internet connections in every room, water planes to Nadi or Suva, deep-sea fishing by motorboat. You choose the catch and the resort workers magic it for you, cheering as they snap your picture next to the improbable marlin or kingfish or shark. He's been that person, hiding from

the sun under the baseball cap decorated
with the resort insignia, believing for a
minute he's a hero, grinning for the camera
like a fool . . .

Despite having hunched over his laptop
for most of the time here he has picked up a
tan too; the skin revealed by his razor is
paler than the rest of his face. Outside the
palm fronds clatter.

When I met Ann she knew ways of saving
money I had never imagined: survival
techniques from a different world. Phone
calls were only ever made from work; there
was a pin jammed into the electricity meter
that slowed its ability to count; friends who
worked in restaurants brought round left-
overs, the lemon tart some famous musician
had been unable to finish, the soggy last of
the minestrone. They ate like princes, these
impoverished artists, on the scraps of others,
and on Tuesday and Thursday nights they got
pissed on free gallery beer at so-and-so's
private view. Where Useless Bill, say, had the
indelible mark of ligger on his forehead, and
would suck dry not only your wine and
cigarettes but every last ounce of your energy,
Ann, with her eked-out pack of roll-your-
owns and the baked potato dinner parties she
laughingly hosted, was not in the same

category. It was Australian hardiness that made her so practical, such a good warmer of rooms. When we moved into the Daley Street house she was the one ripping up carpet, sanding walls, scraping flakes of dirty paint from the banisters. Now that we were going to be parents and now that we were mind-freakingly broke, the car boot sale — garage sale, she called it, although we did not have a garage — was her idea.

Tonia came to help us sort the stuff; she brought her own box of junk to hock off in much the same spirit as healthy sports teams shave their heads if one of their members has cancer. Something was up with her. She wore dark glasses and I kept finding her and Ann in little weepy huddles when we were supposed to be setting up. Finally they painted signs on unfolded cardboard boxes and strung them around the lampposts at either end of our street. The front path was lined with borrowed trestle tables, which were the only items not for sale and possibly the only ones worth buying. I'd hoped for a second-hand-books-on-the-South-Bank sort of effect, but our compiled jetsam made the front yard look more like the sadder stalls around the illegal end of Brick Lane market. Old CDs (no vinyl; I couldn't bring myself to sell that), boxes of *2000AD* comics (I was soon to be a father, I sternly told myself, stifling a grieving sob), Ann's old art magazines, some speakers that no longer worked, saggy-stringed tennis rackets, tools I had inherited from Bridget but did not know how to use, a nearly obsolete VHS player and a second small television, Ann's from before we joined forces. It surprised us both, how many double-ups we still had from our lives before the other existed. This was the perfect time to lose that extra toaster, set of cutlery, electric blanket and double bed. We'd no longer be able to have people to stay, but that was just a plus.

The stress of exposing one's unwanted goods to the neighbourhood was alleviated only slightly by the low regard in which I held most of the inhabitants. Was this how posh insolvent fuckers felt when they had to let the National Trust turn their family piles into history's theme parks? Maybe that's a little grandiose. Yes we're fucking broke, the sale screamed, even though we spend more per week on olive oil than you do on onion rings. Would any of our neighbours have subjected themselves to this humiliation? Ann had paper cups of hot tea on offer, and homemade muffins (spelt flour; from an ancient grain, Ann informed me, and it was certainly ancient in our kitchen). When I came back from buying ciggies, after the first sale (my Brian Ferry box set: a fiver), quite a little gaggle of local mums and kids had gathered. Part of me expected the man to turn up too, but he would surely not be that brazen. And why pay good money for someone's gear when you can nick it for free?

A woman in a hijab gave my great-aunt's armchair an exploratory nudge with her foot. Many of the Muslim women wear sandals even in the cold London spring. Why did they cover the entire body but leave the feet exposed to the weather? I did not know how to go about finding an answer.

'It rocks.' I pushed the armchair to demonstrate. 'In the literal sense.'

'How much is it?' she asked.

'Oh, God . . . isn't there a price on it? Ann,' I called, 'how much for Aunty Pat's chair?'

'Twenty quid,' she said.

'Twenty? That's a bit steep,' I said to the woman *sotto voce*, you and me, we're pals right? 'Fifteen.'

'You'll deliver it?'

'Oh, I don't know about that.'

'Don't worry then.' She turned away.

'Well, can your — have you got — can anyone help?'

She nodded, and took a twenty-pound note from her purse. 'I'll send my son.'

'I think with delivery it's back up to twenty.'

'All right,' she smiled. 'Put a sticker on it.'

Gallery style, Ann had a little box of red dots that she was sticking on the sold items that people weren't immediately taking away. The Christian from next door made the predictable cracks about modern art and somebody should send Charles Saatchi round here, he'd snap up the lot and stick it in the Tate for a million pounds. Tonia smiled thinly.

We made just under four hundred and fifty pounds, about eighty of which belonged to Tonia. Dinner at Nobu, then. Although it was more than we had expected, any elation merely flickered and waned. *Now what?* a small voice whispered. *So you'll get to the end of the month. What happens after that, if you haven't got a job? You start selling stuff you actually like?* Rosemary had still not called. Simon Wright was getting his feet pedicured in LA. I had done everything I could think of, abased myself before every contact I had, to get a job. That's not quite true. Every contact except Hallie.

★   ★   ★

The armchair woman's son was called Hisham. He came the next day, when Ann

262

was at work. We stood in the living room and looked at the bulky orange chair. He was about the same size as me, with a razor-line beard enclosing his chin. I'd never seen him around. The thing must have weighed a hundred kilos. I was only grateful Aunty Pat was no longer in it. Years of her stodge had left a deep well in the seat that proved useful when it came to balancing the chair, upside-down, on our shoulders. The effort of hoisting it buckled my knees. Hisham swore. I apologised. We had to pause and shuffle backwards so I could shut the front door. As soon as I'd done it I realised my keys were still inside. What a fucking idiot. I kept it to myself.

We turtled across the playground in more or less a straight line, watched with amusement by two teenage Asian girls sitting on the swings. One of them called out to us. I felt a lurching thrill, suddenly part of the neighbourhood. We swayed under the weight of the orange beast while we waited at the stained concrete entrance to the council block lift. The air here was cold, as though it came from a place that rarely saw the sun, and smelled abrasively of disinfectant. Inside the lift it mostly smelled of urine. Obscenities were partly visible beneath a newish coat of paint on the three lift walls. From under the excruciating weight of the chair — my neck was on fire down one side, I was doing permanent damage — I watched Hisham's blurred reflection in the steel-finish doors. He looked ahead, eyes loose as though at nothing. For him this wasn't an anthropological excursion to the different world across the way. Outside the lift we scuttled a reluctant circle, neither of us wanting to go in first and backwards.

Hisham's mother was wearing her headscarf still. The armchair fitted quite well into their living room, which gave the quick impression of studio family photographs, the embedded smells of fenugreek and ground coriander, and the glare from the aluminium-framed windows along the far wall. After dumping the chair down my head and shoulders felt as if they were going to float up to the ceiling, away from the rest of my body. The flat faced the playground on the other side from my house. A powerful urge came over me: I needed to see my house from here. We were six storeys up. Disregarding their privacy I crossed the floor of the armchair lady's flat. Our front path was mostly hidden behind the bare plane tree, but there was the house, looking just the same as all the others in the street. Behind it the sloping roofs of more identical houses continued for a block;

unseen behind these, the canal, and beyond that Hackney Marsh. I wondered how long Mrs Armchair and her family had lived here but felt it would be rude to ask, the question too easily implying that they belonged elsewhere.

'Do you ever see that strange man?' I asked.

'Who is that?' Mrs Armchair said. Hisham had disappeared. I wondered how many bedrooms this place had.

'That mentally disturbed man, the home-less one.'

She shook her head. 'It's not a good neighbourhood. Look at all the rubbish down there. The council does nothing. There should be a warden in the park.'

'Yes.' Her feet were hidden by the length of her dress.

'Would you like a sweet?' Some were green, some reddish brown. I took a little white ball and put it in my mouth. It was milky. I nodded and made 'hmm, very good' sounds.

'How is your wife?'

'She's very well thank you, very well.'

'And the baby is due soon?'

'Yes.' Did this woman know Ann?

'You're going to move when the baby is born?'

'No. No, no plans to move.'

She held the plate of sweets towards me again.

'No thank you. I should go. Really we moved here *because* of having the baby. More space.' Perhaps there were fourteen members of her family living in this flat.

On the street outside our house I remembered that I'd forgotten my keys. No wallet, no mobile. I was right outside my door and couldn't get inside.

It was a long cold walk to Ann's work.

She met me at the entrance to the radiotherapy department. 'You twerp.'

'I know. Can you take lunch?'

'I doubt it. Got to show the new girl the ropes.' I remembered — this was the beginning of Ann's last week at work. The baby was due in three weeks. *Don't panic.* The large rectangular waiting room bore some odd similarity to a church hall, or a rest home after lunch but before the ballroom dancing demonstration begins. It was full of mostly grey-haired, grey-faced people sitting singly or in pairs. What I saw was the contrast between Ann's obvious pregnancy, her doubled aliveness, and these ranks of the unwell. She said they never became a group to her, they were all different people with their own symptoms, their own feelings, their completely individual stories. It isn't always a terminal narrative. When people come into the mould room for the first time, when she talks to them or doesn't talk, depending on what signals they give off, as she's recording the surface of their bodies, they're only a tiny bit the illness. Even later, alone upstairs where she recreates those bodies in Perspex, she is struck by the very personal, human nature of the limbs, the torsos, the heads. Soon technology will lighten her workload. Plans are afoot for meshes of four face shapes: three versions of adult heads, plus one for a child; these would be malleable enough to adapt to each patient, the unique forming from the same.

'Can I borrow some money to get home?'

She gave me a tenner. 'Don't spend it all at once.'

What I really did want to spend it on was a pâté roll from the Club Gascon deli, or lunch at the Carluccio's around the corner. The only things left in the fridge at home were Ann's herbal pregnancy doodahs. I felt weak. Maybe Mrs Armchair's sweets had not agreed with me. Maybe I had had enough of borrowing money from my wife.

Andy and I had been back to Victoria Park the night before, after the car boot sale. I needed to go back to the place I was mugged but didn't want to be alone. He offered to hold my hand, increase our chances of being attacked. As we approached the exit gates I could feel my insides churning. How was it those boys still had the power to frighten me? They were supposed to have done their worst. I guess that was the problem — what had happened that night wasn't the worst, and I knew it. I ran faster than usual to beat out the adrenaline. Andy gasped like a baby bird trying to keep up. I had no stamina, had to quit after just fifteen minutes.

'What's happening on the work front?' he had asked as we walked the rest of the circuit, hands on hips, waiting for the stitch to subside.

I laughed for his benefit. 'Mad. It eats people up. I don't know what I'm doing.'

'Mate, you've got to get back to that stuff like your last film.' The naïve council flat romance, horribly simplistic. 'It was all heart, Tom, it was beautiful.'

'It was a flop.'

'But it had heart. It had heart.'

Not, he implied, like anything I had done since. I couldn't tell Andy what I was thinking. Could barely tell myself. Later that night Ann wanted to make love and I couldn't do it. Rome, on a loop.

On my way out of Smithfield I began once more to run, away from the hospital, away from Ann. The streets were busy with the lunch crowd, two long queues outside the Barclays ATM, people ganged up in the doorways of sandwich bars. New growth rustled in the trees. I pushed my legs, my feet hurt in the crappy trainers, the sun beat down hard on my squinting head. The footpath was uneven and unforgiving. New Oxford Street, Tottenham Court Road, Soho Square, beer-drinking men lying desperate, prawn-pink and topless on the grass although as soon as the clouds came out they would freeze. Across Carlisle Street, narrowly missing a black cab, a cycle courier coming from nowhere, Dean Street, Wardour Street, running like a horse in blinkers for fear of seeing somebody I knew, for fear of thinking where I was going. Outside Rosemary's offices I stopped.

Tits-up Cheryl pretended not to notice that I was sweating like a murderer as I recovered my breath leaning on her desk. A tropical microclimate sang between my clothes and my skin. Reef fish swam down my legs and storm-clouds brewed beneath my shirt.

'Where's Rosemary?' I wheezed. 'Can I see her?'

'She's at a meeting.'

'I'll wait.'

'Out.'

'When's she due back?'

'Tom. Make an appointment. This is no good.' She was right. Her small, freckled nose wrinkled. 'Did you *run* here?'

'I know, I know, it's just — fuck, Cheryl.'

'Talk to your agent.'

'Have you read the new vampire draft? What did you think?'

'It's very funny.'

I grew six inches. 'Can you tell Rose?'

'It is so not her thing.'

All of my energy was going into the wrong place. Andy had said he would scrounge some money from the budget for me to come in and talk to the senior school about the film industry. How was I going to do it without either lying or making them cry? I get paralysed with boredom discussing what I do. There is nothing to say and people always fail to understand the process. The worst of them come up with ideas for you. As soon as someone says, 'I've got a great story for you, you won't believe this, you've got to use it in a film,' I know I'm never going to voluntarily see them again.

Cheryl studied me. Her phone rang. We held eye contact as she answered it. One. Two. Three. Her gaze dropped, swept the length of my body. I was here because my wife was going to have a baby. I couldn't be here because my wife was going to have a baby. Cheryl flicked through Rosemary's appointment book making chit-chat with whoever it was on the phone that didn't need to run places. I sat on the pristine white sofa and stared uncomprehendingly at the pages of a magazine.

The school walls were green. Someone I couldn't see said, 'Fish and kettles.' Beer and skittles. My brother. I don't have a brother. Christine. Who's that? The boat rocks as you set foot into it.

'Tom.'

Even I heard the snort from my sinuses as I jolted awake. 'What?' It took a good couple of seconds to remember where I was. The very small boy inside me wanted his mum.

'Rosemary has got five minutes.'

'She's here?'

'Yes.'

Cheryl did not quite suppress a smirk. Rosemary must have walked past me, seen my mouth slackly open, hands holding on to my crotch.

'In you go.'

She always shook, Rosemary, in that divorced ex-drinker way, but she was never nervous. I'd only seen her unseated once, when she had to make a speech in praise of

271

someone and her voice slowed even more than usual as a red welt crept up her neck. Her skin was lightly dappled with age spots and the broken capillaries of her former life as a boozehound. She lit a cigarette. 'Tom.'

'Sorry to just barge in — '

She waved this aside. 'Not at all. I'm sorry I haven't got back to you about your script.'

Oh God, she was going to be polite. The situation was worse than I had thought.

'Rosemary, I realise the whole vampire thing probably isn't your bag. But it did start life as a romance.'

'I remember.'

'Maybe I should have stuck with that but Alan was so convinced . . . ' Her face was unreadable. 'Have you heard from Alan? How's he going?'

'He's good. No regrets.'

'I mean, I was surprised when he decided to . . . have they had their baby?'

'Not yet. Isn't your wife pregnant?'

I nodded. 'Yeah.'

She took a drag on her ciggie with great relish, one of the many freedoms she was afforded as a non-pregnant woman. 'Tom, what happened with that script you were doing for John Halliburton?'

'Oh.' This was unexpected. 'The one set in Fiji?'

'Yes.'

'Well, it didn't work out. My wife wasn't very well and that was bad timing . . . anyway I suspect it wouldn't have . . . in the end we had a different, um, vision for it.' This had been the reason I gave people when we got back from Fiji. Now I blew the dust off it and trotted it out for Rosemary.

'How so?'

'Well, he'd wanted a very commercial script, nothing wrong with that of course, he envisaged it as a kind of action hero story . . . '

'You must have known that when you signed on for it.'

'Not in quite such simplistic terms.' Could I insult Hallie here, even weakly? Was he a friend of hers or a rival? Had it been him I had caught a glimpse of, that day in Marylebone? 'Not that I didn't want it to be commercial, it's just — it seemed more complicated than that. The situation.' It sounded as lame as I felt. The crazy thought that Hallie was hiding underneath her desk flashed through me and I bit my lip to stop from laughing.

'As a screenwriter, Tom, it's important for you to know what kind of animal you are.'

'What kind of animal.'

'Yes.'

'Yes, of course.' Oh fuck, did she actually want me to name an animal here and now? Was there a right answer to this? Would the wrong one — *vole!* — blow it?

'It's hurt you, you know that. In people's minds. You were lucky Alan didn't care.'

I knew. It was not an episode I liked to think about. Abandoning ship. Forcing Hallie to fire me. Holding the marriage in one hand and my career in the other. I'd known it was a sacrifice. But I hadn't known how long I would be paying for it.

'Would you work with someone like Hallie again?'

'Someone like . . . '

A pause. 'With Hallie, in fact.'

'Well really, that would be fine.' It happens so easily. *Yes, officer, I've seen the man.* 'Well, Rosemary, that would be fine.' We were just talking here, I told myself. Ann wouldn't have to know. What would happen even if she did? She'd never have to see him. But still, I resolved to keep it from her, certainly while it was nothing but a possibility.

'Long way from love amongst the ASBO classes.'

Everything was a long way from that one and only credit. It suddenly occurred to me that I lacked the necessary skills to survive, that my version of self was so at odds with the

274

reality of the world that Ann and I would puddle around for ever, our fortunes not rising but dwindling, until we would live in a council flat on the edge of some new town and our former lives would seem to have happened to somebody else. Or, more likely, that Ann would leave me for someone who could support her and help her raise the kid. Wake up, Tom! Wake up! 'Rosemary. I don't know why I'm hesitating. I'd love to work with Hallie again. I'm thrilled he'd consider it. Is he in town?'

'Yeah.'

We stared at each other. I said, 'Thanks, Rose.'

'I'll tell him to give you a call. I'd like to support you, Tom. I admire your commitment.'

It was easiest to gloss over this, out of both embarrassment and not knowing what she was talking about. 'He'd better use my mobile number, there's something wrong with the phone at home.' Namely that Ann might answer it. I wrote it down and pushed it across her desk. 'I think Cheryl's got it, but just in case.'

'Fine.'

'I can't tell you how much I appreciate this.'

'That's fine.' She shut down even further, if

such a thing were possible. I felt sick at the thought I'd disappointed her, failed some test. It was clear she wanted me gone, could hardly bear the niceties of a goodbye. I flushed myself out of there.

* * *

At Ann's maternity leave drinks that Friday I got an inkling of what women have to put up with from each other, the bottomless pit of female knowledge about childbirth. 'Some women experience labour as a real invasion, a violation, like rape,' said Alison, the freckled New Zealand receptionist, in the low growl she reserved for serious announcements. Alison did not have children. Ann and Julie, one of the radiographers, had bets placed on when she would finally come out. They had been waiting eighteen months. Alison lived with her best friend, another New Zealander, who had a boyfriend Alison couldn't stand. Once Ann found her crying in the loos over a fight she and her flatmate had had that morning. 'I hate this bloody country!' Alison sobbed into Ann's neck. 'I want to go home!' 'I know, I know,' Ann said. 'I found it hard too when I first came.' Alison had looked up at her, uncomprehending. 'But you're English.' 'No. I'm not.' Ann explained, and

276

from then on had to avoid Alison's special overtures of friendship, as though they belonged to the same club. The Voluntary Exile Society. Eaters of sausage rolls, drinkers of lager, slaggers off of Empire. She dodged all of the receptionist's meaningful looks and invitations to antipodean party nights, had totally fucked her off, and had to put up with being ignored on the cappuccino round, being last to get her phone messages, and now with Alison's violent theories on childbirth.

'Rape,' Ann said, looking up from her rolled ham sandwich. 'Something to look forward to.'

I snorted. She elbowed me. A social worker I didn't know glared at Alison from her perch on the kitchen bench. 'When I gave birth it was amazing,' she declared. 'Giving life.' She leaned towards Ann. 'Don't listen to anyone who tells you otherwise. You have the power. It's orgasmic. Orgasmic.'

'You mean you actually . . . ' asked Julie, trying to catch Ann's eye.

'Man in the room,' I reminded them. Actually, two, but I wasn't sure Boris the nurse counted. The chief radiographer, very much a man, was too important to make it.

'Amazing,' the social worker repeated, her eyes dim and faraway.

Ann said later she'd wanted to put her fingers in her ears and chant la-la-la-la-la. She hated the way her body had become part of the common property, her private business fair game for all this biological speculation. She couldn't bear to see women her own age breastfeeding in cafés. And here she was after all this time avoiding her body's possibilities, here on the shore of late-blooming mother-hood she had arrived, part of a generational trend, a colour-coded statistic in a magazine article.

'Well,' said the social worker after Alison had gone to the loo ('*Excuse* me. I must just *use the toilet.*' Why was that such an objectionable phrase?) 'They say labour experiences can be heritable. You know, my mother had wonderful birth experiences and so did my three sisters and I. In our culture we so undervalue the maternal line of knowledge, inherited wisdom. If you were in an African village all the grandmothers would look after you during labour and afterwards, rub you with oils, wrap you with soothing skins, teach you the womanly art of breastfeeding . . . '

'This would be after the female circumcision.' I whispered it into Ann's ear.

She shoved me. 'Get another glass of wine.'

'So,' the woman continued, 'do you know

how your own birth was for your mother?'

'I don't. And I can't ask her, she's dead.'

I looked up sharply from the table of plastic cups. It was unlike Ann to be this blunt. The social worker had got to her. Some wine was spilt; I mopped it. Julie caught my eye and asked me about what time to arrive for Ann's birthday party, which was the next night, but I was concentrating on the other conversation.

'Oh, I'm sorry.' The social worker, quietly panicking. 'When did she die?'

'When I was little. I never really knew her.'

The social worker looked stricken, as though she might have killed Ann's mother.

'Not in — ?'

It took a second for Ann to figure out what she meant. 'No no,' she laughed, 'not in childbirth.'

'Come whenever,' I said to Julie. 'After eight.' I took Ann a cup of wine and watched with pleasure the social worker's face as Ann downed it in one hit.

Boris asked me what I was writing.

'Nothing,' I told him, unable to think of a lie. In the four or five days since my conversation with Rosemary, every time my mobile rang my pulse went into overdrive, the tendons of my hands felt weak. Hallie had not called. It was important that I wait for him. I could not initiate the contact, it would involve too much of an apology — and yet I longed for him to ring, longed for the end to the worry of not having work.

'Drugs,' said Julie, who had two children. The wine had made her cheeks pink, she'd lost her volume control and was getting louder. 'Epidural, pethidine, diamorphine, gas. Smash open the cabinet.'

'My drug days are over.' Ann grimaced. 'It's going to be the pain and me, fighting it out.'

'Well I envy you having a break from this joint.' Julie peeled back the halves of her crustless tuna sandwich and sniffed at it before putting it in her mouth and talking through it. 'You know I had to treat an ex-boyfriend of mine last week.'

'That must have been tricky,' I laughed.

She nodded. 'There you go, cancer, that's what you get for dumping me.'

'What did he have? Or can't you say?' Perhaps it was bad form, like asking inmates what they were doing time for.

'Brain tumour.' She burst out laughing. 'Sorry. Ann, don't look at me like that. You must have known a patient or two.'

'No.'

'Apart from that man,' I said. The light outside was fading.

'Which man? Oops!' Julie's elbow slipped off the edge of the table. 'Let's go out.'

'No, we've got to get home.'

Everyone hugged Ann, patted the baby bump, pressed the whip-round present (what was it? Some fancy lotion) into her hands, told her she'd be missed.

'You look after this one.' Boris wagged his finger at me.

I caught Julia by the door as the receptionist was hanging on to Ann's neck. 'Ann must have told you about the man.'

'No. Did she?' Through the alcohol Julie searched her memory. 'A man she knew from Australia?'

'No. Never mind.' I hugged her. 'See you at the party.'

Amongst the usual junk mail, 'You Have Won a Competition,' free pens from Oxfam and reminders from Greenpeace (it worried Ann, this cavalier attitude to paper by a bunch of environmentalists), we got home from Barts to a letter from our mortgage lender. I slid it to the back of the pile and opened it alone, standing in the middle of the kitchen, when Ann was in the bath. We had missed three instalments. I stared at the paper disbelievingly. It was Friday night. Nobody at the bank answered the phone. Nobody could say anything to relieve my thumping heart.

Upstairs the water gurgled out of the drain. I'd fucked up, mismanaged things somehow ... I thought we were sailing close to the wind but to have missed three months' house repayments? The letter gave us a week to make good or foreclosure proceedings would begin. Words that, imagined, had haunted my waking nights since Alan Tranter gave me the flick, were now here, real in my hands, losing the house was *actually* possible. Unless I did something about it. In the kitchen I gulped water but the tension in my temples and my jaw just tightened. My stomach convulsed and I regurgitated water into the sink. My ribs burned down one side. I thumped at my chest. If I had a heart attack and died at least the mortgage would be paid. When I heard the television come on up in the bedroom I reached in my pocket for my phone.

★ ★ ★

The last window bars were fitted the next morning, the day Ann turned thirty-nine. 'Happy birthday,' I joked, removing the blindfold from her eyes to reveal the new-look kitchen, a red ribbon tied around one of the black iron railings. The workmen, two scruffy young opportunists, probably adept at copying keys for their burglar mates and becoming untraceable once your newly secure house has been cleaned out, were waiting for their cheque. Now we had protective bars in every room except our bedroom, which faced the front of the street. Even in our anxiety about the man, we didn't expect him to get a ladder — build scaffolding even, a ladder wouldn't reach — and come knocking on the window. The decision to leave that room alone is just one in a long, long list of actions taken or not taken that I will always regret.

'Darling,' Ann said, 'you shouldn't have.'

'And this is for you too.'

It had been hard to know what to buy for Ann. Because I was an idiot I thought it best to save the big guns for a major occasion like her fortieth. We never celebrated her fortieth. She hung her present — an antique mirror, delicately silvered — in the bedroom. I noticed that she looked to the wall beside it, not in the glass, while she put it up.

'You're so beautiful,' I said.

'Ha.'

For all that I hated having to install the bars, Ann convinced me we were lucky to have the space of our house. The flat in Camden had become a cell by the time we left it; the thought of having a baby there was intolerable. Everyone we knew was obsessed with space, with not having enough and how to get more of it. Andy and Tonia, in their maisonette flat on Redcross Way, had a downstairs neighbour to contend with who played house music all night long and stank out the garden with his aftershave. When we were still in our two rooms in Camden Andy and Tonia were banned from moaning. They were owners — we, in our late thirties even, suffered the insecurity of renting and the humiliation of six-monthly flat inspections by Rip-Off, Shaft & Co, the hateful Theberton Street landlords. Once upon a time we'd been quietly delighted with ourselves for living in Camden, near to Primrose Hill and the park but with all the grunge and credibility of the bands we liked to hear. Then Shoreditch took off, it was Hoxton this and Hoxton that, Ann's art school friends with their Bethnal Green snarls started appearing in magazines, the grimly cool sort I no longer bought but flicked through during a haircut. Somewhere along the line we had become the sort of people who laughed at street fashion rather than followed it. By the same token we no longer wanted to live where there was anonymous vomit on the doorstep in the morning. And we needed space. For years the cramped, filthy conditions hadn't bothered us at all and then, as if a spell had been lifted, we could see nothing else. Ann cried when she came home from work. We lay on the bed and she said, 'Tighter, hold me tighter.' She was afraid of having no money, of never being able to afford anything, never getting ahead. I squeezed her arms into her ribcage, trying to help her breathe out the jitters, and walked the eight steps to the next room to make tea. It was running through my mind to ask around about teaching work, maybe at the National Film and Television School where I had trained, although I was hardly their most illustrious graduate.

'We could move to Australia,' I joked, 'you could marry me and make me a proper Aussie bloke.'

'No,' she groaned from the bedroom, laughing weakly. 'I'd rather rent for ever. They do in Europe.' She came out into the living space and adopted the same position on the sofa, hugging her knees into her chest. 'Why are we so hung up on buying? Why am I? Those unbearable articles in the *Standard* and I fall for it every time.'

It was true, I couldn't understand it or explain it to her. Just as she wanted to be held tightly, she wanted space. Like her ancestors who had been sent to that massive country for lack of space in their own, and who once there huddled on the edges, as close as possible to the faraway rest of the world, the great wide Australian interior too hot, too vast to bear. Space is what we crave and fear. There is nowhere more unsettling than a small town on a Sunday afternoon, the pursed kissing sounds of crickets in all those open back gardens, the hush over the surrounding fields. And this house, Daley Street, which we had bought in a mortgagee sale (it still sits badly with me), what was its great selling point apart from the beautiful shelter of the spreading plane tree outside? Here we were so close to Hackney Marsh, to the openness of those sports fields and the sky that grew wider and higher the further east along the bus route you travelled. Give me land, lots of land, but build me a big fucking fence about it with an entry code and a retinal ID scanner. Ann and I had stood in what was to become our bedroom, the estate agent between us, looking out the window at the scruffy playground across the road and the tower block that rose behind it.

'Nice view,' I said.

'You know it's strange about towers.' The agent turned away from the window. 'After a while you don't see them any more. They disappear.'

★　★　★

After the unveiling of the window bars Tonia took control of Ann. They'd planned a day of pampering, of manicures and massage and God knows what. She drove over in the morning in Andy's beat-up old Saab and whisked Ann off to Stoke Newington. It still amazed me that gentrification had crept this far, that you could get hot oil dribbled on your head in a scented room just off Stokey Church Street, which had always been essentially skanky. I'd picked Ann up from this so-called day spa once, the place was taupe and smelled of those candles that are supposed to remind you of figs or vanilla but really just smell artificial. They fill the air with a gloopy quality, a million tiny particles thickening the atmosphere until, if they could burn enough of them, a fine layer of wax would coat every surface and everyone in range would become a Madame Tussaud's creature, just pretend. When the woman in the white coat led Ann, dazed with relaxation, into the reception area where I was waiting, it was for all the world as though she'd been lobotomised. This is what we count as pleasure these days — paying people to dress like doctors and treat us as though we are survivors of hardships who must be soothed. Have some more me time.

Ann did deserve it. She knew so well how

to talk to the frightened, the ill and the weak about their bodies and what would happen to them next. Tenderly and quickly she laid her muslin strips and spread cool plaster over the bodies of children, of women who were losing their fertility, on the crêpy spotted skin of old ladies who might go at any moment. 'This will feel a bit cold,' she would say, and, 'This will feel a bit tight. It's OK, not for very much longer'. Have you noticed how people talk about 'people', 'people do this, people do that,' without seeming to realise that they are a person too? (I'm doing it now!) Ann never did. People weren't those strange four-limbed creatures over there to her. At least her patients weren't.

While Ann and Tonia were having their fingernails filed and polished I went to Borough Market. We would have chorizo with rocket, soft rolls, a huge dish of langoustines and mayonnaise, radishes and cheeses and *habas fritas* and orange and almond cake for later. This late in the pregnancy I reasoned that the baby could not possibly be brain damaged by some dodgy shellfish; she had as good as had him. I would drop in at Andy's place on the way, which gave me a sort of alibi. I had another errand to run at the market, one that Ann didn't know about.

* * *

Andy was in his dressing gown and specs, his hair sticking out all over his head. Piles of marking were fanned over the kitchen table. I liked their flat. A mural of Tonia's expressionistic birds flew around the walls, brightly coloured cloths were draped over their rickety furniture and Andy was good at tending pot plants. (Gardening: 'heart'; interiors magazines: 'no heart'.) Andy brewed coffee in his stove-top and we took it to their little greened-up balcony, Tonia's bike rammed in one corner, a view of the neighbouring buildings and communal car park below. If you stood on a chair and craned your neck, between two red-brick blocks you could see a gap that was the air above the river. Andy told me he wasn't coming to the party.

'Why not?'

He groaned and drummed his knees. 'Mate. I think I'm moving out.'

'What do you mean?'

'Don't say anything to Ann, Tonia doesn't want to tell her till after her birthday.'

'Andy.' I felt sick. 'What do you mean?'

He scratched his forehead with both hands. 'I've got involved with someone else.'

'You're kidding.'

It had been going on for a few months. A

289

student teacher. Young, of course she was young. Her name was Karma. Karma? This, surely, was asking for it. How had I missed this? I couldn't believe it, and told him so. Tonia was going away for a few weeks, he told me, to stay with family in Castries. During that time he would find somewhere else to live. He jiggled his bare foot between the balcony railings. 'I'm sick of feeling lousy about it,' he told me. 'Karma is amazing.' I mean. He said those words. This was really happening. The smell of coffee, the sun on my legs, the wistful singer-songwriter music from next door made it real.

'Fuck's *sake*, Andy.'

'I've spent all this time trying to pretend it's not going on, that I'm not that sort of guy.' He smiled down at the man washing his car below, sent him a salute. 'All right?'

The man nodded up. 'Beautiful day.'

'It is,' Andy called back. 'It is.' He looked me square in the eye. 'I am that kind of guy.'

After we sat there in silence for a while Andy's mobile rang in the bedroom and he went to take it. I rinsed out the coffee cups in the sink. Was I hurt that he hadn't confided in me? It was so hard on Tonia. Something told me Andy's new girlfriend, this preposterous *name*, would get pregnant before the year was out. Part of me admired his ruthlessness. His honesty. But even as the changed landscape of our friendship unrolled before me, the news just sat on the surface of my comprehension, impossible to absorb. I knocked on the bedroom door frame, waved goodbye at him and made a waggling 'I'll call you' gesture before letting myself out.

At the market I was late enough to skip the worst of the family crowds, which meant banging straight into the tourists. The ruddy Swedes and crass Australians and Americans in pressed chinos and smelly Spanish kids with unwashed hair who'd slept the night at Camden market, and the eager Canadians and the overdressed Italians and everyone, in short, except those too poor to visit London and the French, who had no need of our little British attempt to take food seriously and were there strictly as vendors, stood between me and the food I needed to buy. It was madness, a typically overheated London version of a thing, in this case intended to be a provincial farmers' market, so imagined by all the dreadful types like my parents who spent their summers trying to source the best poultry in Gordes. There's a marvellous *fromagerie* in Coustellet, have you been? Try this olive oil, it's grown by a little man we've befriended near our place in Lucca. Can't you just taste the sunshine! Little men proliferate in my mother's world, they are ever so handy and marvellously clever. Sometimes they even have a name: Little Mark, Little Geoff, Little Pat. One of these days a little man is going to wrap his little hands around my mother's neck and choke her to death. I digress.

Hallie — it was this meeting with Hallie that was my secret from Ann — was not in the pub when I got there. I found a table that wasn't too cornery and waited, my mind variously on Andy and Tonia, on what I was going to say to Hallie and on the food sweating away in the car, the way I had poorly conducted this day. I should have bought the food last but was worried it would run out and by buying it first was demonstrating my allegiance to Ann, yes, I was thinking of her, even in this meeting she did not know about and would not approve of I was thinking of her, doing it for her. The ice around the langoustines would be melting on the surface, maybe puddling a little out of the plastic bag. The cheese, mossy already, would turn. Perhaps I should go back to the fishmonger's stall, ask him to take the shellfish back for a bit. But then Hallie might come in, take offence at my absence, I might fuck it up. On one thing only I was resolute. If he were to offer me a job I would take it no matter what.

Despite this my feet drummed manically on the floor beneath the small round table, as though they knew that I wanted to bolt.

He was big as ever, which is to say bigger than most people, wrapped in an enormous turquoise woollen scarf, his gingery-blond hair above the red Australian face scoping the room, a dinosaur sniffing for prey. Should I say, 'Hallie?' Should I wait for him to see me?

'Tom bloody Stone.' At least it wasn't 'Tom you cunt'. 'Haven't seen you in an age.'

I got the drinks in. These little displays of masculinity are a must. I knew I had balls, I had got Ann pregnant, but I'd resolved not to talk about her. If I didn't mention her then she didn't exist. If she didn't exist then I could not betray her. If I did not betray her then taking Hallie's money was not a disgusting thing to do.

I put the beer on the table in front of him. He stood and hugged me. I hadn't expected to be hugged. It wasn't altogether friendly. It reminded me, as if I needed to be reminded, that he was huge.

'Hallie, I want to apologise for what happened in Fiji.'

A sort of muffled walrus noise happened in his throat. Eyes peered over the slabs of his cheeks. Waiting for more.

'I understand why you had to let me go. It was extremely unprofessional to just — abandon the project. I was in a panic. I am truly sorry for wasting your time like that.'

This was possibly more than I'd apologised to anyone in my whole life.

'All right,' he said. 'Bloody independent film-makers.'

'Ha-ha, yes.' A pause. How to proceed? 'So, how long have you been back in London?'

'Six months or so. I'm over the pond all the time of course. Ran into a mate of yours in LA as a matter of fact.'

'Really?' Did I have a friend in LA?

'TV bloke. Wright something.'

'Oh. Yes.' Had I said anything to Simon about the Fiji thing? Something bothered me.

'You know who else I saw, wouldn't fucking believe it, nearly ran into when I first got back over here, your missus.'

'Sorry?' No — this couldn't be right.

'Yeah, your wife. You got hitched, didn't you? In Fiji?'

Embarrassment clawed at me. 'Where did you see Ann?' It can't have been her. She'd have said.

He thought a moment. 'Someplace — oh yeah, the hospital.' The likely truth of this took me aback ... I was processing it, bewildered, even as he said, pointing to his

294

great corned beef face, 'Skin cancers, got them cut out.'

Now I could see the little patches of brighter, rawer pink, fingernail size, on the side of his nose and near his hairline. Poor Hallie. I imagined him a boy, playing in a burned garden. 'Ann didn't mention seeing you.'

'Nah, well, she might not have. It was from a distance.' He half laughed and took a long drink of beer. Lucky escape, I thought, her not seeing him at Barts. He studied me, as though deciding whether or not to speak. 'So everything's all right then is it?'

'Oh, absolutely. Well, you see,' — how to wrestle this back, there was no elegant way — 'Rose probably told you I'm looking for work.'

He settled, came back into the room. We were men together again, not lost in some emotional hinterland. 'What you got for me?'

I hadn't expected this either. 'Ah. Yes.' Half-heartedly I ran through the vampire pitch, the other, rejected-by-every-one-in-town, ideas. Hallie didn't touch his beer. The only thing on him that moved was his belly, the slow breath of a creature that has mastered energy efficiency. In. Out. I was going to drown.

'The thing is, Hallie, Rosemary said you

might have something. You might need a writer.' I mean, what else would I be doing here? I wasn't after a position cleaning his pool. Yet.

'Did she now?' He chuckled. Wildly I imagined myself the tool in a practical joke, caught up in some kind of reciprocal prank between Hallie and Rose. 'Yeah, I've got a project on the go, needs a redraft. You're not the writer for it, but — '

'Try me.' That phrase always sounded fake.

Now he drank some beer. Sucked his short top lip. 'Nah. I'm perverse but I'm not that perverse. Rose told me you had some hot new project. Were looking for a home.' The last of the beer disappeared down his throat. 'Never mind eh.'

'No I mean it. Whatever it is. Give me a go.' Fingernail crescent dents at the fleshy base of my thumbs later on, when I was washing my hands in the scummy pub basin, avoiding myself in the mirror. Bullshit how in movies people stare at their reflections after momentous decisions — *who am I now?* You know full fucking well who you are, that's why you can't look yourself in the eye, cobber.

'I'm looking for someone to do a character and dialogue job on the Fiji story.'

'What's it called now?' Smoothly, shocked, playing for time.

'*Blood Resort.*'

It was all I could do not to spray beer over the table. He had to be joking.

'To be honest with you fashions have changed. People think they want some politics with their gun attacks you know, some gritty worthy shit. Not my forte.' The whole bombastic project had been well worked up by some American writing duo into, he assured me, a thrilling, edge-of-your-seat ride. Just as I had feared. Now he wanted to bring someone in 'to modernise it, make it a bit trendy, give it the human touches'. Human touches! In this arid world of avatars and high school porn! You were as likely to find love in a strip club as an expression of humanity in anything Hallie had his paw prints on. Mostly, though, underneath my scorn I was afraid. Afraid that if Ann knew she would get ill again. The humiliation of those first days of our marriage still burned. Working for Hallie would be betraying my faith in her, my blind loyalty, a version of what it meant to be married that I now found inconvenient to uphold. Some people called this growing up. Andy would have called it losing heart. But Andy was sleeping with a woman called Karma.

'Listen, mate, if we're going to . . . I will work with you but I don't want any of that bullshit with your wife — I want you to work on the job and just let's get this done. Can you guarantee that?'

He would work with me. He would. A lifeline. Anything else about Ann's problem with Hallie I could find out later. Later, later, later. 'I'll do it,' I said. And fell down the rabbit hole.

I drove home through the City, passing as usual the fuzz questioning some hapless black guy in a car they'd deemed too rich for him. The relief at having a job — even the prospect of a job — made me drive too fast, and there were enough unpaid traffic violations at home already. I hoped like hell Tonia had managed to keep quiet about her and Andy's split. Oh, maybe everything would still be all right! We would not lose the house! I had my second chance with Hallie, could start all over again, find my way back to that career path I had stumbled off ever since Fiji. A whoop broke from my chest. The rare alleviation of self-hate nearly made me cry with pleasure. But something was niggling at me, a prickle in my happiness. Tonia, perhaps.

They all came to the party: the ex-lovers — well, Useless Bill, who must have heard the wine corks popping from across town — and dopey colleagues and girlfriends. The former neighbours from Camden with their own drugs and, even ruder, their own CDs. The poggy New Zullander from Barts with her ruddy lesbian friend glaring angrily at our nice things. Old Slade cohorts of Ann's 'know-wha'-I-mean'ing loudly in their downwardly mobile accents, vying for a perch in *Private Eye*; Tonia making a valiant effort with Alan Tranter of the mid-life crisis and his heavily pregnant wife (how I loved her for this; I came over all emotional and nearly said something to her about the split but not tonight, not tonight); Ann, even huger, drifting around with her pampered glow, radiating a stoned beam though of course she wasn't high on anything real. Tits-up Cheryl tried to get the dancing started about an hour before anyone else was ready. It was hard to take your eyes off her, banging away to Patti Smith, eyes closed, the skin above her hip bones flashing every time she raised her twiggy arms.

The kitchen smelled sharp and garlicky, chorizo spitting on a tinfoiled tray in the oven, but in the living room different perfumes rose and mingled, vanilla and watermelon, the fashionable scents of the day . . . and underneath a quick skunky slash of dark patchouli musk. Oh God it was Kate. The stuff she was wearing was so powerful it was like a talisman, an atmospheric force field to ward off evil magick. Tonia recoiled as Kate approached, turning her face slightly to the side to get away from the smell. Kate offered Simon's apologies, pretending he had a migraine from the red eye he'd caught that morning. She actually said 'red eye'. Simon was contagious.

Ann leaned against the wall and chatted to an old Slade friend as he flicked dismissively through our CDs. Her own work, the clay-and-wax figurines, stood vigil on the mantelpiece and along the bookshelves. She saw the struggles of her artist friends, the compromised lives, still in shared flats at forty-one, still down the Whitechapel local slowly transforming from young thrusters with a sense of irony into bitter old regulars, same as anyone else. Relationships calcifying, babies born to near-menopausal penury, squabbles over the unworthy recipient of the latest British Council junket. It wasn't worth it, and Ann knew that. There were other things she could be doing. In her work she helped people. Self-expression, all that jazz, you could save it for the weekend. If Ann didn't work at Barts and I didn't write for money there wouldn't be this house, wouldn't be the baby, wouldn't be the new wrought iron barrier between us and the man.

There was a cake, organised by Tonia,

whose face glowed above it as she delivered it through the dark to a beaming Ann. I remembered the floating, burning wish papers at Kate's New Year party, and looked around the room for her. She was in the doorway to the kitchen, looking at me through her parted black hair. 'Happy birthday, dear Ann,' we all sang tunelessly. What was it in Kate's eyes, that milky look, the sense of someone pinned in the flow of something, a point of stillness while the air rushed forwards past her like a river. I pulled my gaze away.

'Speech, speech!'

'All right.' The lights came on again. Ann was alight, expansive, she could have floated to the ceiling herself, a human ball of flame rising. She said some lovely things about her friends, about me — frankly it was a bit over the top. Her tone reminded me of something. Tippi Hedren in *Marnie*. We had been to see the re-release a few nights earlier. Now here she was using, unaware it seemed, the soothing cadences of an old Hollywood star, a voice that wore wrist-length gloves and silk stockings: 'Truly, I never dreamed my life could be like this.'

'Hear hear!' Tonia saved the moment. We all toasted Ann and I was nudged into the middle of the room, where I took her arm.

'How to follow that. Well, I must say I'm mildly incredulous, and in awe of Ann for being such a positive person. She could have stayed in Australia, sunning herself on beaches and having affairs with surf gods, but she prefers working in a cancer department, living in the East End, married to an aging loser, no family support, mortgaged to the eyeballs — if this is her life's dream I'm only too happy to help out.' I kissed her cheek. 'Could somebody please turn up the music? I think Cheryl wants to dance.'

'Just a moment.' It was Kate. 'Before you do — I'd just like to say something.'

This was unexpected. Her hair shone like glossy feathers in the lamplight. What was she wearing, aside from that whopping dose of hippie oil? A dress, midnight blue, that skimmed her body and fell all the way to the floor, making no concession to the voguish, casual angles and skinny low-hipped jeans the other women sported.

'I haven't known Ann very long, maybe the least of any of you. But in the time I've spent with her I've been really struck by,' she paused. She knew the word she wanted to say but had to quell the urge to run away and hide. 'Struck by her bravery.' It was a strange choice, but then everything about Kate seemed strange. We slightly rhubarbed through the next toast; the timing was off, everyone had had enough.

Ann beelined Kate and wrapped her in a massive hug. Tonia and I stood drinking together for a bit, both of us rather upstaged by Kate's gesture. I squeezed Tonia's hand. 'You all right, T? I'm so sorry.'

'Don't.' She flashed me a too-bright smile and briskly walked away.

Ann slid down the wall and sat on the floor to take her shoes off. I sat next to her and closed my eyes, my head tilted back against the wall, my hand placed over hers. Of all the good things that happened at that party, this was the nicest. Cheryl danced like a New York traffic cop on speed. I went into the kitchen to do a bit of a tactical clean-up. The art lot shimmied straight out of there. Here, in the first private bubble I'd had all night, the party rolling on regardless, I gave in to this prideful, powerful feeling of having pulled our lives back from the brink. Behind me in the house all of the people who'd ever been important to us talked and danced and drank and posed and argued. It was, I thought then, like the wedding we had not had. Useless Bill came to find me. 'Er, mate, yer wife reckons she's having the baby.'

Kate stayed behind to finish tidying up and help wastrels like Cheryl find mini-cabs. Ann clung on in the back of Tonia's Saab, one hand pulling down on the little handle above the passenger's door, the other gripping my shoulder. From the force with which her fingers were digging in, I'd say the contractions were a bit painful. There was barely time, swept up in the shooshy excitement of it all, to think that this wasn't meant to happen for another fortnight, we had no baby bag ready, no plan in place! But it was, it was happening right now, the baby was calling the shots and Ann and I were hurtling madly through a tunnel into parenthood, into change.

★ ★ ★

Ann was heroic. She squeezed my knuckles till they cracked as she kneeled pushing on that hospital bed. The contractions were an invisible madness, a force that possessed her. There was no such thing as time, no such thing as other people even though the Irish midwife had a medical student in there with us who stank of cheap perfume. Ann rose above it. She pushed and pushed and pushed and pushed ... I wanted to get her medication, help, but just when I thought she might really lose her mind — head rolling loose on her neck, eyes popped — he slithered out on the next contraction. He was perfect with his long eyes sweeping to the edges of his little walnut face, with his beautiful breathing body, the heart fiercely beating under that boxy rhombus of his ribs. Ann collapsed in triumph on the bed slicked with blood and held him to her breast, this tiny naked boy who wasn't really new, who had been with us for so long and had at last appeared in the flesh, at last come into the world, where he belonged. Arlo Stone. The midwife got to work giving Ann some injection or other. Ann was sobbing with joy and relief. Unable to take our eyes from Arlo's round red head we devoured the air around us, we had made a life.

As the days after his birth went on, he lost none of his magnetism. We couldn't take our eyes off wherever he was in the room, he drew everything towards him the way a television sucks up conversation. Neither Ann nor I could be described as naturals. The floppy head terrified me only slightly less than the fontanelle. My oafish fingers were too close to it always, I tried to adjust him in the crook of my elbow like an over-ambitious waitress — he jostled away, the head lolled, aargh — Ann leapt to the rescue, drawing him in close, shooting me hate looks and seconds later crying out for me to come and help her change him. Every time he spat anything out he was changed, the clothes were washed and ironed and folded and on him for all of thirty minutes and off him and washed again and this only stopped when Ann was sleeping, which wasn't very much. The house smelled wetly of organic washing powder and steaming wool, the teapot was continually plugged with the bitter dregs of raspberry-leaf tea, we sat like stunned mullets eating meals my mother had prepared and frozen, taking turns to eat while the other one walked the baby around in a futile effort to stop his seagull cries. Outside of the hungry cries and the nappy change cries, nothing we did seemed to make any difference. Arlo started or stopped of his own accord, he could not be made to go to sleep and he could not be kept awake. One of Ann's colleagues had given her a recently fashionable book about the importance of schedules and routines for new babies, which found its way on to the fire. The spring was cold and blipped with disappointing days, but by the end of April London was in full colourised postcard bloom, frothing through park railings, petals piling up in doorways and corners like the snow of a few weeks before. The house was full of flowers and candles. In the olden days people would go into a church and light a candle for you. Now they just posted you one in a box and left you to do it for yourself.

Clever Arlo survived our ignorance. Bathing him was a strange ritual, one I dreaded in anticipation but always enjoyed at the time. It seemed so hard building up to it, running the water the exact right temperature, peeling the layers off his unhelpful little arms and legs, cleaning up whatever was in the nappy and holding him gently in the water so that he didn't roll away from my forearm and go under. But then — once he was there, staring up at me and kicking with those froggy legs, grabbing at the surface of the water as though he should be able to pick it up, his mouth curling back in that big smiling crescent over his gums — then we could have stayed there for hours. Except the water would go cold and I wouldn't run the hot while he was in there for fear it would burn him.

Sleep deprivation came to seem, in Ann, to have a methamphetamine effect. She baked, she cleaned, she walked the baby endlessly. Even once he was sleeping through from ten until six she was down to four or five hours a night. She vibrated with energy. I took advantage of her complete focus on domestic life to meet with my agent, hustle along the contract with Hallie and beg the bank for a week longer to sort the mortgage payments out. By mutual, silent agreement we did not discuss the money we were spending. Having Arlo had made us rich only in the emotional sense, but it felt also as though we were rolling in cash. He came with us, by cab, to slap-up lunches at Randall & Aubin, where they wrinkled their noses as though he were a bad oyster but said nothing as long as he kept quiet. The daunting unaffordability of the Oxford Street department store's baby section, only weeks earlier, melted away. Oxford Street? Any pallid mass-produced junk from there wasn't good enough for our boy. We wanted French nappy bags and rare Nepalese slippers woven by two-hundred-year-old peasant ladies, we must have handcrafted Brazilian wooden toys. 'I know, let's build him a library, the complete Beatrix Potter in hardback, the full Narnia series, oh look, Tom, at this first edition *Swallows and Amazons* for only 400 quid! Of course he'll never be allowed to touch it but see this green of the cover, isn't it beautiful? Wouldn't it look perfect in his room?' We lived the lives of people we were not.

★ ★ ★

I wore my fatigue with pride. At last I had earned the right to be grizzled unshaven dad picking up my caffè latte of a morning, my marsupial baby cradled in the sling, giving the wife a few minutes' rest. See my virility! I'd often envied these fellows at the local coffee shop, picking up a standing ovation along with their bag of almond croissants. Now it was my turn to share the glory, to feel the love. Oh, and he was easy to love, Arlo, there was no problem there.

Outside the Costcutter you often see tawdry plastic sheaths of flowers strapped to lampposts in memory of a loving colour-photocopied mum or restless young chav who's got in the way of somebody else's crack-fuelled Stanley knife. The carnations sprouting in dirty cling film are a new form of urban decoration, mawkish post-Diana grief. There was one taped to the telegraph pole that day, a blue velour teddy bear hanging off it with a Velcro grip. The sequins around its eyes sparkled in the sun and it was dark where the wet from last night's rain had got it. You'd never seen such a pathetic thing in your life. The thing to do was to avoid reading or looking at the little fact sheet the family had typed about their lost one, avoid at all costs determining which of the two shiny-faced photo subjects, a mother and a small child, was the victim. The bear could have been the toddler's favourite toy, left there by a devastated mother; equally, the family might have left it there to remind the heavenly dead woman of the sweet, clammy hands that still reached for her here on earth.

Ah yes, one *Observer* left, not because there was a rush on them but because the Costcutter man hardly bothered to order them in. The usual tits and admonishments were on display over the other papers. So much money to be made out of peddling resentment. The woman who'd bought my aunt's old chair was ahead of me in the queue. She clucked over the baby, who was looking rather cute in his little white hat, buried in the sling.

'He's just like you,' she said. 'Look, he's scowling.' She mimicked the face back at him. 'Rah!' Arlo was oblivious. 'How is your wife?'

'She's very well, thanks. Thriving on it.'

'Good.' She turned away and paid for her bread and milk. I got change from my fiver for the paper. We walked out together, towards home. Should I keep pace with her? I wondered, would she want to be alone? Would it be rude not to talk?

'How is your son?' I finally thought to ask.

'Very well, thank you. Studying hard.'

'Oh, is he . . . '

'He's studying philosophy at the London Metropolitan.'

'Great. I hear it's making a comeback. Philosophy.' Something I'd picked up from a weekend paper.

'Yes. What sort of work he will get from it, I don't know.'

'Hard for anyone to get work in that field I imagine.' She didn't respond. I adjusted the sling around my chest. 'I'm a great believer in education for its own sake, though.'

'That man, has he been bothering you at all?'

'Oh.' With the thought of him came a wave of revulsion. 'No. Did I tell you about him? Have you seen him?'

'No, never, but your wife has described him to me. He sounds as though he suffers from a mental illness. These people have been abandoned by their families. It's a tragedy. And of course it puts us all at risk. Especially now, with your baby, you must keep a close watch. London is not a safe place.'

I was glad she kept talking, glad of my sunglasses, glad of having the sling strap to hold on to. It had been so easy not to think of the man, the intruder.

Arlo had fallen asleep in the sling, so I scooped him out and took him straight up to his room. A cool draught blew over the top landing; I snuggled an extra blanket (a home-knitted hand-me-down from Kate) over his hunched little back and went to pull down the sash windows in our room. Downstairs, icy fingers of disinfectant jabbed up into my sinuses. Ann had the bright yellow rubber gloves on and was on her hands and knees beneath the table.

'It's so weird,' she said, 'there were all these ants on the floor, so I got the spray from the bathroom but now they're gone.'

'Really?'

'Yeah.' She scuttled out backwards and pulled herself up to standing, breathing heavily. 'Yeah. Just there. A whole swarm of them.' She brushed hair from her eyes with the back of her hand. 'And your mobile rang but I missed it.'

'Thanks.' I checked through the missed calls. *H*.

'Ann.' If she had seen it she would say something. Surely.

'What?' A chipper smile.

I felt drained of blood, white, the way you do when you've drunk too much and think you're going to be sick. 'Nothing.'

★   ★   ★

The weather brought the animal life out in force. As the nights grew warmer we lay awake disturbed by foxes rummaging round the bins and the stray cats fighting. Just after Arlo's one month birthday I was in my study when a terrible hissing sound snatched at the air. I met Ann on the landing, her eyes wide with fright.

'Did you hear that?'

'It must be the cats.'

'My God. It sounded like a possum.'

'Really?'

She shuddered. 'They're disgusting. We had one in the house once. It was huge.'

These instances of her early life emerged rarely. 'What kind of house was it?'

'Sixties. A state house. That's what they call them. My half-brothers used to set traps.'

So this was after her father had remarried.

'Never mind.' She shuddered, lost to some memory. I thought of the mad googly stares of possums I'd seen on nature programmes, their quivering pink noses, almost translucent, those swollen eyes, bald and dark and glistening. Boys and vermin. We paused there on the landing, the held breath of our listening suspended in the air between us. The plane tree creaked outside the window like a sailboat's ropes on a stormy night and the house shook slightly as a lorry trundled down the street. No other sound than that. Her cheek was so soft when I kissed it.

There are two different types of mourners, at least in my limited experience of the great intruder. Some want to understand every medical detail of the dead person's demise, probably in the subconscious desire to turn back time and prevent it. Others appear more stoic; they say things like, 'He's gone now, there's nothing I can do.' I watched my mother, when her father was in a hospice, transform from one to the other. Where are his secondaries, which organs do you expect it to move to next, what happens when it reaches his brain, is he that yellow colour because of his liver, why are his feet swollen, *what can you do?* All her insistent, good-daughter questions slowly crumbled away in the face of the unalterable facts. He was in a hospice. The care was palliative. That was the one thing they could do. And so the relevant, the only question, in my mother's low and modulated voice, became, 'Is he in any pain?' She wept with the frustration of it — I saw her back shaking over by the potted plants in the courtyard — but once, after long days and nights and the frightening beginning of the nonsense talk, he had let go, she didn't want the small print of what had happened. She climbed on to his stiff white bed like a little girl and held his body without fear that she might hurt him any more. He was old, ancient to me then, in his early seventies while I was seventeen and vastly more concerned with appearing clever and getting laid (for me to get one, I needed the other; such was life) than anything else. Until my father phoned, his voice reduced as voices are in such conversations, and told me to come and see grandpa now because it wasn't long. We had been great pals, as he would have phrased it, in my early youth. With all the self-consciousness of a boy aware for the first time of death's reality, on the train to Barnes I remembered the afternoons spent in the glassed heat of my grandparents' sun room. The tiny Earthlike spin of streaky blue marbles along the obstacle course tray grandpa had knocked together, a sloping wooden oblong studded with nails. A plate of buttered raisin scones, the ashtray with the galleon in beaten enamel which swelled around its side. I tried to recapture a more specific scene, something my grandfather might have said, an accidental wisdom, as the train sat waiting for a problem on the line to be cleared. Ploughed fields lay through the dirty, scratched window to my right. My last cigarette sat between my fingers, ready to smoke as soon as we began moving again. Mostly though, which got in the way of thinking of my grandfather, I was thinking, this is it, my first encounter. My first funeral. I had been obsessing for three years about Julia Flyte's assertion, in *Brideshead Revisited*, that Charles is not, will not become, a complete man. It had worried me greatly, Charles's stunted development, or more importantly Julia's opinion of it. It also worried me, though not as greatly perhaps as it should have, that my grandfather had not even yet died and already I was picturing myself in a new suit, comporting myself like a man, a real man, as I stood in front of his funeral congregation and read from 'Corinthians'. Clearly I had not put away childish things (and maybe haven't yet, more than twenty years on). I held it together during the reading, steeling myself as my voice cracked on 'now, face to face'. It wasn't grandpa's face that bloomed within me then but a sense of his presence having been torn out, the bald insult of his death, and my tears (when they did come, as we carried his coffin from the church) were the hot spiky tears of fear and outrage as well as the winded gasps of bereft love.

How comfortable, how privileged to face the genteel death (never mind the yellow, the brain fever, the ghastly smell) of an elderly relative as one is on the cusp of adulthood. Ann was four when her mother died of stomach cancer, and the only saving grace, she said, was that she couldn't remember most of it. There was a hole in her memory, to paraphrase Billy Bragg, where no hole should be.

★ ★ ★

The blossoming trees bestowed their charms over the streets, dripping petals and fragrance under blue skies like painted studio backdrops. My agent and Hallie had agreed the deal for the Fiji project and the agent, bless him, had given me an advance while the contract was being nutted out, saving us from the street. Tonia prepared to fly off to St Lucia so as not to have to be home while Andy moved out. Maybe she would stay there for a while, she said. Her prison work was unsustainable for long. Every visit there filled her with more tales of sadness, women doing things to their own bodies that made you flinch to think about, lives twisted up by abuse, legal injustices, the women's constant burning of their own belongings, prison service sadism, the small moments of release — of being able to say something, of being heard — fleeting puffs of fresh air down a mineshaft. When she came to say goodbye the day before she left, Tonia cradled Arlo and smoothed the constant tears from her cheeks as he gazed at things invisible just beyond her face.

We met Andy at the Tate for Arlo's first exposure to modern art. I was fully paid-up Groovy Dad With Sling as though we were down the market in Nairobi. Ann should have balanced a vegetable basket on her head. Walking over the Millennium Bridge Ann and I talked — in that way you do with a first child, wishing them into the future, when will he crawl, walk, talk, go clubbing? — about how Arlo would grow older between our hands, swinging over the cigarette butts by the river, looking down on the crowds from high on my shoulders while Ann, pregnant with number two, would reach the espresso bar ahead of us, shove her way to the front of the café queue. She was a miracle, talking about having another baby when our first was only six weeks old. I am an only child, and even when young was always wary of other children. Their private conversations, their drunken grip on reality. Being abandoned to a horde of shouting, hearty boys and girls at my mother's friends' garden parties threw me into white panic. These people did not know what they were doing. I sought refuge around adult conversation, learning early on not to impose myself, or sat in empty studies reading other people's guilty pleasures on my own. Every private bookshelf, I discovered, was dotted randomly with sexed-up pulp, or Anaïs Nin or *The Joy of Sex*. They were easy to sniff out; they were the books whose spines were buckled and worn. Reading these books, my breath coming shallower and shallower the older I got, until it was unnatural, rude, to absent myself in this way, and I was forced by social pressure to join in with British Bulldogs and Cluedo, reading and reading and fumbling the pages with thick, moist fingers, unable to lick them and neatly flick the paper over because that was what my mother did and no thoughts of my mother could be permitted in this mesmerising space; transfixed, time slowed and my throat dry, I learned everything I could about what women wanted in bed.

Sitting at a table by the windows, overlooking St Paul's, Andy let slip he'd been made HoD of English at his school, a triumph he'd been reluctant to share while I was an unemployed gimp and this was another example of the universe rewarding caddish behaviour. I pretended to be interested in whatever new exhibition was on but really all I wanted was to walk around with my wife and my son. Ann made an effort with Andy; you'd never know she had cried off and on for a week about the split. After half an hour of stilted conversation in the coffee shop he abruptly stood, knocking over a paper coffee cup with a few drops left in it. Ann, who seemed now unable to leave the house without a small battlefield's supply of first aid and other baby kit, fished in her parenting bag for a tissue, so I saw before she did that a young woman was walking towards us and Andy was moving to cut her off at the pass. This must be Karma. They greeted each other with a kiss on the lips. It was hard not to find this insulting, not to feel that he was doing it defiantly. I elbowed Ann; she raised her head and watched as he guided the woman in our direction. I know she was noticing the same thing as me: Karma looked like Tonia, only younger. Ann's eyes hardened and in seconds she seemed to age in proportion to Karma's youth, to acquire the smiling hostility you see in women of middle years. Karma made a fuss over the baby. We shouldn't have been there.

★ ★ ★

Ann had started going to a mothers' group, where she witnessed one woman breastfeeding another's child while the mother was in the kitchen making tea.

'Nobody said anything! They are all *sick*,' she said, giggling, 'and fat, not that there is anything wrong with that but there is when you wear leggings. If I have to see another giant veiny breast bulging out of a wrap dress . . . if I have to have one more conversation about reflux . . . '

I rather liked the idea of enormous, world-dominating tits bursting out of their frocks, but kept that to myself. While she was out at one of these (soon, she warned, it would be our turn to host) I called Hallie from the home phone. I can't remember what I needed to ask him; only it was strange being back in the world of the Fiji script, but easier to forget about the real lives of those people we had met there, from this distance of a few years. At some point in the conversation I heard the front door closing. She wasn't expected home yet.

'Just a minute, Hallie.' I called, 'Ann? Is that you?'

No reply.

'Sorry Hallie,' I said, 'just hang on two secs.'

'No worries,' he said. 'Everything all right?'

The air on the line suddenly changed, as though it was rushing into the phone receiver from just downstairs. 'Ann, I'm on the phone,' I called. Footsteps up the stairs, pausing on the landing. I didn't want to open my study door, to break the spell.

'Mate, call me back,' said Hallie, and he hung up.

'Ann?' I spoke into the receiver. 'Ann, are you there?'

There was nothing, just breathing. Then — away from my telephone ear, I just had time to register, from out by the stairs — a sudden tumble and clump. I ran out of my office. She was below me, in the landing corner. The phone was still in her hand. Her neck was at a funny angle and her whole body was folded in against itself like a piece of origami. 'Are you all right?' I skidded down, just saving myself against the wall from falling on top of her. 'Oh my God, are you all right?'

Slowly, wincing, she straightened herself. I patted her arms, her body, held her chin. She was in shock. 'Ann, Ann.' What was it you had to look for in concussion? She put her hands to her head. Her knees and palms were carpet burned. We heard the baby start to cry from the bottom of the stairs.

'Is he in the pram?'

She tried to nod and winced. 'Yes.' Blood was smeared over her front teeth.

'You've cut your lip.'

She ran her tongue up under her top lip, patted at the gum with a finger. 'I don't think so. My gums are fucked, it's the breastfeeding.' A small laugh. 'Nobody tells you you have the baby and *then* fall apart.'

'What on earth happened? Can you stand up?' I helped her. Her hands gripped the banister. 'Stay there.'

I brought Arlo into the kitchen and held him in the crook of my elbow while I made sweet tea. This knack of doing things single-handed was one Ann and I had lately mastered. Ann limped in and sat down. 'God, that was so weird,' she said.

'Are you sure nothing's sprained?'

'No, no, I'm just a bit freaked out, that's all.' She sipped her tea. Arlo whimpered. 'No darling, Mummy just needs a minute.' He began to cry again. 'Oh please Tom, can you deal with him?'

'Shh, shh,' I jigged him on my knee. Usually she hated to see me do this and quoted doubtful statistics about the amount of time men spend rarking children up and women spend trying to calm them down. 'Boo,' I said to him, pulling out my sure-fire silly face. 'Boo.' Come on Arlo, I thought, this is my full repertoire. Please stop. I held him close and rocked him a bit. The sobbing subsided, and in its place a warm hum of satisfaction spread through my chest.

Later I tucked the duvet over Ann and

drew the curtains so that our bedroom walls fell into a soft grey. 'Take it easy,' I said, 'you should catch up on some sleep.' I went to go but she held on to my wrist.

'Who was on the phone?'

'When?' Stalling.

'When I got home. I went to call Tonia but you were on the phone and then I heard someone else.'

'Just work, a work thing, a guy who wants a short film script. Why were you listening in?'

'I wasn't listening in, it was just that I went to make a phone call and then — '

'Why didn't you hang straight up?'

'What are you working on? You're working on something, what is it?'

'I'm working on a dozen things. Throwing it all at the wall so something will stick and I can pay back the credit cards.'

'Don't shout at me.'

'Sorry.'

She turned away from me. I realised she was shaking.

'You've got an inner ear infection. I'll make an appointment at the doctor's.'

'No, no, I don't want to take antibiotics while I'm breastfeeding.'

It was more than my life was worth to suggest we give Arlo formula. Ann had joined the mad and swollen ranks of breast milk propagandists, and believed that if anything other than her own milk passed Arlo's lips until he was at least eight the result would be bow legs, a hump on his back and a predilection for torturing puppies. 'OK,' I said. Being in that room with the sunlight shut out reminded me of the last time I had been ill. 'How about I call Kate?' How about, I was thinking as she lay gazing at the wall, the white-on-white-striped duvet cover rising and falling, over her breasts, how about we brave the terrifying issue of post-childbirth sex some time soon?

★ ★ ★

The next morning was mirror-bright. Downstairs light danced through the windows — so streaked and dusty they might have been pawed at by a giant sponge — and shone silvery on to the empty kitchen, everything abandoned just as it had been when Ann fell. Welcome to the *Mary Celeste*. Kate arrived in a flurry of hand-picked flowers and baby toys. After she kissed me hello she held my wrist and said, 'Are you going to be here all day?'

'I guess,' I said. 'If Ann's still sick.' Ann was up, but in her nightie. I was due to meet Hallie in town that afternoon.

'I might need to talk to you,' Kate said.

I shrugged. 'Fine.' Sure thing, crazy lady, I said inside my head. Arlo and I read the paper in the kitchen while the women consulted. Ann didn't have a temperature but had insisted it made her too sweaty and restless to have me sleep in with her, so she had kept Arlo by her side and I'd had a grumpy night on the fold-out sofa bed downstairs. This new parent business was catching up on us. We were fools to have gadded about so soon after Arlo was born. This was why people in pale blue tracksuits went for weeks without washing their hair and subsisted on delivery pizza. Because it gets you in the end, I thought, that exhaustion. The new life sucks up more than its share of household energy, it strips women of calcium and men of perspective and pays out in heartmelting gurgly smiles, for which you would suffer the loss of all your looks.

Kate had brought her own green tea, and a calming something-or-other for Ann. She blew the steam away and looked at me over the cup with the expression of someone who is carefully choosing her words. 'Ann isn't sure you'll want to do this.'

'What?' I pulled Arlo down on to the kitchen floor and began to change his nappy. The hostility of the gesture was fully intentional. Since when did this woman become an intermediary in my marriage? I glared at Ann. 'What is it?' She was scratching in the time and date on a temporary resident parking card for Kate.

Kate spoke: 'She wants me — with you both — to conduct an exorcism of the house.'

'A what?' Ghost house Hackney.

Ann went out to put the voucher under Kate's windscreen.

'Since that man was here, trying to break in, we feel there's some kind of bad vibe that hasn't quite been cleared. It's a simple ritual, no Catholic juju.'

'Just Scotch commune juju.'

'Yeah. MacTavish oojebaba.'

'You're going to turn me into a sheep and fuck me.'

Kate stared at me, then burst out laughing. 'I can't believe you just said that. That's Welsh people, anyway.'

'What do you think, Tom?' Ann called on her way back down the hall towards us.

'Look. Say I agree to it. Because if I don't believe in something, what does it matter, right? When would you want to do it?'

'We could do it now.'

'What about Arlo?'

Kate thought for a few seconds. 'You've got a sling?'

Kate went off to the front room to organise her eye of newt and toe of frog and so that Ann and I could have the kitchen. Our relationship was comic, I suppose. Inside it we were two people screaming; from the outside we just looked like a couple of clowns in mad wigs pulling funny faces. In her witch's kit Kate had a pamphlet that told us a little bit about the process. According to the italic type, printed on cheap, pale-pink paper, we were standing in a 'dwelling that is host to harmful spirits, causing sickness'. 'Do you really believe this?' I asked Ann. 'Come on.' On the bench I arranged the vials of witchy homeopathic crap she was taking — Grey Spider Bush Essence, Fringed Violet, something else I forget — alongside her bunches of bay leaves, the cones of sandalwood incense that had proliferated on every windowsill in the house, a crumbly chunk of frankincense from our bedroom. Exhibit A.

'What are you doing?' Ann said.

'You told me this stuff was for pregnancy, breastfeeding. Not,' I read from the pamphlet, 'for driving out negative influences . . . repairing aura damage . . . what the fuck, Ann?'

She snatched the page from my hand and gathered all the stuff on the bench into a pile. Kate's footsteps creaked on the floor above our heads. We sat on the kitchen floor for what felt like a long time. She leaned against the side of the sink cupboard, her legs out in front of her like a doll's, white paper flower hands in her lap. The pamphlet lay on the linoleum between us.

'What are these negative influences?' I asked. 'Who's that — me?'

'Tom.' She laughed. 'You centralise yourself in everything.'

I don't know about Ann but those long minutes were the closest I had ever come to contemplating life without her. In that hot kitchen we sat on the lino and I imagined the next steps. Telling our friends. Telling my parents. Selling the house, splitting the funds. Finding somewhere smaller for Ann and the baby. A flat nearby for me. Negotiated visits. A gradual shrinking of intimacy. The multiplication like cancer of the things we didn't know about each other. Life as I never wanted to live it.

'We may as well,' she said. 'Please.'

She was so slight. With my arm around her I could feel the ribs through her T-shirt. Arlo, hammocked across my chest, sucked his fist.

'OK.' I said. Everything flipped. We could chant, ring bells, have the fucking exorcism, save ourselves together or both go completely fucking nuts. Her knuckles gripping my fingers tight, we pushed our foreheads against each other like animals.

'I love you,' she said.

'Thank God,' I said, 'for that.'

Kate asked how much we knew of the house's history. All blank to me, apart from the poor fuckers who had to move out when the bank foreclosed on their mortgage and we swooped in, the desperation of first-time buying rendering us carrion eaters.

'Well,' Ann said. 'I have looked in the council records . . . '

'Really?' I asked in a passive-aggressive voice that masked the aggressive-aggressive way I actually felt. 'When?'

'When I was pregnant.' She wasn't going to wilt. 'I took a couple of days off work.'

A gelatinous silence blew up like a big jellyfish between us, filling the room, pushing love to the edges.

'Did you find anything relevant to the phenomena you have experienced?'

'Whoa whoa whoa.' I looked up into the corners of the ceiling. 'Is this — are there cameras in here? Am I being punked?'

Ann ignored me. 'People have died here, of course, it's a Victorian house, but the things . . . that have happened . . . haven't had any kind of human form.'

'The insects, the smell.' Kate might have

been reciting a shopping list.

'Ann,' I ventured, feeling that togetherness was one thing but we still had to explore all the options, 'do you not think that the, ah, swarming insects might be a little bit of an acid flashback?'

She gave me a hard stare. 'I'm not saying none of this is my fault.'

'I'm not saying that it is.'

'Many people I see have experimented with drugs,' Kate said soothingly.

'I bet they have,' I muttered.

'It can be the spirits' way of weakening the vessel, or the visitor opportunistically attaches itself to a consciousness already altered.'

I wanted a drink. It was eleven o'clock in the morning.

Kate got down to the business of exorcism. It is embarrassing in the extreme to recollect marching round the house after her and Ann, trying to shoot white light out of my hands as though they were spray guns. In the upstairs stairwell we formed an unintentional bottleneck that left us all red-faced and cross. Arlo squawked and Ann took a turn with him in the sling. Later I tried to make her laugh by doing a Bodie and Doyle roll and bursting into the bedroom with my back flat against the wall, but she didn't crack. After that we had to go outside while Kate lit incense in every room. The day was fresh, the sky very blue above the black surface of the playground. A translucent red plastic bag scudded about on the ground, pinky and glowing, full of air like a lantern of finely dried skin. Our God-bothering neighbour strolled by, a woman we were on nodding terms with, pushing her toddler in one of those three-wheeled buggies that, like our hand-me-down from Kate, looked like Darth Vader's wheelbarrow.

'Glorious day,' she said.

'Isn't it,' Ann replied. I pushed the gate open and wandered across the road to breathe, feeling the pressure of it all tight in my chest. I should have been working and we were shut outside our house while inside a woman with soft toys in the back windscreen of her car performed an exorcism in the living room. All right, they weren't her own soft toys, but nevertheless. A hand touched the back of my neck.

'Are you OK?' Ann twined her fingers into mine.

'Yes.' I smiled at her. 'Let's make scary faces at Kate through the windows.'

The front door opened. Kate looked pinkish and slightly warm, as though she'd been having a quick Hoover. 'Come in,' she said. 'Tom and Ann and Arlo Stone, welcome to your home. Spirits begone!'

The peppery scent in the house from the bunches of herbs was not unpleasant. 'It's a bit like being a casserole,' I said, 'but it's better than the smell of mould.'

'Did you get a plumber in?' Kate asked.

'They couldn't find anything.'

'A mouldy smell is a common manifestation.'

'Common to Hackney,' I said. 'East End drains.' *Manifestation.* Were we really allowed to talk like this now?

Kate rummaged fruitlessly but persistently in her large satchel bag until I had a vision of her being swallowed up by it and had to ask her if she wanted help.

'Do you have any bay leaves? Even dried ones in a packet, you know, for stew?'

I showed her the little bush we kept outside the back door for cooking.

'Bay spirit, I ask your forgiveness for picking you to help purify this home,' she said, before clipping off a couple of leaves with our kitchen scissors. I found Ann in the hallway and told her that if I put Kate in a film script nobody would believe it.

'I don't know, they don't seem to have any trouble believing in vampires, or that there are college students out there who are still virgins.'

'How much longer is this going to take?'

'We have to believe in it. There isn't any point otherwise.'

'OK.' I leaned in to kiss her hair, my hand sliding round the swell of the sleeping baby. So good that he was now out in the world. She rubbed her cheek against mine, her mouth towards mine, and it might be the fantasy of memory but I feel at that moment, that instant, we were as close as we ever were.

'All done,' Kate beamed. Ann heaved herself up to standing with a grunt and went upstairs to put Arlo to bed. I poured three large glasses of red wine and passed one to Kate.

'Thirsty work,' I said. 'Will you stay for lunch?'

'Can I ask you something?' Her voice was low.

'Yes?'

She leaned in the open back doorway. I could smell curry being cooked next door. Kate gave a quick sigh. She looked sick.

'Are you OK?'

'Simon says you're working with that man again. John Halliburton.'

Fuck. Chink chink chink the pieces clicked into place. Hallie seeing Simon. Simon talking to Kate. The next step would be Kate telling Ann. I had no option here but honesty.

'Actually, Ann doesn't know about that. She and Hallie didn't get on. You know he fired me from the project in Fiji.' She nodded. 'Ann wasn't well. We'd just married.' While I spoke I'd moved right up to her, against the facing door-jamb so I could speak as quietly as possible and all in a rush. Put this fire out now. 'You mustn't say anything. We've been broke. We've nearly lost this house. I want to tell her further down the track.' In the pause that followed I could hardly breathe for fear Ann would come downstairs.

'No.' Quickly, so I wasn't sure what I was hearing. 'It's what he's saying about her.'

'I'm sorry?'

Kate shook her head, eyes reddening with tears. 'He's saying terrible things about her. To Simon. Just last night at some fucking dinner party in Santa Monica.' She never swore. Her voice was forced, urgent. Last night? Then Hallie was still in LA?

'Like what?'

'It isn't true. But you've got to make him stop. You can't work with him. He's a drunk and a power freak Simon says, and — '

Ann was in the room. 'Wow.' She strode over to Kate and kissed her on both cheeks. 'I don't know what you did but this house feels fantastic.' Her beaming face turned towards me. 'Doesn't it? Can't you just feel it,' her fingers twinkled in the air like stars, 'all tingling and clean?'

'Yes.' I passed her a glass of wine, though she was being a bit of a purist about alcohol because of the breastfeeding. Food had become like fuel to her, something she shovelled in her face disregarding its taste, only interested in how many nutrients it would pass on to the boy. 'Cheers.'

After Kate left Ann insisted she would be fine at home now, that I could go off up west and 'do whatever it is you have to do'. She kissed me on the mouth. 'Thank you for today.'

'That's all right.'

Hallie's UK mobile was going straight to answerphone. On the drive to his Soho office gas bubbles kept rising in my throat. What had he been saying about Ann? What would I say to him? The afternoon was steaming hot and I was slightly fuzzy from the wine. The back of my shirt stuck to the car seat. In a traffic jam I went to phone through the congestion charge payment but discovered I'd left my mobile at home. In Biro I wrote a reminder on my hand to pay it when I got back: 'c.c.' Idly I tried to turn it into a lightning bolt like Ann's scar. All the while what Kate had said was churning in my gut. I parked in Soho Square and sat in the car for a minute trying to get one thing to stay in my head instead of this tide. People drank on the scorched grass in the sunshine. A young woman with towering hair crossed the road past me, hand in hand with her girlfriend. The Soho buildings hummed with heat, white castles behind an impenetrable shimmer.

Hallie's office was in a refitted Georgian building, upstairs from a mirror-and-chrome media club on Shaftesbury Ave. I walked up the four flights, past the waves of conversation and laughter coming from the club rooms. Knocked and pushed on the door to Hallie's reception. Introduced myself to his receptionist for the third time; she never remembered my name but when I told her, 'Tom Stone. I'm meeting Hallie at four,' she said, 'Oh, we've been trying to get hold of you. Hallie's stuck in Los Angeles. And actually from there he's got to go to Sydney so he won't be back in London till,' she flipped through a large black desk diary, 'the end of next week. And he's got . . . ' she went on, trying to find an alternative date for our meeting.

I cut her off: 'Did you leave a message?'

'No, somebody answered the phone. Your wife? She said you'd already left.'

'Right. Thanks. Do you have a number for

Hallie in Sydney?'

She wrote it down. I put it in my jeans pocket. The thing that had been bothering me since the day Arlo was born became clear, a bubble rising to the surface. About six months ago Hallie saw Ann at the hospital. I was amazed when my voice floated out of my body just as it always sounded. 'Can I ask you to find something for me?'

She still had last year's desk diary. It sat on top of the current one, lines and columns filled and colour-coded with all of Hallie's very important life.

'This is just, you see I had a meeting with Hallie last mid-October, and I need to be accurate about the date for my accountant and I've lost my diary. After our meeting he went on to an appointment at Barts' — I waved my finger vaguely around my face indicating Hallie's skin cancers, and she nodded. 'Is it in the diary?'

She found October. Pages divided by the hour, by meetings and phone calls, lunches, screenings, all in different coloured pens. My hands were slippery. There would be nothing there.

'I can't find you . . . '

'Really?'

'But here's the hospital appointment.'

2 p.m. on 16 October. *I left work early.*

Because of . . . this guy that's been following me.

'He had a different meeting that morning though.' She slammed the diary shut, looked at me hard.

'Ours was lunch,' I said. 'Thank you. Thanks very much.'

I don't remember walking down the stairs. 16 October, the day of the derailment. That *Evening Standard* headline: 'THE WAKING NIGHTMARE'. *Because of . . . this guy that's been following me.* What was in that pause? Hallie. Hallie was. Kate asked if she knew the man and Ann said, 'No. But I recognise him.' 'Black or white?' asked Simon, and in that moment she made her decision. In that moment she made him up.

Along Old Compton Street everyone strolled in the middle of the road, meandering with Friday evening happiness. The punchy smell of sausage came from I Camisa. American tourists consulted with each other in the doorway at Valerie's: 'Is this the place?' Up Frith, past Bar Italia, a swan-like woman at a table outside, black-aproned waitresses taking orders, groups of young men with matching beards and haircuts. I wondered if Ann knew what she had done. If she even knew the man was her invention.

I was back by my car. Suddenly it hit me

and I ran to a rubbish bin and threw up into it. Another fucked-up guy in Soho Square. *Somebody answered the phone. Your wife?*

The wedding night is lit by kerosene torches. Candles float on the pond amidst gardenia blooms; cones of citronella incense burn to ward off bugs. Bare-chested men with leaves circling their upper arms entertain the wedding party: fire-walking, dancing, drumming. Night insects fly into the torch flames, *tzzt*, drop to the ground. Ann lies on a tapa cloth in her wedding shift with Vincent Desjardin's suit jacket slung over her shoulders.
Hallie is at her side with the kava bowl.
'Married on my dime!'
Looking at her sideways.
'You Australian?'
She has to go. Get away. Her legs jelly. Through a group of people she sees two men helping Tom as he tries to walk on hot coals. She wants to reach him but she is pinned down by the numbness of the drink. Something muffled, like the sea, booms inside her head.
'What sent you to London?' he asks.
'I have to go.'
'You all right?'

340

She scrambles up. Gravity is intensified. She pushes, pushes herself slowly up, away from his heaving chest, the slab of his face. The suit jacket falls off her as she rises. He's holding one end of it in his fist. Another hand is on her calf. A moan rises from her. Her torso sways. *Let go of me.* Does she say it out loud? *Let go of me.* Something else is at work. A turning over, the stretching and yawning awake of the small clay woman she carries inside, the life she has suppressed. He laughs. His voice comes out high, excited.

'I do know you. Ann — Ann thing — I knew your brother. You were a bloody . . . and here you are with Tom bloody Stone! Of all the people.' With one grunting hoist he is upright and next to her, his thick fingers around her arm. He strokes her scar and whistles long and low. 'Botch job.'

Ann's arm burns under his grip, burns with trying to get it away. Tears prick her eyes. She has to get away from this man. The shut-down part of her mind is making sound now, it is a low scraping sound and she doesn't know why. She mustn't know why.

'Please,' she says, 'don't tell Tom,' without knowing what she means.

Above them somewhere the moon is

watching. Tom hops and shouts by the rosy coals. Men either side of him laugh like thunder.

'Ah, fuck it.' Hallie moves his hand away from her arm. 'You know what, you got old.' The walrus man squats on the ground at her feet and she still doesn't know what he is talking about.

I got home too late. Ann's hair was gone. Her skull was peaked at the back, terrible and bluish in the half-light, her eyes enormous.

'What have you done to your hair?' I tried to cross the threshold but she pushed me back. 'Ann. Ann. What have you done?'

'Sshh!'

'What?'

She held up a hand, palm towards me. 'Someone's in the house. Upstairs. I think it's him.'

I shoved past her into the hall. 'Where's Arlo?'

'Asleep.'

The door slammed behind me. Startled baby cries cut down in waves through the ceiling above us. I ran up the stairs and halfway to the top floor could see that she had put a chair under the handle of the nursery door. Arlo would be all right. I had to keep Ann safe. She was behind me, at my back. I turned and shrank from that mad head. Her body was young, skinny in jeans and a T-shirt. 'Where is he?' I said. 'Where's the man?' My hands shook. I opened the bathroom door and recoiled at a mass in the corner — an animal, I thought, a feral cat — but it was Ann's hair. Where were the scissors? Find the phone. The scissors and the phone. Through the half-open door to my office I glimpsed the white glow of the computer screen. Papers scattered. My shadow fell into the room before me. The film script, the Fiji script I was doctoring was in pieces on the desk and on the floor. Ripped diagonals, big rough-edged triangles of type-spattered white. The computer was open to a 'Final Draft' document that had bursts of letters on it as though someone had pounded the keys at random or with fists: 'B; 1 fds; 1,, v, 1, .cfcvf.x..x.['. Ann was breathing at my neck. I couldn't stand it. Upstairs was cold. Somewhere the windows were open. I had to call Kate. A doctor. Kate. '*Mehhh*,' Arlo bleated from behind his bedroom door, '*mehhh, mehhh, mehhh.*' A few streets away a siren dialled up and then down. Ann breathed. I wished she would stop staring at me. The red parachute of fear blooming, blooming in my chest. The weak, paralysed wrists and legs of a bad dream. The wolf's head, the bars, Ann's sexless clay men, these things were supposed to protect us. In Ann's birthday mirror all I saw was her head behind me, stripped of its hair and the forehead short somehow, truncated. Her eyes had gone. Just gone. I took her skinny wrist. Above us Arlo's squawks got louder, closer together. The 'where is everybody?' cry, the 'why am I alone?' cry.

'Come with me.'

She followed me downstairs. I flipped cushions and opened drawers looking for the telephone. Our banisters, our stairs and our walls looked alien. A dream dolls' house. Component parts of places you once knew. Find your way around. My mind swarmed dense and stupid. I was at the kitchen door and as a reflex fired the light switch. Blinked the split second of ghost silhouettes, green man-sized oblongs — one by the table, one by the sink, another in front of the door — away from my eyes. A glass on the bench, there, and the rubbish bin standing in the corner, there, and the table and chairs and the space under the table and chairs. A metallic taste spread through my mouth.

'Where's the telephone?' I turned and faced her. Made myself look in her eyes. She'd lost all sense of space, was so close to me, lips lightly parted. Rosemary's phrase ribboned through my head: *what sort of animal you are.* Say it. Just say it. 'Who is the man?'

Her blank stare.

'Who is the man?' I shouted it. 'There is no man.'

Nothing.

'We're going to call the doctor. There's no man here.' The relief of saying it was immense. Why hadn't I called a doctor on her before? I would no longer take responsibility for this. I picked up one of her clay figures, felt its weight in my hand. Put it back on the table. She was breathing rapidly. 'Ann? Where is the phone? Did you talk to Hallie? Is he the man?'

She opened her mouth. 'Arble andel egin lud.'

I slapped her. She cried out. From the top of the house came a sharp corresponding scream. Arlo. Ann twitched, turned. Her breath shuddered. A moan came from her body. Arlo screamed and screamed. In that swollen moment a knife divided me. What if she had been telling the truth all along? What if the man was there? Shut in with Arlo. The man was there. Arlo's screams suddenly subsided and the quiet dropped on my head like cold water I saw his small pale face the man's filthy hands and

I took the stairs two at a time, pulling Ann, stumbling, behind me, losing her somewhere halfway —

yanked the chair out from beneath the door handle of Arlo's room breathed deeply, calmly as I opened the door. 'Stay back.'

Ann slowly, robotically walking up the stairs. 'Stay over there.'

Arlo was on his back in the cot, crying feebly. The room breathed silently in a slowly rotating circle around me. No man's form emerged magically from the wall behind the alphabet poster, no crouching figure hunched in the corner shadows by the cot. Behind the door, nothing. He is he isn't hitting my head mad. What was I capable of thinking? 'Ann!' Hating her. 'NO ONE HERE.'

I scooped Arlo up and felt the white curdled sick down the side of his head which was wetting the sheet. His soft auburn hair was sticky with it. I needed now to get her, to bring her beside me down into the bathroom where I would wipe Arlo clean, Arlo who was whimpering now in my arms, I would fix him up and find the phone and call the doctor — these were the half-thoughts, the plans forming beneath the skin of my mind as my body moved through space towards where I had left Ann.

Between Arlo's room and ours something announced itself in my vision. Something wrong with the space that at first I could not identify. The scent of stocks in the vase in our bedroom, exhaust fumes and rubber, the hot evening air of the street far below billowing through to the landing. With damp, smelly Arlo pressed to my shoulder, I took a few steps into the bedroom. The curtains blew 'No'

Arlo had never taken a bottle. Everything near us was shut by the time his hunger became the most pressing thing. He had slept most of the afternoon, exhausted by the chaos, then woke and wouldn't stop his piercing cries. The police liaison woman wouldn't leave the house. I hadn't left the house. I had let them take Ann away without me, without Arlo. Andy spoke very loudly at the policewoman. He apologised and drove down to Boots at Liverpool Street station and got his car clamped while he was buying formula. He came back in a taxi with the bottles, the unwieldy steriliser, I remember, like the one we already had been given by Kate, nappies in all different sizes. He had clearly been weeping but I was looking at him through the wrong side of a magnifying glass so there was nothing I could say. The poor baby's squalling was so desperate he couldn't take the bottle at first. We made it too hot, then we made it too cold, then we worried that if we warmed it up again there might be bacteria and he would get ill and the thought sliced my head: if anything happens to Arlo . . .

Kate walked in as the baby was nearly finishing the bottle. He was flushed and drowsy in my arms. She looked at us and walked straight out of the room again and I could hear the sounds of somebody trying to harness a sob. The policewoman who was the community thing or whatever you call it person went into the hallway after her. She was really very nice that woman, although she knew less about babies than I did. I suppose I could have asked for someone else. But I thought of Ann gritting her teeth through the labour even though the med. student had been wearing this stomach-turning perfume, not asking her to leave because she thought the girl had to learn somehow. She would have let the policewoman stay, and so I did.

There were procedures. Identification. Removal to the coroner's control. A day later the post-mortem. In the booklet that the social worker left behind it said, 'If you do not want to know more about the post-mortem, you should skip this section.' A man with springy grey hair and bad dandruff told me, in that pallid phrase, that 'she never regained consciousness'. Surprising what you can be grateful for.

★ ★ ★

I hate 'Death is nothing at all.' I would like to kill Henry Scott-Holland, if he weren't already dead. 'I have only slipped away into the next room' — he makes it sound like you're going for a cup of tea. You're not coming back. 'Whatever we were to each other, that we are still.' Except here. Except together. 'What is death but a negligible accident?' Accidents can be prevented. I could have prevented this. It was holiday season. We held the funeral until Tonia could get a flight back from Castries.

★　★　★

Ann's things were still in the bathroom cabinet for a long time. Her claggy mascara, her flat-smelling pregnancy body oil, the citrus soap that goes so rich and foamy in the shower. 'Sixteen quid it cost,' she told me in shocked amusement after one of her shopping sprees, 'sixteen pounds for a bar of soap! I bought it by accident, the shop girl was so sweet and look how she wrapped it up, there was this Notting Hill type behind me and I just couldn't bring myself to say — er, no, I thought it said *six* pounds, I've made a mistake. Even six pounds! Oh God, what was I thinking.' No mention of the rest of the spending, which I didn't know about until the bank statement came. The soap was a bargain compared to the other stuff that needed paying off. Three pairs of trainers because her feet got bigger in pregnancy and never shrank back. Two pairs of Costume National heels, same reason. Hair dye. Hairspray, hair lotion, something called serum, all organic because of the breastfeeding. New maternity bras because the ones she bought just before Arlo was born turned out to be too small. Tops that were easy to breastfeed in discreetly. Skirts and trousers to fit her newly skinny waist. Special cream for stretch marks, oxygen something for her eyes, peppermint foot lotion, and the soap. The soap she started using. Everything else, even the shoes, she drove in black plastic rubbish sacks of remorse to the Marie Curie charity shop in Highbury Corner. I remember watching her from our bedroom window as she loaded the car, I didn't know with what. Some old crap, I'd thought, impressed by her strong arms, her energy. Then after she was gone the items appeared on the credit card bill.

★　★　★

You can save a lot of time if you don't shower. It's hard to quantify, but there are so many little daily routines we perform that just swallow the hours. You might think a solo guy like me, after Ann died, had lots of time on his hands. Baby's with the grandmother, wife's gone. It's the opposite. There was never enough time. There could be no minute away from my desk that felt useful. It wasn't just that Ann was there, every day, waiting for me on this computer that I never turned off, that gently slept when I slept and sprang to life, Ann in its memory, when I touched the keys, in the morning when I couldn't lie in bed, in the night when I couldn't stop being awake. The fear of dying consumed me, the fear of knowing it, as Ann must have known it, somehow, that she would not see her boy again. Her neck broke. I did not want to know more about the post-mortem. I kept thinking that I must not, cannot die. The fear was with me every day and night. Arlo, small Arlo with his cap of reddish hair, couldn't be any more alone than he already was.

★ ★ ★

Kate came to the house to pick up some of the hand-me-downs Arlo had already grown out of; another friend of hers was having a baby. It was autumn, four months since the funeral. Arlo was with my parents and I was packing to move down there for a bit.

London, living on our own, wasn't really working. 'I'm in Islington,' she said from her mobile phone, 'how long will it take me to get there?' Maybe she came from the hairdressers, she had that newminted look about her. Had definitely dyed the grey from her hair since the funeral, was wearing her denim skirt with the nervy energy of women who drink and don't eat.

She'd brought a casserole in a Tupperware box. 'I'll just put this in the freezer.'

'Thank you.'

There was no room in the freezer. It was full of soups and lasagnes, things people had made for me. I was grateful. I still ate takeaways. Arlo was just having his first solids, but I couldn't join him on the pumpkin purée. I had cleared away the worst of the bachelor excesses, the pizza boxes and mouldering coffee cups, and turned some peaceful music up in the living room. She said she wanted tea but when she saw my glass of wine she changed her mind. 'I'm driving,' she said, then, 'oh, fuck it.' We sat on the kitchen floor. It is easier, ground level. We drank a bottle and she told me about her kids, what they were up to, the new school year and Titus had won some scholarship or other, they had tutors of course, they were being pressure-cooked, it wasn't a childhood at all. 'I never know,' she said, 'I have no bearings any more. I don't ever know if I'm doing the right thing.' A little silty circle had formed in the bottom of my wine glass. It was nice to listen to someone else talking. 'I keep seeing birds everywhere. That's something Ann said, she said there's a bird that perches on the walkway over the railway tracks down the road, a big brown bird. She thought it was watching her. Birds see everything, don't they? They look down on us and see everything, that's what I told her. Not just her.' Kate looked at me, her mouth dragging down at the corners, and covered her eyes with her hand. 'She said it was more like birds swooping in her head.' For a minute or two she cried. I held on to her ankle until she took a couple of shuddery breaths and stopped. 'How's Arlo doing?'

'I'm going to Wiltshire. To my parents'.'

'To live?'

'No. Tomorrow.' My mother's idea; she was worried about me, a vague puffy pressure I dimly felt emanating from the south-west at all times. 'How's Simon?'

She laughed, and went on for a bit too long in a slightly unhinged way.

'I should get the Moses basket.' It was in the hall. I couldn't face getting it.

Everything about that day Kate had

dropped off the things — the day Ann thought the man broke into the house — came back to me in a flood, as though I was right there again on the landing with Ann, not here on the kitchen floor, drunk. Ann pale, afraid. I said to Kate, 'I don't think Hallie was making it up. About Ann.'

She nodded. 'I don't think so either.' Her voice frayed. 'Tom, I blame myself. I blame *myself* for what happened.' The air around her head was coming unstitched.

'We all did it.' The silence stretched out. She stood up. She walked towards the door. Not the long way, which she could have taken, round the other side of the table. Past me. I reached for her legs. They flinched and went rigid when I touched them, carved out of smooth brown skin like furniture. My fingers ran up her calves and pressed into the pulpy dip at the back of her knees. She breathed out, a gentle sound. I swallowed the urge to put my mouth on her skin.

'Ann told me what you like to do,' she said. What was she talking about? It took me a moment to understand. A black freckle lay right on top of her knee, begging to be wiped away.

'No.' I lifted my head. It was heavy as a medicine ball. 'What she liked to do.'

Kate looked down at me steadily. 'Oh.'

I heard her walk down the hall. The sound of the door closing. Her car engine as it revved up. The neighbourhood was in the room with me, littered asphalt, chewing gum splodges, infested puddles. Swings creaked on their rusting chains, the bitten black rubber of the seats smelling as strong in the dry air as a hot car tyre. Kate, buckling herself in while behind the chicken wire wall of the basketball court someone watching her thumped a ball against the ground, again and again and again. 'Be careful', I wanted to say to her. After the street fell silent I went and double-bolted the front door.

★ ★ ★

Under the clean skies of Wiltshire I had time to myself while Stella took Arlo off for walks in his buggy, to show him what life was truly like (no one raised in London had a real childhood, she declared) and to meet various local *éminence grises*. Once I went with them and we passed a drunk man lying in a ditch beneath a giant camellia hedge and as I slowed down to check if he was alive my mother said through her teeth, 'Keep moving.' In the hours at my disposal, having called a halt to anything that looked like work, I cruised the Internet in dad's freshly painted study. They didn't have broadband — searches were excruciating. But I was in no hurry. There were nearly three million entries for 'Ann Wells'. School reunions, family gatherings, I looked at as many as I could. She wasn't hiding there.

When everyone was asleep I stayed up late watching television. Cried in front of a documentary on Australia. Their Prime Minister, a grey man refusing to say sorry. Guilt and blowflies. In the ad break my mind drifted to a trip through Tuscany with Ann and Tonia and Andy. Ann floating through this walled town or that piazza, hips and knees jutting like a racehorse, her whole body sensitised, eyes unfocused in a sort of post-fucking glaze. Then I thought of the lone women standing on the outskirts of town, maybe five minutes' drive away by a lay-by or a wood, Moroccan women standing there alone beside their portable stereos, waiting to be picked up.

'When you think,' Tonia had said, 'that they wouldn't let me in to St Peter's because my sundress was above my knee.'

'You see,' said Andy, repeating two of his favourite sayings, 'the bigger the front, the bigger the back. No heart, Catholicism.'

On a concrete wall down some street in a suburb called Botany the Australian telly programme showed the burned-out aftermath of a race riot, a concrete wall stained with graffiti, the Nazi-style SS. The letters were faded to grey. Like Ann's scar, except there were two of them. The vandal must have been interrupted from the far end of the alleyway. The tail of the second S tapered off at a leftward angle and in a dying line it connected with the tail of the S before it.

N.A.M.W. 07.07

She lies on the bed in Fiji. There is the persistent turning sound of a doorknob. There is a girl in the room. The girl sits on the bed and listens to the sounds on the other side of the door. Her body is stiff. She needs to pee. Fourteen years old. Face puffy with forming, spotty, red. The laughing drawling voices of her brothers outside the door, her brothers' mates. She scrapes a fingernail down the cut mark on her leg. It's funny because a while ago she was drunk and slid down the stairs to the landing showing the holes in her tights to everybody and now she doesn't feel drunk. There's that boy, the one they call Horse, the one she likes. That boy asking if she knows what a blowjob is. Everyone laughing. Making her show them on the bottle. She doesn't know his real name, just the name they call him, and she repeats it to herself, inside her head, so conscious of her itchy poisoned skin. She picks at the raggy bits around her fingernails. That boy might like her.

Ann crawls from the bed to the bathroom and throws up into the toilet bowl. When there is nothing left she retches. She takes the nail scissors and drags them across an old scar on her leg. Breathes. Her head clears. Her body that knows what it knows stays there and her mind rises up like burning paper into the world without memory. She pulls apart.

Desjardin unlocks the door with the master key. He stands aside to let Tom into the cabin. Tom thanks him and closes the door behind, hears the crunching of footsteps as the Frenchman walks away. The room is hot and dark. He says, 'Ann?'

She's in bed, muffled beneath the sheets. Twitches away at his touch.

'You're boiling.' He crosses to the air-conditioning unit on the other side of the room. When it clicks and hums she hunches further beneath the sheets. 'Cold.' Her voice is croaky.

'Are you ill? We only got hitched! You don't have to take to your bed.'

She doesn't say anything.

Calmer now, gentle. 'What's the problem?

Let's go and see the nurse. You knew I'd
have to work when Hallie showed up.' He's
by the bed again, stroking her leg. It's rigid
under his hand.

'I want to go.' Her breath smells viral,
metallic. He puts on the bedside light and
sees scabs around her mouth, cold sores
that have come up in the night.

'Let's go to the nurse.'

'We have to go. We have to leave.'

'Don't be mad. We're going in a couple of
days. I've got to work. Come on, they must
have some kind of flu medicine here.' She's
floppy when he pulls her arm. He shakes
her. Her head lolls around. 'Ann!' He throws
her wrist back down on the bed and walks
away, frightened by the heat rising in his
chest.

When he comes back he has brought the
nurse, a middle-aged Fijian woman who feels
Ann's forehead and says, 'Oh yeah, oh
yeah.' She gives Tom a bottle of powdered
antibiotic and tells him how to make it up.
He thanks her and when she goes he puts
the powder in the bathroom. Ann doesn't
move from the bed. She gets hotter and
hotter. The antibiotics have no effect. When
Tom says he'll bring Hallie to see what's
wrong she says 'no' over and over again.
Desjardin calls by. 'Everyone's concerned,'

he says. Ann sleeps. Tom tries to go back to work in Hallie's bure but can't concentrate. He should get Ann home. Not to Suva, their next scheduled stop, three days there with Hallie. To London. Hallie makes no effort at sympathy. He's fucked off and he lets Tom know it. Man's wife's a time waster. A distraction.

Two days after the wedding Tom steps out of the shower and startles. Ann is in the bathroom, naked, a thin red line running down one long thigh. The scissors are on the glass bathroom bench.

'Did you cut yourself?' He reaches down. Touches it gently. 'Ann.'

'*Please*. I want to go.'

He shivers from a drip of fear. For her? Everything he has worked to set up? Could he do this? He holds her, suspicious of the rising excitement inside, the thought that he could abandon everything to prove how much he loves her. He breathes out, strokes his hands over her hair.

★   ★   ★

They don't talk on the plane. One day, Tom thinks, he'll probably laugh about how he went to Fiji with his girlfriend to write a hit film and came back married, sacked and in debt. He'd told Hallie he was leaving early with Ann and as he expected Hallie had fired him. Part of Tom thought, fair enough. Man can't handle his wife. Part of him felt sorry for every poor fucker who didn't have Ann to handle. Beside him, she sleeps in a lorazepam cloud.

★   ★   ★

The girl sits on the bed worried that she might wet herself. Her brothers and their friends laugh outside the door. The one she likes has told her to wait there. He's going to come in soon. She fingers the side of her cheek, a painful spot there, and waits.

The doorknob turns, it turns and it sounds like a cork slowly being pulled from a bottle.

It was tough taking Arlo back home to Daley Street. I had put it off for weeks, just lying for hours on my parents' conservatory floor with him, rolling balls across his line of vision as he giggled and squeaked and the cardboard world gradually suffused again with life. He changed so quickly, coming more and more into himself, his eyes clever and dark like Ann's, her same habit of gazing into the middle distance, in conversation with things we couldn't see. I brought him into bed with me whenever he cried at night, a pillow on one side of him to stop him slipping off the edge. On the nights he didn't cry I woke him up and brought him into bed anyway.

I wasn't drinking any more. I rang my agent and told him I had quit Hallie's project and that I needed another job. Maybe scripting wildlife programme narration, that would be about my speed. Hallie was away, nobody knew where. There was one rumour about cancer and another one that he'd been asked to head up one of Australia's main television channels.

Arlo batted with his legs at a second-hand baby gym my mother had wheeled out of the parish toy library even though we weren't members. Birds wheeled over the garden. I watched my father through the conservatory glass. He was shaking his foot around to try and get something off the end of his shoe. Yes, wherever he was, Stella wasn't far behind, and she appeared now in her long blue dressing gown, talking to him in dumb show, probably remarking on his stubby little legs. 'Short men must never sit on tables,' she had said the night before when I was doing just that, waiting for Arlo's bottle to cool down. 'Your feet don't reach the floor.' She had also said, 'You can't stay here for ever, Tom. You have to go back to London at some stage.'

'Well actually, Dad and I saw a house for sale in the village this afternoon.'

We had, on the walk back from showing Arlo the ducks, stopped to look at a low, pink-plastered cottage next door to the chemist, prettier inside than the front led you to believe, with a flat lawn at the back and views from the bedroom windows over that lawn and down to the river. Dad stayed downstairs with the unwieldy buggy and the bouffanted estate agent while I stood at the window in the double bedroom and watched the sky for a minute. Neither of us said anything about it on the way home. When I told Stella the look on her face made me laugh.

'It's all right. I'm not going to move here.'

'You know we'd love it if you did, I just don't know that you'd be happy here, you're such a city person really.'

'Mum.'

She softened then. I realised I should call her that more often. 'We're going back to London. I've just been thinking, that's all.'

My father had the shoe off now and was still shaking it, his stockinged foot held delicately. Poor dad, something nasty from the birdbath had got on to his fingers. He kept trying to throw his hand away in slow flicks but the desperate semaphore wasn't working. Then he leaned right over, delicate as a ballerina, the leg without the shoe pointing up into the air, and wiped his hand on the dewy lawn. It was coming up that was hard, and there was a windmilling wobble at halfway, but he regained his balance and when he'd got upright again he looked around and smiled at the garden. He couldn't get the smile off his face.

★ ★ ★

Arlo and I got to Daley Street at night. The place was lonely, its big FOR SALE sign posted outside. Andy had been fielding all that and it was about time I took over. The wolf's head looked grave, the enemy's relic of victory from a battle the house had lost. I kept up a one-sided conversation with Arlo as we entered the hall, switching on lights, grateful for his beating pulse in my arms. Dust lay over the table and the mantelpiece, over the kitchen benches. There were small leaves around that must have blown under the back door. This I kept locked, despite an old fruit smell that hung sweetly and unpleasantly in the air. Cats scrambled and yowled outside. I should have let the place out before I went away. Not for the first time

I thought of Ann's father, the elusive Mr Wells, who I had not tried to trace. One day Arlo will want to know him. I can wait.

We watched television until he fell asleep on my chest. I kept the set on low all night, lying there on the sofa not sleeping, feeling that Arlo's easy breath was the pump that kept my breath going, that his little body starfished over mine was a form of protection. Above us the second storey of the house loomed cavernous and black all the way up into the wild dark sky. I watched the closed living room door.

On the bed the girl waits. She likes this boy, she doesn't mind waiting. She waits. She waits. Fourteen years old. She sits on the side of the bed and waits. Picks at a cold sore. Shaves her head. The doorknob squeaks as it turns.

She sits on the bed and watches herself burst through the door and into the room. The speckle-headed blank girl with unsaid words behind her face is in a mood to hurt somebody.

B; lfds; l,, v, l,. cfcvf .x..x. [

I took Arlo to Borough Market to see Tonia. In a corner of a large shared table at the coffee place she bounced Arlo on her knee, her gaze glued to his face, a tissue bunched up to her mouth. Christmas was coming, with a chill in the air that brought edges, shapes and colours into focus. I'd spoken to Andy that morning; one of his college mates had a private drama school; there was a new part-time position teaching script work that he wanted me to apply for. It was too early to be away from Arlo, though I was grateful to him for thinking of me. Things weren't going well with Karma, he said. 'Well then,' I told him, 'stop wasting your fucking time.' Tonia held Arlo by her cheek and was talking to him in a low, secret voice, and he was smiling.

'You should have a baby,' I said.

She pretended not to hear. I thought of Bridget. There was a tender spot there, a sore tooth of guilt or affection. I owed her an apology, perhaps. Down the table a little girl swore at her mother and pushed her hot chocolate over. 'You are a horrible child,' said the woman beside them, whose trousers and bag were covered in brown milk. Tonia passed a pile of paper napkins towards them but the mother was in a paralysis of embarrassment and the little girl was still shouting. People in the queue stood and stared and the order taker was frozen in the gesture of handing somebody his change while she was staring too. A wave of missing Ann roared up my body. She would have loved this, she would have laughed and felt compassion for the mother and been appalled by her all at the same time. Her slanted glance next to me. Its absence was almost as hot as its reality. Her elbow, sly at my ribs. That Ann.

'Excuse me,' I said to Tonia, reaching for the baby. 'Sorry. I've got to go.'

'Are you all right?' Everyone standing now, making way, the spilled flood still being mopped up as I pushed past.

★ ★ ★

Because of the Olympics I sold Daley Road for a stupid amount of money and we lived for a while in a rented place near Tonia and the river. Somewhere around then Andy moved back in. About a year after Ann died (a year that, aside from Arlo, passed like featureless linoleum under my feet as I stood doubled over by the freezer section in the supermarket) I bought this place in Muswell Hill; my parents helped me out. Good schools. I ran into Kate outside the vegetarian café and she told me her news, loudly, in the way of people who have had enough of

keeping their voices down. I kept expecting
her to remember the children and check
herself but she didn't, and they looked bored
and fake-tough as though they'd heard it all
before. Simon was usually in the States. He
wanted to marry someone out there. He and
Kate had never married so everything
happened very fast. He used to think
marriage was a bourgeois conspiracy. Now he
wanted his children to be ring-bearers while
he exchanged vows on a beach with a
barefoot script development girl called
Tamara. He told Kate one night when she
was in the bath. She stood dripping and
threw an electric toothbrush at his head.

'Didn't I darling?' she said to Ruby. 'At
Daddy's head!'

'Mum.' Titus tugged at her arm. 'Come
on.'

'Got him right here!' She smiled at me
manically and said, 'That's our bus! Call me!'
And she hitched up her skirt and with the
children ran between the North London
shoppers as if darting through trees in a
forest.

Now she comes over sometimes, with the
kids, to my house. Arlo always likes that. I like
Titus and Ruby too — they have a heavy
burden in life, what with their fruitcake of a
mother and a narcissist father who rocks up

every few weeks with basketball-coloured skin and the latest Playstation. They were visiting last week when, for only the second time since Arlo and I moved here, Tonia popped in. She phoned from outside the house. I opened the door as she was locking up her bike.

'You look great.' I kissed her cheek. 'Really well.'

In the kitchen she kicked her shoes off and we made small talk about the revamping of the canals, the prices at Fresh & Wild, the new bar across the road. Kate made tea, and I saw Tonia pause for a minute, noting how familiar she was in my kitchen. She dropped her eyes to mine. I shrugged. It's nothing, but I couldn't help smiling.

'So we saw that new film the other day,' she said. 'By that guy you know. Joe Baxter?'

'Yeah, I heard that was out.'

'Not very good.'

She was just saying that, but I loved her for it. 'How's Andy?'

Tonia nodded. 'All right. Good, actually. More on top of things with work.' He was deputy head now.

'I'd love to see him.'

'Yep.' She tugged at her hair. 'He misses you.'

'And you guys?'

'Yeah, fine. You know, it's always . . . Oh my God.'

'Dad?' Arlo was in the doorway, his face quivering. 'My thing from the Aquarium broke.' His eyes went from me to Tonia, his chin crinkled and I could see he was deciding whether or not to cry. He liked to cry, lately, which someone told me was normal in five-year-old boys. Not that that stopped me worrying.

'Hello Arlo,' said Tonia. 'Do you remember me?'

He glued himself to my legs. The rims of Tonia's eyes had reddened. I forget how like Ann he is.

'We're having a party next Sunday,' I told her. 'Whose birthday is it?' Arlo said something muffled into my leg and held up five puppety fingers for us to count.

'Then we're going to Australia,' he said.

Tonia looked at me, her hand to her mouth. 'Really?'

Kate opened the French doors on to the small overgrown garden. 'Titus, Rubes, we've got to get going.'

'Just for a visit.'

Slowly Arlo wandered over towards Tonia's chair. He stopped a foot or so from her. The wind chimes Ruby had made at school started their pretty clonking sound as a breeze blew in from the garden. Kate began to pick up her children's stuff, which was strewn everywhere, and I went up to my study for a photograph I wanted to give Tonia. Ann's head is still there but I've moved it to the top of the book-shelves, where it gathers dust. In the absence of trophies and awards it will have to do. I've stopped trying to know *how* to remember Ann. I had the chance to find out and I didn't see it and despite what I seem like, I know what that makes me. Now on a good day it seems enough just to remember.

★ ★ ★

The sea surrounding Sydney is a thick rich blue, the odd rusty freighter sitting low, like a giant canoe, on its surface. The cliffs dwarf you even from the air; they must have towered sickeningly over the convict ships. There are the city's towers in the distance and, closer, a huge ugly oil refinery, giant vats crouching on the land, flames leaping from pipes. Arlo and I staggered off the plane half dead from the flight. It was bliss to arrive in this foreign place, papery as ghosts, shabby with the stains of airline food, anonymous. The birds outside, rosellas, sounded like chattering Italian kids welcoming the dawn. The eucalypts were lofty as the umbrella pines in Rome but larger, those trees that in the summer crackle and ignite. Out through the glass walls we could see lush crimson and yellow flowers, rhododendrons, sprinklers hosing showers of light.

I sat Arlo on our suitcases on the trolley and wheeled him laughing through the glaring white terminal till he spied the bright orange car-hire logo. We waited behind a young couple who couldn't decide whether or not to pay the higher daily rate for the insurance. It was morning and the black glove scent of espresso beckoned through the air from a coffee stall across the way. On the wall behind the car-hire man a large round clock with a red second hand ticked. 'Dad?' asked Arlo and I realised that the honeymoon couple had gone and the man, a young man with his black hair gelled in many different directions, was waiting for me to speak. Behaviour was required. Passport, credit card, driver's licence, name. Arlo was hooked somehow around my neck, his fingers hot down the back of my T-shirt. I unpeeled them and lowered him to stand on the floor. The car-hire man was still waiting. Dumbly I shook my head, unable to let go of his bewildered gaze or to find words through the overpowering sense that something was missing. I had expected Ann to meet us off the plane.

ACKNOWLEDGEMENTS

Some years ago I received generous and timely assistance from the Royal Literary Fund. In 2006 I held the Buddle Findlay Sargeson Fellowship, which enabled me to finish this novel.

* * *

I would also like to thank Suzy Lucas, Becky Shaw, Peter Florence, Brita McVeigh, Karl Maughan, Leanne Pirie, my agent Georgia Garrett and editors Mary Morris and Gillian Stern for their steadfast and astute encouragement; Geoff Logan for the guide to radiotherapy mould room practice; and for opening up the world of screenwriting — though neither Tom nor I could pull it off! — I am grateful to Juliet Dowling and Stephen Cleary. Finally, special thanks to my publisher, Alexandra Pringle.

We do hope that you have enjoyed reading this large print book.

Did you know that all of our titles are available for purchase?

We publish a wide range of high quality large print books including:
Romances, Mysteries, Classics
General Fiction
Non Fiction and Westerns

Special interest titles available in large print are:
The Little Oxford Dictionary
Music Book
Song Book
Hymn Book
Service Book

Also available from us courtesy of Oxford University Press:
Young Readers' Dictionary
(large print edition)
Young Readers' Thesaurus
(large print edition)

For further information or a free brochure, please contact us at:
Ulverscroft Large Print Books Ltd.,
The Green, Bradgate Road, Anstey,
Leicester, LE7 7FU, England.
Tel: (00 44) **0116 236 4325**
Fax: (00 44) **0116 234 0205**

THE STORY OF A MARRIAGE

Andrew Sean Greer

It is 1953 and Pearlie Cook, a dutiful housewife, finds herself living in San Francisco; caring not only for her husband's fragile health, but also for her son who is afflicted with polio. Then, one Saturday morning, a stranger appears on her doorstep and everything changes. All the certainties by which Pearlie has lived are thrown into doubt, as she struggles to understand the world around her, most especially her husband, Holland.